Murder Is Uncooperative

Murder Is Uncooperative

Merrilee Robson

Merrilee Robson (signature)

NORTH STAR PRESS OF ST. CLOUD, INC.
St. Cloud, Minnesota

ISBN: 978-1-68201-031-0

First edition: September 2016

Printed in the United States of America.

Published by
North Star Press of St. Cloud, Inc.
P.O. Box 451
St. Cloud, MN 56302

www.northstarpress.com
www.merrileerobson.com

For Stuart

CHAPTER
One

Finding an apartment can be murder.

I'd looked at three that day.

The first had just been rented. The ad for the second had described it as having "spacious rooms." I thought it might work for my father's wheelchair. What the ad failed to mention was that those rooms could only be reached by climbing three flights of stairs.

The third was a basement suite, chilly even on a warm September morning, with a smell of mold I was sure was not going to go away.

Later, disappointed, I trudged slowly up the stairs of our rented townhouse. I could hear my son crying before I even opened the door.

My father was lying on the floor, blood from his head spattering the black and white tiles.

Ben threw himself at me, and I hugged his sturdy little-boy body as I sank to my knees next to my father.

"Grandpa fell," Ben choked out between sobs. "And his head is all bloody, and he won't talk to me."

Dad's face was pale and his white hair was streaked with blood. I desperately touched my father's neck, looking for a pulse.

I'd taken some first aid training, but I wasn't really sure if I could detect a pulse. My own heart was thudding too loudly.

I was relieved to see Dad open his eyes and move his legs.

"Becky!" he said, making a move to get up. "Thank goodness you're here. Ben . . ."

"Dad, don't move," I said. "We need to get an ambulance." I grabbed a wad of tissues from my purse and pressed them gently to where the blood was flowing from the wound on my father's head.

"Grandpa, are you better now?" my son asked. "Does your head hurt?" Ben passed me the portable phone he'd been clutching, and I was surprised to find myself talking to an emergency dispatcher.

"The ambulance should be right there," the woman told me. "Is your father still unconscious? The little boy said he was bleeding."

I could hear sirens now. I remembered to thank the dispatcher as the ambulance pulled up in front of the townhouse and two paramedics joined us in the tiny hall.

They knelt beside my father, carefully checking for broken bones. One of them removed the wad of bloody tissues.

"Nasty gash," he said. "We'll need to take him to the hospital to get that looked at." He eased Dad onto a gurney, then turned to look at Ben. "You did a fine job calling us."

Ben had been watching the action with fascination. The attention from the paramedic made him suddenly shy, and he grabbed my leg and looked up at me.

"I called 911," he said, "and the lady talked to me. She said I should open the door when the ambleeanse came. I know you said not to let strangers in the house, Mommy. But Grandpa still wasn't awake, and the 911 lady said it would be okay. I was glad you came home, Mommy." Ben's voice started to tremble. I could see tears gathering in his brown eyes.

"We would have been able to trace the call anyway," the paramedic said, "but the dispatcher said he told us his name and address and everything. He was crying, but he did great for such a little kid."

2

"We learned at pre-school," Ben said proudly. "And Mommy and Grandpa and I practiced with my toy phone. Because my daddy doesn't live with us anymore and sometimes Grandpa and I are all by ourselves."

"You did good, buddy," the paramedic told him. As he climbed into the driver's seat he said, "We'll be taking him to VGH Emergency," referring to the closest hospital. "Drive carefully if you want to come and meet him there. You seem a little shook up."

I wanted to head right out. But I knew that visits to emergency rooms usually involved long waits. I really didn't want Ben to spend hours in a chaotic waiting room, exposed to all sorts of germs and seeing the evening's casualties as they were brought in.

But I needed to be with my father too.

Well, Ben did have two parents. I grabbed the portable phone to call my ex-husband.

Of course I got Dave's voicemail.

Hearing the voice of the man I once loved still gave me a shock. His message sounded so warm and cheerful too.

"Dave, it's Rebecca. I've got a bit of an emergency here. We're all okay but Dad had a fall and needs to go to the hospital. I was wondering if you could take Ben for a while, maybe overnight. I don't know how long it will take for Dad to get checked out. I don't want Ben up till all hours while we wait around.

"Um . . . I guess we'll head over to the hospital now. I don't think I can have my cell phone on in there but we'll be at VGH emergency. I'll check messages when I can. Talk to you later."

Going anywhere with a four-year-old was never easy. I gathered up the bag I kept for any excursions with Ben. It held a warm hoodie, a complete change of clothes, wet wipes, a basic first-aid kit, a few storybooks and toys, a small pillow and blanket. I added some juice boxes, a banana and raisins, grabbing the keys to Dad's blue Toyota from the bowl on the kitchen counter.

I tried to keep myself calm and to sound cheerful as I strapped Ben into his car seat. "Let's go see how Grandpa is doing."

The emergency room reception was packed with people. Several generations of an Indo-Canadian family conversed quietly together. The women's clothes made bright splashes of pinks and greens in the otherwise drab waiting room but the worried looks on their faces told a more somber story. A young man in a soccer uniform sat with his leg elevated on one of the chairs, with an ice pack on his knee. A pregnant woman walked up and down, an angry, pained look on her face. A man walked beside her, trying to talk to her, but she wasn't answering him.

I was told my father was being X-rayed. The receptionist directed us to some uncomfortable chairs with stiff plastic seats. An unpleasant smell of disinfectant tried unsuccessfully to cover up something nastier.

"Where's Grandpa?" Ben asked. "I thought we were coming here to see him."

"The doctor is checking him. We'll see him when they've finished."

"Mommy, will Grandpa be okay? His face looked funny when he fell. I was scared."

Well, that was the question, wasn't it? I assumed my dad's arthritic legs had given way on the stairs. His joints were damaged and he was often in a lot of pain. While he could sometimes walk, he was finding it harder and harder to get around. The wheelchair he used to resort to only on really bad days was being used more and more often. But our townhouse had lots of stairs. That's why we needed to find a new place to live.

But how badly had he hurt himself? There was definitely a head injury, but what if he'd broken something? Or what if he hadn't just tripped and fallen? What if he'd had a stroke? Or blacked out for some reason?

My father was still relatively young and reasonably fit despite his debilitating disease. But there were any number of things that could go wrong. He wasn't ready to move into a care facility but he needed someplace where he could get around without difficulty. I worried about him being alone when I was out. He didn't know many of the neighbors in the townhouse project. We really needed to find someplace else to live.

By the time we saw my father, he'd been X-rayed, scanned, and given almost a dozen stitches. An intravenous tube ran into his arm and a thick bandage covered the wound on his head. But he seemed much better, alert and able to talk with us.

I lifted Ben up onto the hospital bed, where he snuggled up next to his grandfather, patting his face and giving him a soft kiss on the top of his thick bandage. My father wrapped his arm around my little boy and kissed him back.

"The scan didn't show any serious damage," the emergency doctor told me, "but he's got a nasty cut on his head. We couldn't identify any fractures but there are a number of contusions that will likely cause him some pain."

The doctor frowned at the chart in his hand. "I gather he fell down some stairs," he said. "I'm very surprised that a man in his condition is living in a home with stairs."

Tell me about it, I almost snapped. While Dad had his IV fluids and I'd been plying Ben with regular snacks, I hadn't eaten anything since breakfast.

"Yes, I was just looking for another apartment today," I replied.

"That's good," the doctor said. "We'll keep him here overnight anyway, but I wouldn't feel comfortable sending him home to a place with stairs. It really isn't safe."

We stayed with my father in his curtained cubicle in the emergency ward, talking quietly until Ben and I had reassured ourselves he was okay. Ben was snuggled up beside his grandfather, and his breathing was starting to become slow and regular. I could tell Dad needed to rest too.

So when the nurse came into Dad's cubicle to examine him again, I got up to go. I leaned over to kiss him goodbye and to pick up my son.

"I should get Ben home," I said. "And you look like you could use some beauty sleep yourself. We'll come back again tomorrow."

"You get some rest too, Becky. You look tuckered out. Oh, and I never got a chance to ask you about the apartments you looked at. Were they suitable?"

"Not really," I told him. "But I'll look again tomorrow. I left a message at that housing co-op I applied to when I broke up with Dave. I think they have wheelchair-accessible apartments and they're supposed to be affordable too. It looks nice from the outside."

"Hmmm," my father said. "Nice place with really low rent? It sounds too good to be true. Are you sure there's nothing wrong with that place?"

"I think they get government funding to help keep the rents low. But they have a long waiting list."

My father looked a little sad. "You know your mother and I were really looking forward to retiring early, but now I wish we hadn't. We thought it'd be our only opportunity to travel before my old legs got too bad to move around. But if we hadn't taken early retirement, I probably would've had more money to help out."

I touched his hand. "Dad, at least you had a bit of time to enjoy retirement with Mom before she died. Don't worry. We'll be fine."

Dad's pension was lower than it would have been if he hadn't retired early. And my income had taken a hit lately, too. I was sure we'd be fine, as I told him, but finding an affordable home would really help.

Before leaving the hospital, I checked the waiting room to see if my ex-husband had managed to get there. No sign of him, and he hadn't answered my message either of the times I had stepped out of the hospital waiting room to check my voicemail.

I carried Ben to the car and strapped him into his seat in the back. Then I turned my cell on and called Dave's number again. I got his voicemail.

"Hi, Dave. They're keeping Dad in the hospital overnight and maybe a bit longer, but he seems to be okay. I'm taking Ben home. Talk to you later."

We'd been in the hospital for hours but it wasn't that late. The days were growing shorter, but this early in September there was still light as we left the hospital emergency room. The traffic was fairly heavy with people heading into downtown Vancouver for a Friday evening.

How long had it been since I'd had an evening out, I wondered. Certainly not since the divorce, and probably not for a while before Dave and I split up.

I carried my sleeping son to the rented townhouse and managed to get the front door open without waking him.

My father's blood still stained the black and white tiles in the front hall. I planned to clean that up as soon as I got Ben to bed. I carried him up the steep, narrow stairs to the top floor, where he and I shared the small bedroom.

Dad had offered to give us the larger bedroom on the second floor when Ben and I had moved in with him, but that would have meant dealing with even more stairs, and we knew that wasn't a good thing.

I lowered Ben into his bed and started to remove his shoes.

"Ready to brush your teeth, kiddo?" I asked, smoothing the blond curls off his forehead. Ben didn't budge. With all the drama this afternoon, he'd missed his nap and the long wait at the hospital had exhausted him. He kept sleeping as I took off his pants and shirt and only muttered a little as I lifted him to pull the covers over him and tuck his favorite stuffed toy, a purple plush cat, beside him. His real kitten jumped up on the bed and curled up on his other side.

I headed back downstairs and looked in the fridge for something quick to eat. I was exhausted, but I was also starving.

I was startled by the phone.

"Rebecca Butler?" a friendly voice asked. "It's Les from Waterview housing co-op. You were asking about a three-bedroom that's wheelchair accessible? We have one coming available. Do you want to take a look at it?"

CHAPTER
TWO

I was early for this appointment. The five-storey brick building looked well maintained. The dark-blue paint on the front door shone. The large windows at the front were clean, the beveled glass sparkling in the autumn sunlight. A square of grass in front of the building was neatly trimmed and framed by shrubs, with some pale pink and yellow roses still in bloom.

I pushed the doorbell.

As I waited, I checked my reflection in the glass doors. My light-brown, chin-length hair was tidy. My khaki pants and a moss-green linen jacket that brought out the green in my eyes were both neat, ironed, and free of stains. I hoped I looked like a good tenant, someone who would pay the rent on time and take care of the place.

The glass also reflected the view of the street. I saw a woman coming up behind me. Probably in her sixties, though it was hard to tell, she was pushing a shopping cart filled with bottles, cans, and bags stuffed with who knows what. Even though the day was warm, she was dressed in a heavy gray coat and gloves. The hem of her skirt had unraveled at one side and drooped beneath the hem of her coat but I could see she had made an effort to pin it up with a safety pin. I guessed she was one of the many people who lived on Vancouver's streets.

I reached into my pocket, searching for some coins to give her. But she wasn't asking for spare change.

"Don't go there; don't go there," she was saying. Many of the street people suffered from mental illness or drug addiction. I held out my hand to give her a dollar but she just shook her head. "No, don't go there."

I pushed the doorbell again.

"Hi, it's Rebecca Butler," I announced to the crackly sound that greeted me through the intercom. Not everything was perfect in this place. "I have an appointment."

A buzzing told me the door was being unlocked, and I pulled the handle. The homeless woman reached out as if to grab me but she moved away when a young woman leaned out of a doorway in the hall. The door hissed shut behind me.

The young woman who had answered the door was in her late teens or early twenties, and tall, with her hair in long dark curls. She had a pale oval face and lush, plump lips. She would have been stunning, except for her frown and a slightly dazed look in her large brown eyes.

"I'm sorry. We've been having trouble with the intercom," she apologized. "Can I help you?"

"Rebecca Butler," I repeated. "I have an appointment with the building manager to see one of the apartments. I'm afraid I'm a bit early."

She wrinkled her forehead.

"Maybe 505?" she asked. "But that's a three-bedroom. Are you . . . ?" She was looking past me, obviously expecting to see a husband and a couple of children. "Les is with some other people," she added. "I'm not sure . . ."

I wasn't about to be put off by a teenager. I imagined another family upstairs, signing the lease on the apartment meant to house my son, my father, my kitten.

"She has an appointment, Ruthie," a cheery voice interrupted her from down the hall. "I see people who have appointments, remember."

A garden gnome was walking quickly towards us. At barely five-foot-three, I'm used to men towering over me. But he was even shorter, with sturdy legs and an oddly long torso. Dark curls circled a large bald spot on the top of his head, matched by a short beard. He smiled reassuringly at the young woman before turning to me.

"Rebecca?" he said, reaching for my hand. "I'm Les. Sorry to keep you waiting. Welcome to Waterview Housing Cooperative. Let me show you around."

The elevator that took us up to the fifth floor was free of the graffiti and mess I'd come to expect in my search for a new home.

The apartment was perfect.

The building was old but it had large windows that filled the apartment with light. A faint smell of fresh paint lingered on the creamy walls. Polished fir floors glowed golden.

The living room had a large bay window, with two smaller windows on each side. I imagined an overstuffed armchair, or maybe a small, round table, where I could sit writing and drinking tea. The windows looked out onto a quiet residential street lined with mature maple trees, their leaves still green this early in September, but with the promise of autumn color to come.

I checked each of the bedrooms and the large closets. The kitchen was spacious, with lots of storage. The window looked out on a fenced-in playground. I could see kids my son's age climbing on playground equipment. A glass door led to a small balcony with room for a small table and chairs. An older woman on the next deck gave me a friendly smile as she watered her tomato plants and flowers. The yeasty smell of baking bread floated over from her open window. The smell instantly reminded me of my mother, and I had to blink the tears from my eyes.

"How much?" I asked, my voice cracking a little.

I couldn't believe the answer. It was $100 less than the basement suite I'd looked at the day before.

"Do you allow pets?" I asked the manager.

"A cat or small dog would be fine."

I could have kissed him. Rental places that allowed pets were hard to find. But I couldn't give up my son's kitten. Especially after all the changes Ben had already gone through in his short life.

"Yes," I said. "Yes, I'd love to live here."

After showing me apartment 505, Les showed me around the rest of the building. The "Waterview" part of the name was a bit optimistic. Perhaps there had been a view when the building had originally been built, before the trees around it had grown so large. But it was in a friendly neighborhood, close to a park, a community center, and a good library. Grocery stores were within walking distance on Commercial Drive.

"This is a great building," I told the manager. Up close, he had dark tufts of hair sprouting from each ear. These wiggled each time he moved. I tried not to stare. With his wide, lopsided grin and energetic way of talking, he was attractive in an oddball way.

"It's an old building, but we've just finished renovating everything," he said, gesturing around the wide lobby. "The hallways were wide already and the apartments were a good size, so we were able to adapt some of the apartments for people in wheelchairs."

He pointed to the doorway of the office. "See, no sills. And see how wide the doorway is. We've designed it so all the public areas are wheelchair accessible."

"My father will be living with us, and he uses a wheelchair. But my son and I will be living here too and we . . ." My voice trailed off. I could see the sunny apartment slipping away from me.

"That's the beauty of this place," the manager said, curls bouncing as he gestured in a way that seemed to indicate the whole building. "It's not an assisted living facility or anything with medical care. Most of the disabled people who live here can get along fine without any help. And only some of the people who live here have disabilities. But it's all wheelchair-accessible. "

His enthusiasm was contagious and the design of the building was impressive. I really wanted to live here.

We ended the tour back in the office where we'd started. The young woman, Ruth, was slumped at one of the gray desks, tapping at the keys of a computer. She had put on a pair of glasses with thick plastic frames.

The office was a complete shambles. File folders and stacks of paper made unstable towers on each of the three desks. More towers of storage boxes lined two sides of the room, almost reaching the ceiling. The boxes obscured the one window in the room.

All the chairs, except the one that Ruth was sitting on were stacked with more files and papers. She was staring intently at the screen of her computer, ignoring the papers piled on either side of the screen, as if this chaos were normal.

"As you can see, organizing paperwork is not one of my strengths," Les said, looking a little sheepish. "But it's not normally this bad. We just cleared out a storage room so it could be painted. I think we can throw a lot of this stuff out, but we just need some time to sort through it."

He pulled a form from the top of a stack of paper a foot high and handed it to me.

"Let's see," Les was saying. "You originally applied for a two-bedroom. With your father living with you, you'd qualify for a three-bedroom. Let's just update your form here."

I stepped towards the desk to find a flat surface I could write on, and tripped over something on the floor.

I bit back a curse as I pitched forward. I managed to avoid falling. As I tried to steady myself, I dislodged a stack of books and papers from the corner of the desk. The edge of one binder landed on my foot with a thud I knew would leave a bruise.

Les and I both bent down to pick up the papers I'd displaced. I saw that what I'd tripped over was a large metal plate that had been lying flat on the floor.

Picking it up, I found that it was quite heavy. It was a square brass plaque announcing the opening of the cooperative over thirty years ago. A sharp corner had left a large scrape across the strap of my brown leather sandal and blood was welling up from the corner of the coral-painted nail on one toe.

"Oh, I'm so sorry," Les said, taking the plaque from me and placing it against the wall. It was out of the way there but looked like it could be knocked over quite easily. "Are you all right? Ruthie, can you get the first aid kit?"

I grabbed a tissue from my purse and blotted the blood on my toe. "It's just a scrape," I told him, but I could tell it was going to hurt for a while.

As I bent over to apply the bandage, I quickly pushed the plaque so it was wedged behind a pile of boxes and wouldn't immediately drop on the floor again.

"Are you sure you're all right?" Les asked. "I'm so sorry. That's normally bolted on the wall outside," Les said. "We just took it down when we were painting and having the brick cleaned."

"I'm fine," I said, ignoring my throbbing toe. "And I'd really like to live here. I think the apartment would be just great for my son and me. And my father would love it. But how many people are looking at the apartment?"

"We do have quite a few people on our waiting list," the manager admitted. "Lots of people would like to live here. But, see, we're here to help people in need. And you're a single mom, right? Little kid? Disabled dad? Not much money? You sound like a person in need. Of course the membership committee has the final say." My heart fell, and then rose again as he winked at me. "They do listen to my opinions."

As I left the building, I saw the homeless woman waiting on the sidewalk. I must have been limping a little. She stared at my foot and, when I looked down, I saw that blood was seeping from my toe.

"Don't go there," she said, her voice croaking. "Bad things happen."

"I'm fine."

"Take this," she said, pushing something into my hand. It was a small, tarnished pendant on a chain. Dirt covered the medallion face, but it appeared to have a picture of something with wings. "Guardian angel," she said. I tried to hand it back to her but she backed away. "Take it," she repeated. "You need it."

CHAPTER
Three

A month later, I finished unpacking the last box in my new apartment. It already felt like home.

The movers had helped place the heavy furniture, and I'd been able to arrange smaller pieces in a way that made them look like they belonged there.

Dad had the biggest bedroom, with space for him to turn his wheelchair. I took the second bedroom, which was oddly shaped but had a small nook perfect for my desk. It was near the window and would get morning sunlight, making it an inviting space to work.

Ben's toys and books were unpacked in his room and his kitten was asleep on his bed. Dad had taken Ben out to explore the new neighborhood.

Les had told me that a spot in the co-op's underground parking was included in the rent, but I hadn't yet picked up the remote that would open the garage door. I made a mental note to do that before the office closed today.

I was happy with how things looked. The green loveseat and chairs my mother had picked out for their retirement condo nestled in a corner of the living room. The oak bookshelves fit against one wall as if they had been made for that spot. I was heading for the door when I heard a knock.

It was Les, smiling widely and looking more than ever like a garden gnome. With him was a silver-haired woman who looked to be somewhere in her early sixties.

Les was holding something out to me. "I realized you hadn't picked up the remote for the parking garage, and I wanted to make sure you had it. And I wanted to introduce you to Gwen, the president."

The woman was tall and slim. Her thick hair was pulled up in an elegant twist and secured with a silver pin that matched her dangling earrings. She was dressed in a linen tunic and pants in different shades of lilac. Her soft leather sandals were a deep violet.

"Oh, I'm so pleased to meet you," I said. "I just love it here. Les has told me that everyone is really friendly."

I saw the woman meet Les's eyes, and the manager shrugged slightly. "Well, we just wanted to make sure you were settling in," Gwen said. "I hope you'll like it here. And you'll get to meet everyone at the meeting on Monday. You did get the meeting notice?"

I nodded.

"Great, well, we'll see you at the meeting," Les said. "Just check with the office if you have any questions. Oh, and we wanted to give you a copy of the occupancy agreement you signed before you moved in." He handed me a document about fifteen pages long. I remembered that most of it seemed pretty straightforward. I had agreed to pay my rent on time, to report any maintenance problems promptly, to keep my apartment in good shape. As Les had explained before, I would be expected to attend members' meetings and to participate in some committee work around the co-op. The document stressed that everyone would try to be considerate of their neighbors, but it outlined a dispute resolution process if I had a problem with the co-op or with one of the people who lived there.

That didn't seem likely, I told myself. I was going to love it here.

"Oh, by the way," Les said, turning back. "I noticed on your application form that you were interested in gardening. It's pretty short notice, and I'm sure you just want to settle in first but the garden committee is having a bit of a work party tomorrow morning. Just some fall clean up, a little weeding and leaf raking. If you want to join them, they're starting at ten o'clock."

"I'd love to," I answered.

THE SUN STREAMING through my uncurtained bedroom windows woke me up early the next day, even before Ben was starting to stir. As I headed past his open bedroom door, I saw that Ben's kitten was awake. I quickly picked him up before he started meowing for attention. The gray-striped kitten was small but he was vocal when he wanted something. Ben called him Maui. Maui was a popular vacation destination for Vancouverites who could afford the trip. It was also the name of a Hawaiian demi-god. But Ben had named him after the sound he made. The spelling was my idea.

Holding him close to my body, I moved to the living room and sat down with the kitten on my lap.

I would need new curtains or blinds in here, I decided. The windows were wider than the ones in the condo. When Mom and Dad had sold the home I'd grown up in, they had rented that place. They planned to travel a lot, but they wanted someplace large enough for family dinners, for Ben to stay over.

Then Mom found a lump in her breast.

I looked at my watch. It was a delicate gold band that had belonged to my mother. It felt odd to see it on my wrist, but it somehow felt like she was close when I wore it. I sometimes thought I could still smell her perfume, a faint whiff of Chanel. It had been almost a year.

I blinked back the tears and stood up. I could hear Ben getting out of bed. It was time to get him ready for the day, and time to feed the cat.

Ben was scheduled to spend the weekend with Dave, so I wasn't surprised to see my ex-husband's number when my cell phone rang.

"Did you need the address again?" I asked, figuring he needed directions to the new place. "We're just off Commercial Drive."

"Um, sorry Bec. I'm not going to be able to make it." I didn't detect a lot of regret in my ex-husband's voice. "It's a work thing."

Dave was a sports reporter at the newspaper I used to work at. Games were scheduled well in advance, so he usually knew when he would be working. But sometimes things came up unexpectedly. That was the nature of the job.

"So, when are you going to get here?"

"Well, I'm not sure how long this will take. It might be better to just skip this weekend. Let me talk to Ben."

I knew Ben would be disappointed, but I was pleased Dave was at least willing to break the news to Ben himself. He hadn't been the most mature parent, and he usually left it to me to convey bad news. Dave was the fun parent, the one who took his son to hockey games and to the water park, the one who bought remote-controlled trucks and other expensive toys, who let Ben eat all the hot dogs he wanted.

I was the parent who cleaned up the vomit after the hot dog fiasco, who bought the batteries to make the toys run, who made sure Ben had dry clothes to change into after going to the water park, who made sure he ate vegetables.

It was clear that Ben looked forward to the time with his father.

"Daddy!" he cried, grabbing the phone eagerly. "Are you almost here? You should see my new room. Where are we going today?"

The look on my little boy's face broke my heart. "But when can you come here, Daddy? I want to show you my new room. And Maui wants to see you."

Tears were gathering in Ben's brown eyes as he listened to his father. He handed the phone back to me and rushed to his room.

Dad came out of his room as I followed Ben down the hall.

"Problems? Need any help?" he asked.

I smiled at him. "Thanks, Dad. I think I need to deal with this myself."

Ben was sprawled across his bed, crying in the abandoned way children have.

"Why doesn't Daddy want to see me?" he asked.

I silently cursed Dave for putting me in the position of having to explain. "Daddy said he had to work."

"All weekend?" Ben was a smart kid.

"I guess so. But, guess what, Benjy-bear? That means we get to spend more time together. So you can come help me do some gardening and meet some of the neighbors. How about that?"

Ben was a good-natured kid. He soon dried his tears and was smiling again.

He put on his shoes, and we went out into the hallway. As we were leaving our apartment, I saw someone heading to the door on the other side. She was a small Asian woman in her sixties, her chin-length dark hair heavily streaked with gray.

"Hi," I greeted her. "Are you one of my neighbors? We've just moved into the co-op. I'm Rebecca Butler."

I stuck out my hand, smiling in what I hoped was a friendly manner.

The woman scowled and hurried past me to the door on my left. She opened the door and slammed it shut behind her with a bang that echoed through the hall.

CHAPTER
Four

I was disturbed by the way the woman had acted. But maybe she didn't speak English, or maybe she wasn't a neighbor after all, just someone visiting. She'd had shopping bags and looked like she belonged, but I thought there must be some explanation for her rudeness. I put it out of my mind.

We headed down to the lobby. Les had said that was where everyone was meeting before starting work on the garden.

It was right on the dot of ten o'clock when we got off the elevator and stepped into the lobby.

We were the only ones there.

From what I'd heard about living in a co-op, I'd expected dozens of people. Had I got the location wrong? The office was closed on a Saturday, so there was no one to ask.

Had they already started work? Maybe everyone had arrived there early and was already in the garden.

I went outside to see if I could find anyone working in the yard. No one was there. The co-op's grounds didn't look like they needed too much attention. The large maple trees in front of the building had scattered some golden leaves on the front lawn. But the lawn itself was neatly trimmed, and I couldn't see any leaves in the flowerbeds that lined the building.

The only thing that marred the appearance of the building was a rusty white motor home parked directly in front of it. I remembered seeing it when we moved in, but it had been parked further down the block on that day. Today, it was parked in a spot that would be a real problem for anyone wanting to move in or deliver something large.

The door to the motor home was hanging open. I couldn't tell if that meant someone was inside, or if it was broken. The door looked like it might drop off its hinges at any moment.

I looked around for anyone from the co-op. I did see the homeless woman I had met on the day I applied to move in. She was across the street staring at the building with a scowl on her face. She didn't have her shopping cart with her but I was sure it was the same woman.

I had tried to simplify our move as much as possible so I had given away a number of things I thought we wouldn't need in the new place. The small pendant she had given me was dirty and tarnished but I was reluctant to part with it. I wasn't superstitious, and didn't really believe that the good luck charm had helped us get into the co-op. And it was filthy and likely covered with germs.

But it seemed churlish to throw something out that the woman had pressed on me so urgently.

So I had cleaned it. When the charm was cleaned, the detail of the image was much clearer. It was an angel, the wings finely etched and long hair curling around a delicate face. The carving was much better than I would have expected from a cheap trinket. I had used some silver polish on both the charm and the chain and discovered that both were made of sterling silver. They were beautiful.

I felt dreadful, thinking that a homeless woman had unwittingly given me something that could be valuable. So I was pleased to see her now.

The woman gestured to me, indicating she wanted me to cross the street. I glanced down at Ben. I didn't want my son to be unaware that some other people weren't as fortunate as we were.

But I still wasn't sure I should introduce him to a woman who seemed to have some mental health problems. Could she be dangerous?

Ben pulled his hand away from mine as he noticed a car pulling up to the curb. "Daddy!" he yelled and ran across the grass.

As Dave got out of the car, I saw a sudden look of surprise on his face. He recovered quickly, bending down to catch Ben as he hurled himself into his father's arms. "Daddy, Daddy, you came after all!"

Ben took his father's hand and pulled him toward us, chattering all the time. "Hi, Dave," I greeted him. "Didn't you have to work after all?"

"Um, yeah, Bec." He was blushing a little. "Um, I hadn't realized that this was where you'd moved to. I guess I didn't recognize the address. I'm just here to pick up a colleague. I can't stay."

"Daddy, we're going to rake leaves," Ben was saying. "Do you know how to rake leaves? Can you show me how?"

Dave bent down to his son's level. "I can't stay, Ben. I told you I had to work."

"But I want to show you my new room. And Grandpa and Maui want to see you. Can't you stay, just for a minute?"

"Sure, for a minute. Why don't you show me this new room of yours?"

I opened the front door for them but didn't follow them back upstairs. Something was going on with Dave and I wanted to think about it. "Dad's upstairs, so he can let you in. Ben, you show Daddy the way to our new place."

The woman who had given me the pendant was gone. I was about to cross the street to look for her when the front door opened and a woman hurried out.

She was pretty, probably in her late fifties, with dark hair and a round, rosy face. She was dressed in an outfit that was very similar to one Gwen, the president, had worn yesterday. Her loose linen pants and T-shirt were a lavender shade, covered with a short-sleeved knit top in a slightly darker shade. Silver earrings, set with amethysts, hung from her earlobes, and rows of silver bangles clinked together on one wrist. The outfit was similar to Gwen's but somehow it looked very different. The loose flowing layers had glided over Gwen's tall, thin frame. Similar wide-legged pants made this woman look shorter and wider than she actually was.

But her warm smile made her look lovely. As she approached, I could smell a sweet, flowery scent.

I had thought about what to wear to the work party. I wanted to make a good impression on my new neighbors. But it seemed silly to dress up to do garden work.

I had settled for beige capris and a T-shirt in a spring green. My canvas slip-on shoes were the same beige as the capris, with some light green trim. I had kept some of my mother's gardening equipment, and I managed to find a pair of gardening gloves and a trowel. I didn't have a rake, but I assumed the co-op would have the appropriate equipment.

"Are you here for the gardening work party?" she asked. When I nodded, she went on, a little breathlessly. "You just moved in to 505, right? I'm Mariana. I live next door."

As I introduced myself, I realized she was the woman I'd seen on her balcony the day I first looked at the apartment.

"Have the others already started?" I asked. "Les said the gardening committee was organizing the work. Are they out back?"

"Oh, Rebecca . . . I think Les gets a little enthusiastic when he talks about the co-op. He really likes the idea, but I think his view of the co-op is more what he wishes it would be, rather than what it's really like."

"So, what's it really like?" I wondered.

"Well, this work party? It's probably just us."

"Just us?"

"Yeah. Gwen, the president, might come. But the others? Probably not. You see, we have a lot of members living in this building, more than a hundred. But a few of them moved in when the co-op first got started more than thirty years ago. They're loyal members, but they're getting older. They're not coming out to work parties the way they might have done in the past. And some of the newer members just want an affordable place to live. They're too busy or just not interested in doing much around the co-op."

"Oh. It's just that Les described it as a real community, with everyone involved. He made it sound so special."

"Well, like I said, Les sort of looks at the co-op through rose-colored glasses. It's not really like that. But it's not really a problem for the work party. We hire people to do most of the maintenance. But some of us like to do some gardening, and we do a bit around here from time to time."

She smiled warmly. "I always wanted a real garden, more than just balcony plants. I enjoy that. But I'm sorry if you got the wrong impression. You don't have to do this if you don't want to."

My mother had loved gardening. I hadn't shared that with her when she was alive, but somehow I wanted to learn more about it. Besides, it would be great to be outside.

"It's a beautiful day," I answered. "Let's go and garden!"

Mariana showed me where the rakes and gardening equipment were stored. There was even a child-sized rake Ben could use. By the time we returned to the front yard, Dave and Ben were back. Both looked pretty subdued.

Dave muttered that he had to go get his colleague and went back inside the building. I introduced Mariana to my son. Ben looked down at the ground, a little shy with strangers.

"You look like a pretty strong guy," Mariana said. "I bet we'll be able to get through the gardening in half the time, with you helping."

"I help Mommy and Grandpa a lot," Ben answered. "I am strong. You want to see my muscles?" Ben flexed his arm, showing off his biceps the way his father had shown him.

"Wow, you *are* strong. Well, let's put you to work."

It was still early in the season, so there weren't a lot of fallen leaves. But we set to work with vigor.

Ben spent most of his time raking up small piles and scattering them again, but we soon managed to create a reasonable pile.

"You know what the reward is for guys who rake up piles of leaves?" Mariana asked my son, who shook his head. "They get to jump in the pile!"

She demonstrated, hopping onto the edge of the pile, scattering only a few of the leaves we'd gathered.

Ben was more enthusiastic, throwing himself in the center of the pile and tossing the leaves around him. He did that a couple of times. Mariana and I raked the pile back together after each of his jumps.

"You're pretty good with kids," I said. "Do you have children?"

She smiled. "My son, and one grandson. But they're back east right now, near Ottawa. I don't get to see them as often as I'd like to but I'm hoping they'll move back to Vancouver soon."

Ben was still jumping in the leaves. "Come on, Mom. You try it," he was saying, when his father returned.

"Daddy!" Ben yelled. "We're raking leaves, and then we can jump in them. Want to watch me jump in the leaves? It's Mommy's turn now, but then you can try it!"

There was a woman with Dave. The colleague he had mentioned, I assumed. She was what my father would call a pocket Venus. She was tiny, barely five feet tall, with soft waves of very light blond hair falling to below her shoulders. Her eyes were large and surprisingly dark, almost black, with delicate brows arching over them and thick eyelashes that surely couldn't be real.

She was simply dressed in jeans and a T-shirt, but the jeans were obviously designer and fit her curves closely. She looked delicate, but her fitted T-shirt revealed deep cleavage and breasts anything but elfin. They looked as artificial as her eyelashes, I thought snidely.

I knew I was being catty. This woman made my own body—which I had considered slim, fit and not un-sexy up to that moment—look boyish and angular. I also felt huge, which was an unfamiliar experience.

I gave myself a mental shake and smiled a greeting at her.

"Bec, this is Cara," Dave was saying. "Cara, Rebecca's my ex. She just moved into this building."

Cara shook my hand, smiling prettily. "What a coincidence, you moving into my building. Dave's mentioned you, and he's certainly told me all about your big boy here." She smiled at Ben, who ignored her. I guess her charms only worked on men once they reached puberty.

"Ben, say hello to Cara. She works with Daddy."

I thought I saw a look of surprise on Cara's face, but I was focused on my son. Ben usually had pretty good manners. My father had taught him to shake hands, much to the amusement of some of his friends. But today he just muttered, "Hello," over his shoulder and went back to raking leaves again.

Calling to his father to watch him, he took his small rake and industriously raked the pile back together quickly.

"This is Mariana, one of our new neighbors," I told Dave. "I guess you already know her." I said to Cara.

"Oh, yes, I know Mariana," she said. I thought she started to frown, but then she dimpled again and waggled her fingers at her. "Hi. Sorry, I couldn't join the work party but, as you see, I had plans. Glad you've got some help." She glanced across the lawn at the rusty motor home and then looked back at Mariana. "Why is that thing still here?" she asked, looking at the vehicle with distaste.

Mariana shrugged. Dry leaves were starting to pile on the roof of the vehicle, making it look like it was going to turn into compost, not drive away. "It's not supposed to be there. It's too big to park on the street. I guess Les will deal with it on Monday, if it's still there," she said.

"How long have you been at the *Sun*?" I asked Cara, referring to the paper where Dave worked. "You must have started after I left."

I thought she was taking a long time to answer a straightforward question, but we were interrupted by Ben.

"Mommy, Daddy, you can jump now. I raked the leaves up again. I did a really good job!"

"I can see that. But we should get on our way," Dave said. "See ya, Bec. Goodbye, my man," he said, bending down to Ben's height. "We'll do something real cool next weekend, I promise."

"Okay, Daddy," he whispered, looking down. He went back to his raking.

"Umm . . . He was supposed to have Ben this weekend," I explained to Mariana, "but he has to work."

We went back to raking, but the mood was spoiled. We started to bag the leaves for the compost bins behind the building.

Dave and Cara headed to the black sports car he had bought when we split up. Ben chose that moment to burst into tears, and I bent to comfort him. Looking over his head, I noticed that Dave was rolling a bright pink suitcase with hard, shiny sides.

Dave might have been heading out of town to cover a tournament or an away game of a local hockey or football team. And maybe the paper would send two reporters, but it seemed unlikely. I suspected that Dave wasn't working at all this weekend.

We were divorced, and what Dave did didn't matter to me. But I would be angry if I found he was missing out on time with his son to spend the weekend with a woman.

Dave loaded the pink suitcase into the trunk and helped Cara into the car with care he had never shown me, even when we were first dating.

I leaned over to give my son a hug and didn't see Dave drive off. But I did hear the door of the motorhome slam back with a loud crash. I looked up to see a large man climbing down from inside and rushing towards us.

"Guess you didn't know I could hear you and that other bitch talking about my motorhome, eh?" he yelled. "I don't know why you people can't learn to mind your own business."

He swung the toolkit he was carrying in a large arc, barely missing us. I jumped back, but Mariana didn't flinch. She answered him more calmly than I would have thought possible. "Now, Aaron, you should know why people are upset about it, but you can talk to Les or the board members, if you really don't understand."

"Yeah, like that's gonna happen," he snarled. But he did keep moving, storming past us and into the building.

"Who was that?" I asked, my voice trembling a little.

"Oh, Aaron. He lives in the co-op. And he owns the motorhome, as you can probably tell."

"I thought he was going to hit you."

"Oh, he mostly just yells," she said, calmly. "He can make a lot of noise, but I've never seen him actually hit anyone. And he'll usually back down if anyone stands up to him. Notice he didn't come out while your husband was still around."

She laughed, but when she turned to look at the motorhome parked on the street, her face turned white.

"Are you all right?" I asked. "That was upsetting. And it's getting hot out. Maybe it's time to go inside."

"No, I'm fine. I just thought . . . But it's been . . ." She had been staring intently at the street, but she looked back at me and managed a faint smile. "Yes, you're right. Let's just take these bags around back. I think it's time to go in."

CHAPTER
Five

On Monday, Dad was feeling well enough for a short walk and decided to check out one of the coffee shops on Commercial Drive. The street had been the center of Vancouver's Italian community and had been known as "Little Italy" for many years. Now it had a more eclectic ethnic mix, but it still boasted many Italian restaurants, delis, and coffee bars.

After Dad had headed off with his walker, I used his car to drop Ben off at the pre-school he attended three times a week. I decided to do some grocery shopping before going home. I'd avoided buying too many things before the move, so we wouldn't have so much to pack. Now we were running a bit low on essentials. It was time to stock our new cupboards.

With the car loaded with supplies, I thought I'd use the underground parking garage Les had mentioned. I hadn't bothered with it during the weekend but now I grabbed the remote door opener Les had given me. The door moved as smoothly and evenly as everything else in this well-run building. Les had assured me that the parking spot we'd been allocated was close to the elevator. I appreciated that. It would be easier for Dad. And, as the mother of a young son, I was often carrying a sleepy boy, bulky toys, or bags of groceries.

I was driving slowly, carefully looking at the numbered parking spots, when I suddenly realized I was heading directly toward the bumper of the rusty motor home I'd seen earlier on the street. It was filling a parking space, jutting out further than any of the other vehicles in the parking garage. In fact, I was lucky there hadn't been another vehicle coming out because it would have been hard for two cars to pass in the space that was left.

The RV also spread out into the two spaces on either side, which were both vacant, either by design or because nothing larger than a bike could have squeezed in beside the motor home. I was driving past, still checking the numbers on the parking spots, when it dawned on me that one of the spots the motor home was occupying must be the one Les had assigned to me.

I climbed out of the car, peering under the bumper of the motor home to check the number painted on the floor of the garage. Sure enough, that was the one Les had written down for me. I checked the spot again. There was no way I could squeeze even our small Toyota into the space left by the motor home. The spot I had been given was right next to the elevator, which was great. But that meant that it had the cement wall of the elevator shaft on one side. Even though it was quite a wide space, designed so that a driver or passenger would have room to get out of the car and into a wheelchair, there was just no room for the car.

I headed back out to the street but wasn't lucky enough to find a space in front of the building again. I finally found a spot a block over and lugged my shopping bags up the street.

I was feeling the strain on my arms and vowing to work out more. When I reached the building, the office door was open. I stopped in the doorway to see if the staff were there. Ruth was slumped in front of her computer again, frowning at the screen. I set my bags down to rap on the open door to get her attention. She looked up and frowned at me the way she had looked at the computer.

"Yes," she asked, "can I help you?" Her tone told me she wasn't entirely sure she wanted to, even if she could.

"It's the parking spot," I said. "Les gave me the number of the spot but there seems to be a motor home taking up the space," I said.

"There's a motor home in your parking spot?" She looked at me quizzically.

"Not in my spot, in the one next to it. But it's blocking my space."

"Oh, well, if it's not in your space . . ."

"But I can't use my space," I replied patiently. "Unless I got the number of the spot wrong. I just wanted to check." Why was the co-op employing this woman? She always seemed completely clueless.

"Is there a problem, Ruthie?" Les's rubber-soled shoes were quiet, and I hadn't heard him coming into the office.

"She says there's a motor home in the way but it's not in her space. I don't know what she expects us to do."

"I just wanted to check if I have the right parking spot—" I started to explain, when Les interrupted me.

"The motor home's in the parking garage again! He knows he can't do that."

He was almost yelling, but I knew he wasn't mad at me.

He turned to Ruth. "Remember we talked about Aaron's motor home? I've told him he can't park here and Gwen's talked to him too. I'll write him an official notice, but can you put it on the agenda for the meeting tonight, Ruthie? We could probably use a refresher on the occupancy agreement. Everyone gets a copy of the rules, but they tend to ignore them if it's not convenient."

"You got a reminder about the meeting, right?" he asked. "You should've received a printed notice, then a reminder by email."

"I did get a printed notice, but I don't think I saw an email. But that's okay. I put it in my calendar."

He turned back to his assistant. "Ruthie, didn't I ask you to add Rebecca to the co-op email list when she moved in?"

"Oh, sure." She smiled, pulling out a blue file folder from her desk. I noticed the folder had a neat label with my name on it. "I have her address right here."

"Did you add her to the list? It won't do much good in a folder on your desk."

"Oh, okay. I'll add her to the list." She turned back to her computer, putting the folder down and returning to what she'd been doing, not at all concerned that she had messed up in her job. It was no surprise that the members didn't attend meetings and work parties if they didn't get notices.

"Don't worry," Les said, as if reading my thoughts. "I usually take care of that myself."

"Well, thanks for clarifying about the motor home. So this is the right number of the parking spot?" I showed him the slip of paper he had given me last week.

"Oh, that's the right spot all right. Right beside the elevator. I wanted it to be convenient for you." Les's normally cheerful face was grim. I wouldn't want to be the owner of the motor home.

The rest of the day was rushed. I had to finish a project for a client, so I needed to put in a couple of hours at the desk in the corner of my bedroom before picking up Ben at pre-school. It was a very different workspace from the bustling newsroom where I had worked before Ben was born.

I had wanted to work as a freelance writer and editor after Ben's birth, so I could spend more time with him. I liked being able to plan my schedule around him. I had developed a number of regular clients, and was busy enough some times. But the decision had seemed like a better idea when Dave and I were still together, with the benefit of one full-time salary. And the slowdown in the economy had just made things worse. My income was a little too precarious sometimes.

I had asked about returning to the paper, and looked for other jobs. But newspapers were struggling, and there weren't any spots available. I was still hoping some of my contract work might turn into a full-time job. I really liked being able to spend time with Ben, but I worried about not being able to pay the bills. At least moving into the co-op was a real help.

Before the meeting, I managed to find the occupancy agreement Les had given me and read through it again. The co-op's rules seemed reasonable—trying to guarantee that a lot of people could share a building in relative peace. No loud noise late at night, park only in your designated spot, report any repairs needed in your home to the office as quickly as possible.

I felt a bit better prepared when I headed downstairs to the meeting room. Dad was looking after Ben, so I was alone as I stepped into the elevator. I was a bit worried about the issue of the motor home being raised at the meeting. I didn't want to start off on the wrong foot with my new neighbors. And I'd seen how angry the man who owned it could get. But Les had said that the motor home had been a problem before.

A few people were drifting into the meeting room as I got there. A table had been set up at the front of the room and someone had placed chairs in rows. I was glad that this meeting was taking place so soon after I moved in. Les had told me that the whole membership only met four times a year. The board of directors and committees met more frequently but this would be my best chance to meet more of my new neighbors.

Gwen, the president, moved away from the front of the room and headed toward me. "I'm glad to see you again, Rebecca," she said.

As the members started arriving for the meeting, I could see that the co-op was home to a population as diverse as Vancouver's. A young couple arrived, the woman carrying a sleeping infant. They looked very young, maybe still in their teens. The baby was adorable, with a crop of dark curls that matched his mother's, and the longest black eyelashes. His skin was a charming brown that blended his mother's dark skin with his father's lighter tone. I smiled at them.

A woman who looked to be in her eighties or even nineties pushed her walker ahead of her as she walked slowly to the front of the room. Two middle-aged women chatted together in Cantonese.

"My father's looking forward to meeting more of the other members," I said to Gwen "but he's staying with my son tonight."

"Oh, didn't anyone tell you? We pay for childcare so members can attend the meetings." She glanced over at the young couple with the baby. "Anna and John know that very well but they aren't ready to leave baby Jordan on his own yet. You know how new parents are. I hope he stays asleep. They live near me and he can certainly make it known when he's unhappy."

She smiled at the young couple in an indulgent way. "Anyway, we have teenagers in the co-op willing to do baby-sitting. The staff should have given you a list."

I suspected that this was another one of Ruth's tasks that she had neglected. I didn't say anything, but Gwen saw the look on my face.

"Right, well there is something about the childcare policy in the occupancy agreement but I guess that's a lot to absorb all at once. Just ask Les for a copy of the baby-sitting list next time you're in the office. I'll mention it to him too. Distributing information to members is supposed to be Ruth's job but . . ."

A man about my own age approached us then. He smiled warmly at me and introduced himself as Jeremy, the vice-president. He was tall, with wavy chestnut hair and a short beard of a slightly lighter red. He was wearing a thin blue sweater that matched his blue eyes and emphasized his broad shoulders. I hadn't really looked at men since Dave and I had split up, but I found myself enjoying talking to him.

Then he asked Gwen a question about the evening's agenda, and they got into a detailed discussion about the meeting. I left them to find a seat.

I noticed the Asian woman who lived in the apartment next door to me. I smiled at her and said hello, but she just ignored me. I looked about the room for someone familiar.

Dave's colleague, Cara, was just coming in. She had been friendly enough. I intercepted her near the door.

"Hi. It's Cara, right. We didn't get much of a chance to talk when we met. I just moved into 505. What unit do you live in?"

"Why do you need to know that?" Her voice was sweet and she was smiling, but it didn't seem a friendly smile. "Want to keep tabs on Dave? Really, Rebecca, you have to give up on him. He's not coming back to you, no matter what you think."

I was stunned into silence for a moment. Then I could feel my face flush. "I think you might want to ask Dave about who left whom," I said, trying to keep my voice calm, "and you might want to ask him why."

I turned away from her and saw my neighbor, Mariana, just taking one of the chairs. She gestured to me to join her, and I sank gratefully into the folding metal chair beside her.

"How are you doing?" I asked. "No ill effects from the yard work? I was worried we'd tired you out doing all that raking. And having that man yelling at us was certainly unpleasant."

38

"I'm fine," she assured me. "I'm just sometimes surprised I can't do as much as I used to. I guess I'm getting old. And we're all used to Aaron. It's just that I thought . . . but it's been a while. I really hoped . . ." She shrugged and her voice trailed off. "How about you?" she asked, shifting in her seat. "Are you settling in okay?" she asked. "Meeting the other members?'

"I was trying to talk to our neighbor," I said, indicating the woman who lived on the other side of us. "But she always just ignores me. Doesn't she speak English?"

"Oh, Naomi speaks English as well as you or me. It's just that she's mad at you."

I looked at her in surprise. "I've barely spoken to her . . . just to try and introduce myself. What could I have done?"

"Oh, not you specifically. She would have been upset at any-one who moved in. Her daughter applied to move into the co-op. Naomi thought it'd be really convenient if she could move in next door. Naomi looks after her granddaughter a lot. But it's just her daughter and the little girl. They need a two-bedroom. They wouldn't have got that apartment, even if you hadn't moved in. Naomi should get over it. I'm sure a two-bedroom will be available soon."

"But couldn't they have moved in anyway, even if the apartment was too big, to be close to Naomi?"

"Oh, the co-op's quite fussy about that. Because the housing is government subsidized, they try to make the most of it. Even long-time members are supposed to move to a smaller unit if their children leave home. I'm in a three-bedroom myself. But I think I told you my son and his family are planning on moving back to Vancouver. They'll be living with me, for a while anyway, so Les isn't pressuring me to move."

I remembered reading about that in the occupancy agree-ment I'd looked at before the meeting. There was a section on over or under-housing, explaining what Les had been talking about when he told me that we "qualified" for a three-bedroom apartment. You were over-housed if you had fewer people living there than bedrooms in the apartment, under-housed if there were more people than bedrooms. The policy explained that the co-op would try to house people in an apartment of an appropriate size.

"Well, I guess the policy makes sense," I said, "but I don't understand why Naomi is so mad at me." The president called the meeting to order just then, so I didn't get an answer, but I vowed to make friends with my neighbor.

Les had joined Gwen and Jeremy at the table at the front of the room. They started by briefly introducing me as a new member. A few people smiled at me but others just looked at me blankly. From what Les had said, I had expected a friendlier group. But I was starting to realize that this wasn't quite the community Les had promised.

There was a printed agenda, but Gwen asked if anyone had any other business to add. Several people put up their hands, but she called on Cara first.

"I'd like to talk about getting a dog," Cara said.

"The co-op allows one pet per household," Gwen said. "You can have one if you don't already have a pet. We don't need to discuss it."

"But, I do. I already have a cat. But my daughter wants a dog now."

"Well, that would be against the co-op's policy," the president replied patiently.

"I just want to talk about it," Cara said, her voice trembling a little. "Can't we just put it on the agenda?"

I saw Jeremy lean over to Gwen and say something to her softly.

"All right," she said, sighing loudly. "I'll add it to the agenda."

Several other people said they had announcements about community events they wanted to make at the end of the meeting. They were added to the list, and then Gwen moved into the meeting agenda.

After approving the minutes, the financial statements, and other routine business, we reached an item called "parking issues" on the agenda. Les got to his feet.

"This isn't an item I'd normally talk about in a meeting," he began. "But I've tried to deal with this issue with the member, without reaching a solution. I thought it might help to bring it up here. It's about the motor home."

The man I had seen coming out of the motor home jumped to his feet. I hadn't noticed him sitting a few rows in front of me.

"This is completely inappropriate," he shouted. "I told you I'm going to move it. I've told you over and over again."

"Aaron, you keep saying you're going to move it, but it's still here. It's too big to leave on the street in front of the building. It takes up too much space. We've had complaints from the neighbors. And now it's in the parking garage where it's blocking other members' parking spaces. I've tried to explain the problem to you, Aaron, but you don't seem to listen. I thought it might be helpful for you to hear from some of the other members."

There were nervous mutterings from some of the members, but no one spoke up.

"See," the man screamed, pointing his finger at Les. "No one else minds if I park there. It's just you setting up rules like a little dictator. I've told you and told you that my son wants to use the motor home on some land he has. It'll be great for us to use in the summer. He'll move it later on. It doesn't seem to be bothering anyone else."

The man sitting next to him touched Aaron's arm and said something to him. But Aaron ignored him. He was spitting as he yelled at Les. He kept shaking his fist at the manager. If he had been standing closer, I'm sure he would have punched him.

Everyone in the room was sitting in silence. I guessed they were either too shocked or too afraid to say anything. Gwen coughed nervously but didn't intervene.

I hadn't planned on saying much at my first meeting. I had wanted to get used to the co-op and understand the issues before taking an active part in the meetings. And I didn't really want to take on the large, angry, red-faced man. But his tirade against the manager seemed out of line.

I raised my hand a bit and got to my feet.

"Um," I started. Very eloquent start to my first co-op speech. "Um, hi. I'm Rebecca. As you know, I just moved in. And, the thing is, I can't use my parking spot. The motor home takes up half of it and my car won't fit. I don't know much about how the co-op works but it seems to me that I should be able to park in my spot."

I sat down, my legs shaking. Mariana reached over and patted my hand.

"Nicely done," she whispered.

The man had turned to glare at me when I got up. Now he started yelling at me.

"You!" he shouted. "We all know whose side you're on. And we know why!"

"That's quite enough, Aaron," Gwen interrupted. I wondered why she hadn't said anything before. Surely, verbally abusing the staff of the co-op was unusual. But the co-op members were acting like this went on all the time. Most of them looked uncomfortable, but no one looked as shocked as I was at the man's behavior.

"I've had enough of this," Aaron said. He pushed past the other people in his row and left the room. The man who had sat beside him—a short, thin man with wispy blond hair—got up and hurried after him. Gwen sighed again.

"The co-op policies are quite clear on what size of vehicle the parking garage can handle. We've heard from Aaron and Rebecca. Does anyone else have any comments they want to make?"

Now that Aaron had left the room, the other members were much more outspoken. Several expressed outrage that the motor home had been around for so long. Anna, the young woman with the cute baby, got to her feet.

"I think the co-op should send a letter to Aaron telling him to remove the motor home by the end of the week. And we should have it towed if he doesn't." There were mutters of agreement.

"Do you want to make that a motion?" Gwen asked.

"Uh, would my name have to be in the minutes?" Anna asked in a soft voice.

Gwen sighed again.

"That's generally how we handle motions."

"Then no."

I was starting to get the picture here.

"Is it always like this?" I whispered to Mariana.

"Pretty much," she whispered back. "Some people know how to get their own way, either through bullying or making emotional appeals. Most of us just want to live here without any trouble, so we just try to avoid conflict, whatever the rules say."

"But doesn't that cause problems?"

Mariana smiled. "Yes, that can cause problems."

I raised my hand.

CHAPTER
Six

"I'll make the motion," I said. This wasn't how I'd planned on introducing myself to the co-op. I'd planned on feeling my way around, getting to know a few people, maybe joining a committee, making friends with my neighbors. This felt a lot like warfare.

But I wasn't inclined to let a bully get his way by shouting and intimidating his neighbors. And besides, I needed my parking spot.

I was pleased when Jeremy seconded the motion.

After asking if anyone else wanted to say anything, Gwen asked for a vote.

"All in favor?" Quite a few hands went up.

"Opposed?" No one raised their hands. The co-op members might not want to stand up to Aaron, but they didn't support him either.

"Motion carried," Gwen announced. Turning to Les, she asked, "Can you draft a letter to him? I can sign it tomorrow. Next on the agenda is Cara's request to add a dog to her household."

Cara stood up and smiled at the people in the room. "Well, it's just that my daughter saw this teacup poodle puppy she really wants. Her father's willing to buy it for her, but he doesn't want it to stay at his place. So I wondered if the co-op could bend the rules just a little." She smiled again. "She's just crazy about that little dog."

Gwen was doing a lot of sighing in this meeting.

"Cara, the rules are very clear. We allow only one pet per household. That's what the members voted on."

"But if the members voted for it, we could change our minds, right?"

Les leaned forward at the table. "There are procedures for how the co-op sets rules. If you want a change, there has to be proper notice given. And there would have to be good reasons to change the policy. But we could add it to the agenda at the next meeting, if you want to."

"But that's months away," Cara said, her voice shaking. "Are you saying my little girl can't have the pet she wants?"

"She already has a pet," Les replied. "You already have a cat."

I suspected Cara's daughter had lost interest in the cat when it stopped being a cute little kitten. The puppy would probably suffer the same fate. Maybe waiting until the next meeting would solve the problem.

But Cara wasn't giving up. "Are you asking me to give up my cat? I can't believe you'd do that." Tears spilled down her face. "What kind of a person are you?"

"No one's asking you to give up your cat," Gwen explained. "The rules just say you can't have a dog too."

"I can't believe you would be so mean to a small child." Cara was openly sobbing now. The woman next to her was patting her shoulder in a comforting way.

"I move that we let Cara have a dog and a cat," she said. "It's only a small dog, anyway."

I was surprised when Jeremy seconded the motion.

"All in favor?" Gwen said. Hands shot up.

"Opposed?" Mine was the only hand that went up. Mariana looked at me and shrugged.

"Did people just vote to break the pet policy because she cried?" I asked her quietly.

"Yes," she agreed. "As I said, you'll find that people can pretty much get their way with anything, if they approach the membership the right way."

"So none of the rules are really followed?"

"Les does his best to keep us on track. And Gwen does realize we have rules for a reason. But she doesn't like conflict. Sometimes it's just easier to go along with what people want. Then, when we realize there are too many pets in one small space and there are complaints, we'll have another meeting and vote to allow only one pet per household. We've been through this before."

The meeting ended shortly after that. The young woman named Anna hurried up to me.

"It's Rebecca, right? Welcome to the co-op. That was so cool the way you stood up to Aaron."

"I'm surprised people put up with that kind of behavior."

She laughed. "He yells a lot, and it can sound quite scary. People don't like to stand up to him. But I don't think he'd really be violent. Kevin can usually calm him down. He's a real sweetie. We all love Kevin."

Seeing my puzzled look, she went on. "The guy sitting next to him? That's his partner, Kevin. Kevin mostly comes to meetings. Aaron doesn't come all that often. But I guess he knew we were going to talk about the motor home. People are getting quite fed up with it. He had it in the parking garage before, and we had so much trouble getting our van around it. I hope he finally moves it."

She grinned at me. "Well, I should get Jordan home. But I'm really glad you moved in here, Rebecca. Maybe we could get together some time. I hear you have a little boy too."

"Yes, Ben is four," I answered.

"A bit too old for a play date with Jordan, then. But we could still get together, couldn't we? You could, you know, maybe answer some parenting questions if I need advice?"

"Sure, that'd be fun," I answered. Anna seemed so young. She couldn't have been more than nineteen or twenty, and possibly younger. But it would be fun to get together some time.

She hurried off and I looked around the room. Gwen and Jeremy were still at the front of the room, talking to Les. Mariana was chatting to some of the other members, so I headed home on my own. But as I was opening my door, I heard the elevator and saw Naomi getting off. I really wanted to make friends in the co-op. I felt like I was making a good start with Mariana and Anna, but it bothered me that Naomi seemed to dislike me for something really not my fault.

I hoped I could clear things up.

"Um, hi, Naomi," I started hesitantly. "Can we talk? We seem to have got off on the wrong foot, and I'd really like to be a good neighbor."

"I have nothing to say to you," she said. "I don't like your type."

"But you don't know me. I'm sorry your daughter didn't get this apartment, but I really didn't have anything to do with the decision."

"Well, my daughter wasn't willing to sleep with the manager!"

I was dumbfounded. "Of course not. Did someone suggest that? That'd be completely inappropriate."

"Well, that didn't stop you."

"What did you just say? Why would you even think that? I'd never sleep with Les to get an apartment, and I don't think he's the kind of man who would even suggest it."

47

"That's not what he said," she answered and slammed her door in my face.

I went into my apartment, but I couldn't help thinking about what Naomi had said. Had Les really implied I'd slept with him to get the apartment? Or had he propositioned Naomi's daughter, holding out the promise of the apartment if she agreed? Both seemed unlikely.

I wondered if Les or Gwen were still downstairs, clearing up after the meeting. Maybe they could explain why Naomi had said what she had. Or perhaps they could give me some advice on how to get along with my neighbor. I took the elevator back down to the office.

The meeting room was deserted. At first glance, I thought the office was closed, but then I saw that the door was slightly ajar. I pulled it open and peered in, calling Les's name.

I almost tripped over one of the storage boxes that had lined the wall of the office, waiting to be put into storage.

The boxes, which had been stacked neatly against the wall, providing some order in the chaotic office, were now scattered in piles around the room. It was as if some giant toddler had used them as building blocks and then had a tantrum, throwing the boxes around and piling them in random heaps.

I looked around the room, wondering if I could start piling the boxes back against the wall in some sort of order or if I should call someone to help.

What had happened here anyway?

Knowing Les's odd method of storing things in the office, maybe this was his idea of organizing things.

Then I noticed a pair of denim-clad legs sticking out from the largest pile. The legs were twisted at an odd angle, ending in a pair of scuffed brown suede shoes.

CHAPTER
Seven

I stood still for a moment, not quite believing what I was seeing. Then I grabbed one of the boxes and tried to shift it. The thing was heavier than it looked. I needed help.

I looked around for the office phone but couldn't see it anywhere. I started for the door when I remembered I still had my cell phone in my jacket pocket.

"Police, fire or ambulance?" the 911 dispatcher asked.

"I need an ambulance," I told her. "There's been an accident."

I gave the address, then ran down the hall to pound on the door I thought was Gwen's. "The office," I gasped when she answered the door, wiping her hands on a dishtowel. "I need help."

"Rebecca, what on earth . . . ?" But I was already running back down the hallway. Gwen followed. She still had the dishtowel in her hand when she got to the office, but she dropped it when she saw the legs under the pile of boxes.

"Oh, no, I think that's Les."

We were able to shift the heavy boxes together, lifting them off quickly and piling them to the side. But when we pulled the last box off him we could see that he wasn't moving and that blood was pooling around his head.

"Do you think someone broke in?" she asked. "There's stuff all over the place, but there usually is. All these boxes."

"Maybe he was trying to get something in one of the boxes, and they fell over," I said.

"I knew this office wasn't safe. I should have done something. But every time I brought up how cluttered the office was, Les would just say he was going to get to it soon. He had a million excuses. He was going to sort through the stuff and get rid of it; he just needed to get the storage room painted. Now look!"

"I called the ambulance, but we should probably do something."

Les was lying face down and I could see a huge wound on the back of his head. Blood stained the fringe of dark hair that circled his bald spot and trickled to the floor. I know head wounds could bleed heavily, even if they weren't serious. But this looked like a lot of blood. I picked up the dishtowel Gwen had dropped and pressed it against Les's head.

She shuddered. "All that blood."

I could hear Les taking raspy breaths. Then they were drowned out by the sound of an approaching ambulance, and I sighed with relief.

Gwen looked a bit greenish. "I'll go let them in."

I was relieved when the paramedics took charge, loading Les onto a stretcher and wheeling him out. They moved quickly, and I worried about the serious looks on their faces.

The elderly woman I'd seen at the meeting peeked out from the door of one of the ground floor units. She was wrapped in a bathrobe, and wisps of her hair stood up like she'd just woken up. She had a scared look on her face.

"We've had an accident, but everything's been taken care of," Gwen assured her. "You can go back to sleep."

Gwen still looked too pale.

"Do you want to go back to your place and sit down? You look a little shaky."

She shook her head.

"I guess we need to notify his family. They'll want to be with him."

"Does he have a wife and kids?"

"You know, I have no idea. Les has worked here for longer than I've lived here, but he never really talked about himself. We must have some contact information in the files," she said. "Can you help me look?"

The filing cabinets were unlocked. Gwen frowned at that. "These are supposed to be kept locked. Ruth usually handles the filing, but Les might have been looking for something," she said. "We just need to find the staff records."

We each took one of the file cabinets. I found a file marked PERSONNEL. I handed it to Gwen, and she started to leaf through the sheets of paper.

"Oh, here it is," she said with relief. "And he does have an emergency contact listed. Oh, that's odd." She looked up. "He's listed an emergency contact, but the person he's listed is Ruthie."

"He's related to Ruth?" I asked.

"Well, not that I knew, and that wouldn't really be appropriate. He supervises her work. But she was hired before I got on the Board, so I don't know. Maybe he just listed her because he doesn't have family nearby.

"Anyway, I guess I need to call her and let her know." She looked around the room. "It probably would be a good idea to clean up this mess, but I just can't handle it right now. I'll just lock up and we can deal with it tomorrow."

She was just locking the office door when I saw Mariana coming down the hallway.

"Did something happen?" she asked. "I heard a siren." Then she gasped. "Oh, my goodness, Rebecca, are you all right?" She hurried toward me.

I looked down to see what she was looking at. My pants and T-shirt were streaked with blood, and the palms of my hands were covered with it.

CHAPTER
Eight

I looked down at my hands in horror. "I . . . no, Les was the one who was hurt."

Gwen grimaced. "I think there was blood on the boxes we moved." She looked at her own hands and wiped them off on her jade green sweater, smearing it with small streaks of blood. "You were closer to him, trying to stop the bleeding." She gulped and looked for a moment like she was going to throw up. "I better call Ruthie," she muttered and hurried down the hall toward her apartment.

Mariana looked at me with concern. "Are you really all right?" she asked.

"I'm not hurt but it was a shock finding him like that."

"What happened? You said Les was hurt?"

"I don't know. Gwen seemed to think someone might have broken in. I suppose someone could have got in and thought there might be money in the office. But I don't know how you would tell if anything's missing. I think maybe the boxes fell on him."

I realized I was shaking.

"Oh, you poor thing," Mariana said, stepping toward me. She put a comforting arm around me and I leaned into her. Her scent was something powdery and floral, not the Chanel my mother had favored, but I was instantly reminded of the hugs my mother had given me whenever I was feeling down.

Great, I thought, *anything bad happens, and I want my mommy. When am I ever going to grow up enough that this stops happening? Probably never.*

"Let's get you home," Mariana was saying, steering me toward the elevator. It was comforting having her with me. "I could make you a cup of tea. That's always helpful after you've had a shock."

My dad opened the door when we reached my apartment. "That was a long meeting," he started to say, and then realized I was covered in blood. "Becky, what happened? My god, are you all right?"

"There was an accident in the office," Mariana was saying.

"I'm fine, Dad," I said, interrupting her. I remembered my manners enough to introduce her to my father.

"I live next door," Mariana explained. "I was going to make her some tea."

"Oh, Mariana, thanks, but I'm okay. I just want to have a shower and go to bed. Thanks for looking after me."

Dad put his arm around me and pulled me into the apartment, thanking her before closing the door.

I leaned against him. Even if I couldn't have my mom, I still had my daddy. That would do.

I headed for the bathroom and started the shower. I stripped my clothes off, knowing I would never wear them again. I could probably wash them and get the blood out but just thinking about it made me shudder.

Actually, everything was making me shudder. I was shaking uncontrollably. I got into the shower and scrubbed myself until my skin was red. I knew everyone tried to avoid blood because of fear of disease. But I wasn't really thinking of that.

I was pretty sure that, despite my first aid and the care of the paramedics, Les wasn't coming back.

I went to bed after that, but I kept replaying the scene in the office over in my mind. I was still wide awake when the phone beside my bed rang. I grabbed it before the sound could wake up Dad and Ben. It was Gwen.

"Oh, Rebecca. It's awful. Ruth called to tell me Les didn't make it."

I felt tears in my eyes. "I'm so sorry. He was such a nice man. Maybe if I'd found him a bit sooner."

"Don't even think that," Gwen interrupted me. "You did everything you could. But that's not why I'm calling. There's a police officer here. He wants to talk to us about what happened."

"A police officer? But wasn't it an accident?"

"Well, remember that I thought at first someone might have got into the building. I suppose Les could have found someone breaking into the office and they pushed the boxes on him to get away. Anyway, he told me they investigate any sudden deaths that aren't expected. I'm sure it's just a formality. But they should be able to tell if someone broke in. He just wants to talk to us about what we saw."

I got dressed and went down to the main floor again. I gulped when I saw the boxes, Les's blood staining some of them.

The officer with Gwen looked young to me. He took statements from both of us.

"So you found him?" he asked me. "You were the one who made the call for the ambulance. I believe you said it was an accident?"

"That's what I thought. The office has boxes piled all over it. I thought they'd fallen on him."

"But you thought someone might have broken in?" he said, turning to Gwen. "Is anything missing?"

"Who could tell?" she said, gesturing to the mess. "It's always complete chaos. We keep some petty cash in here but not a lot. I could check the files to see if it's still there. But Ruthie would probably know more than I do. She's the one who handles the bookkeeping. That's Ruth Jacobs, the office assistant."

He checked his notes. "Ah, yes. We talked to her at the hospital. I have her contact information."

"She would normally be here tomorrow at nine o'clock," Gwen continued. "But when she phoned about Les she asked for a couple of days off. I think she's some sort of relation, but I don't know what."

"That's okay," the officer said. "We won't want anyone going into the office until we've finished our investigation. I'll seal it up after I leave."

"So you *do* think someone broke in?" Gwen was saying. "This is a nice neighborhood, but I know there have been break-ins in the area. And sometimes homeless people get in, looking for a place to sleep."

I thought of the woman who had warned me about the co-op the first day I came here. She had been right that bad things happened here.

"Was the lock damaged?" I asked. "Here or the front door? How would someone get in?"

"Well, Les wouldn't have locked the office door if he was working. And the front door, well, we were having trouble with the intercom, so sometimes people just buzz people in if they're expecting someone. I think Les had it fixed, but maybe it's broken again. Or people will prop it open if they're just going out for a minute. They're not supposed to, but it happens."

"We'll look into that," the officer was saying. "So you two were both in here tonight?"

We answered a few more questions before he left. He seemed to be asking a lot of questions for something I still hoped was an accident.

CHAPTER
Nine

I don't think Les's death really hit me until the next morning. I had barely known him, but he had been considerate and helpful to me. And he seemed such a dedicated employee. It would be a real loss to the co-op.

I'd taken Ben to pre-school and had come back to do some work in my home office. I had a couple of assignments to complete for two of my corporate clients. One had asked me to draft their annual report from material they had given me. The reports they had asked me to use were full of jargon and odd bureaucratic phrases that might have meant something to the staff members who wrote them, but not to anyone else. They were hard to read, but I enjoyed the challenge of trying to keep the meaning, while turning the language into something a layperson would understand. The other assignment was a bit more fun—a couple of articles for an employee newsletter.

Not exactly the investigative stories I had wanted to do when I started journalism school. But the work paid the bills and I still took satisfaction from turning a bit of jargony nonsense into prose that anyone could understand.

I hadn't completed as much as I had planned, thanks to all the disruption of moving. So I settled down to finish as much as possible before it was time to pick up Ben from pre-school.

I was so deeply into my editing work on the annual report that it took me a moment to realize someone was knocking on the apartment door. Glancing at my watch, I saw that I'd been sitting at my keyboard for over three hours. *Good time for a break*, I thought, heading to open the door.

I was pleased to see Mariana and even more pleased to smell the scent of warm chocolate. She was holding a plate of cookies. "I was doing some baking and thought you might like these," she said, "or at least I thought your little boy would."

"I think we'll all like them," I said. "They smell wonderful."

"Good. Are you doing all right? I know last night must have been rough."

"It was," I admitted. "But worse for Les. What a terrible thing to have happened. You heard he didn't make it?" She nodded. "Look," I said, "would you like to come in? I could make some tea."

"If you're sure I'm not interrupting. Some of us do tend to drop into each other's homes all the time, but I'm sure you have lots to do."

"Well, I'm ready for a cup of tea, and I'd love to have your company. I really appreciated your help last night. I was pretty upset."

"I can imagine how awful it must have been." She followed me into the living room. "Oh, this is charming. It's funny; most of the units have the same layout, but everyone decorates them differently, so they each look different. That loveseat looks like it was made for this room."

"Hardly. We're not in the custom furniture income bracket. But I was glad it fit so well. And the bookcase is exactly the right length for the wall. That was lucky. They're both fairly new. My mother bought them when she and my dad sold their house and moved into a townhouse. Their old furniture was too big for the new place."

Seeing her questioning look, I said, "She died last year." I felt tears gathering in my eyes again and quickly changed the subject. "I'll just get the tea on. And let me unwrap these lovely cookies."

Mariana had brought the cookies over on a plate covered with a linen tea towel. I thought for a moment about the towel I had pressed to the wound on Les's head and shuddered.

"Gorgeous plate," I said, as I removed the covering. The plate was made of delicate china and the soft pink and blue flowers looked hand-painted.

"It was my grandmother's," she said. "I inherited her china and some of her other things."

"Then let me put these on one of my plates and give this back to you," I said quickly. "Ben's a good kid, and pretty careful with things. But you know a four-year-old and a kitten are just not a good fit with family heirlooms."

As if on cue, Maui came trotting into the living room. His nose twitched at all the unfamiliar smells—Mariana's perfume, the cookies, the still-new smell of the co-op apartment.

"What a sweet kitten," Mariana said, holding out her hand toward Maui. He backed away.

"He's pretty shy around strangers," I said. "He usually hides when people come over. He and Ben are good buddies, though. My two babies."

I put the tea and cups on the low coffee table in the living room and went back for the plate of cookies.

"Is Ben with his father today?" she asked casually. "Or out with your father?"

Aha, I thought, *I see the reason for the cookies*. Mariana was about my father's age. And my father was very good-looking, with a full head of silver hair and very dark eyes. Despite his arthritis, he was still pretty fit. Several of the women in our old townhouse complex had seemed to be interested.

"Ben goes to pre-school a couple of days a week," I answered. "And Dad has gone to the pool at the community center. Swimming is one of the exercises he can do even when his arthritis is bad. It's nice to have a pool so close."

"Oh, it is," Mariana agreed. "That's one of the things I love about this neighborhood. I'm often down at the community center to use the library. I've been working out at the fitness center too. And I love the pool. I'm there a lot. Maybe I'll run into your father there sometime. I like to keep fit."

Looking at her comfortably rounded body, I questioned her fitness level. But I was willing to bet Dad was going to run into Mariana at the community center a lot. I didn't think that he was over my mother yet. But there was no denying Mariana was a lively, fun woman. And she was pretty. Her round face had very few wrinkles, and her dark hair, though obviously dyed, was shiny and thick. Her dark eyes were warm and friendly.

The outfit she wore seemed too elegant for visiting neighbors. Today she was dressed in a slim, long cotton dress in green, with a darker cardigan. Sandals in a soft, dark-brown leather completed the look. Hardly the outfit I would have chosen to bake in, if I even owned such a pretty dress.

I wondered if the gorgeous outfit was for my father's benefit, or if she just dressed beautifully all the time.

Mariana's green sweater reminded me of Gwen's last night. I shuddered again as I remembered her wiping her bloody hands on that sweater. I was willing to bet she would never wear it again. I had thrown my own bloodstained clothes in the garbage as soon as I could strip them off. I hoped the blood hadn't transferred to Mariana's clothes when she comforted me.

I was just pouring the tea when someone else knocked on the door. Because the outside buzzer hadn't rung, I was expecting it to be Gwen or someone else from the co-op. I pulled open the door with a smile on my face.

I'd never before seen the man at my door, but he was certainly pleasant to look at. Black hair, cut well enough to show just a hint of wave. Olive skin that had spent time in the sun this summer. A strong nose that wouldn't have looked out of place on an ancient statue. Cheekbones to die for. And golden eyes like an eagle.

He was wearing a beautiful gray suit, unusual in this casual co-op. It stretched over his broad shoulders but didn't hang loose on his slim torso. I wasn't much of a judge of men's clothing but the suit looked made for him. Or maybe he was just the perfect size.

Well, if the co-op has guys that look like this, I might start dressing up too, I thought. I looked up at him.

"Rebecca Butler?" he asked. I nodded, still smiling.

That was before I noticed that the young police officer I'd met last night was standing behind him. And that the man I'd been ogling was holding police identification in front of my face.

"I'm Sergeant D'Onofrio. I just have a few questions I wanted to ask you."

"About Les? Sure. And this is my neighbor, Mariana Cole. She was there last night too."

"Yes, I have you on the list," he said to her. "But I'd like to interview you separately."

"Oh, sure," Mariana said, standing up. "I just live next door. Come over when you're ready."

The officers declined the tea I offered them but did sit down so they weren't towering over me.

"You and Ms. Gwendolyn Arsenault found Mr. Walter?" D'Onofrio began.

"Mr. Walter? Oh, Les. I didn't know his last name. I've just moved in to this building a little while ago. No, I found him. I went to get Gwen after I'd called 911."

"I gather you told the emergency dispatcher that there had been an accident. You asked for an ambulance but not police. Can you tell me why you thought it was an accident?"

"Well, I just assumed. The office's been a mess every time I saw it. I just thought the boxes had fallen when Les tried to get something out of them or move them."

"And yet, when Ms. Arsenault came into the office, she thought that there had been a break-in or that someone had been in the office. Do you know why that was?"

"Gwen did say that. I guess there had been some incidents in the past. I didn't know about them. As I said, I'm new to the building."

"I've been told that Mr. Walter was instrumental in helping you move into the building. Yet you say you didn't know him." D'Onofrio was frowning.

"Well, he was the person who took my application and showed me around the apartment. He seemed like a good manager who really cared about the co-op. And he was always willing to be helpful."

"I've also been told he gave you preferential treatment for this apartment and a parking space."

I frowned. "No. I've been on the waiting list for a year. And then my father needed a wheelchair-accessible apartment. We were lucky to get this place. But the only other family I've heard about was smaller and didn't need wheelchair access. I guess there must have been others. But I'm sure the process was fair."

"And the parking space?" D'Onofrio asked.

"I don't know. A parking spot in the underground garage comes with the apartment. Les mentioned something about wanting it to be convenient for my father's wheelchair. I don't know if anyone else wanted that spot. I certainly didn't ask for any particular parking spot."

"So you're saying there wasn't any particular relationship between you and Mr. Walter?" he continued.

"Yes, that's what I'm saying. I just met the man. I know he listed the office assistant as a contact in his personnel file but I don't know what their relationship is."

He glanced at his notebook. "Did you notice if Ms. Arsenault had blood on her clothing when you went to get her?"

"When I went to get her? No, of course not. Surely you don't suspect she had anything to do with this."

I remembered Gwen wiping her bloody hands on the sleeves of her sweater. But that had been later, after we'd been trying to help Les.

D'Onofrio's golden eyes looked at me the way I imagined an eagle might look at his prey. "And Ms. Cole? Did she appear to have blood on her clothing?"

"I don't think so." I remembered Mariana hugging me in the hall. "Well, maybe from me. I got some blood on my clothes when I tried to give Les first aid."

"Yes, I gather, Ms. Butler, that you were completely covered in blood."

I gulped. "There . . . there was a lot of blood. Head wounds seem to bleed a lot. Anyway, I was trying to stop the bleeding before the ambulance got there. Gwen had a tea towel. I think she was doing dishes when I went to get her. I used it to try to stop the bleeding. I don't know what happened to it."

"We'll find it if it's still in the office. What happened to the clothes you were wearing that night?" he asked.

"I . . . I threw them out. They were covered in blood." I could feel tears gathering in my eyes. "I never wanted to see them again. Even if I'd washed them, I'd always think about Les."

I thought I saw a glimpse of sympathy in his eyes. But he went on. "And these clothes, you put them where?

"In the dumpster out back." He wrote something in his notebook. "They might still be in there. I don't know when the garbage gets collected."

He made another note in his book and looked at me again.

"Can you tell me why you were in the office so late at night?"

I could feel myself blushing. "Um, I wanted to ask Les something. And it wasn't really late. The co-op meeting had just finished."

"Is it true that you had gone down to talk to Mr. Walter because you had just heard that the co-op members believed that you had used sexual favors to get your apartment?"

Sexual favors? That sounded oddly quaint. I might have laughed if I hadn't been so embarrassed. I could feel my face getting even redder. "I don't know what *all* the co-op members believe. But, yes, Naomi, my neighbor, told me she had heard that. It was nonsense, of course."

"And I believe she told you she had heard this from Mr. Walter. And you wanted to confront him about it."

The word "confront" caught me. "No." I could hear my voice shaking. "I just wanted to ask him what he'd heard and to talk to him about it. I'm starting to get the impression there are problems in this co-op. I don't know how that rumor started. But I don't think it was Les. He was a nice man."

There were tears in my eyes now. Ever since my mother died, I found I was much more emotional than usual. A symptom of grief, I suppose. And sometimes, if I started to cry, I found it hard to stop. I didn't want to lose it in front of this police officer.

The golden eyes regarded me with what looked like suspicion. "You seem very upset about someone you didn't know very well."

"I found him. I don't know about you, but I don't see dead bodies every day."

I wasn't sure what to think about the look he gave me. "We'll want you to come in to make a formal statement," he said, "and we'll need to take your fingerprints so we can compare them to the others we found."

We made arrangements for me to go to the station in the morning. I was sure the fingerprint ink would be black, not blood red, but I couldn't help feeling that, for some time to come, my hands and my memories would be stained with the effect of Les's death.

CHAPTER
Ten

Ben had pre-school again the next day, and it was mid-morning by the time I'd dropped him off, done some shopping, and made it back to the co-op.

I saw Gwen at the door of her apartment and stopped to ask how she was doing. The loss of the co-op's manager was going to put quite a burden on the president.

Her eyes were a little red, and she looked pale. But I was relieved to see that she smiled at me in friendly greeting.

"I'm all right, Rebecca," she answered. "I was just so upset about Les. Now I'm the president of a co-op without a manager. I just don't know what to do."

I saw that she had a couple of large cardboard boxes on her dining table, with papers and file folders scattered across the table surface.

She glanced at them too.

"I'm trying to get some co-op work done. There are probably more important things I should be doing. The co-op has bills to pay, and we'll have to keep track of who has paid their housing charges. I hope Ruth can handle some of that. But I'm trying to get this done. It's some work on the co-op's history. I started this before Les died. He kept talking about putting together a history of the co-op. He wanted to do it, but he never had time. So I offered to take it on. And now I'm thinking I could make it a sort of a memorial for him. But I just don't know where to start."

I could see tears in her eyes again.

"Listen, Gwen. Would you like me to help? This is the kind of thing I do. I mean I'm a writer, and I used to be a reporter. I'm pretty good at pulling together a jumble of information and writing something that's easy to understand. I'd be happy to go through that stuff and see what I can do with it."

She smiled in relief. "Would you? Even if you could just sort it out, that'd be a big help. I just have these two boxes. There are probably lots of others that need to be gone through. But if you could just start with these, that'd help. And if you're willing to sort out the others and actually write the history, it'd be marvellous."

She started shuffling the papers on the table and dumping them in the boxes, as if she couldn't get rid of them fast enough.

When she had filled the first box, she handed it to me.

"One is probably enough for you to carry," she said. "When you get through that, you can come back for the other one. I can't tell you how glad I am to get rid of this, Rebecca. Whatever you can do will be appreciated. I know there are more files," she added. "I did ask Ruth to look for them. But they're just a bunch of old pictures and files from the co-op's past. The co-op's financial statements are more pressing. Anyway, thanks for taking this on. Let me know if you find anything you don't understand."

I was starting to realize there were many things about the co-op I didn't understand. I hoped these boxes would help me understand the tensions in the building better. If someone was pointing the finger at me for Les's death, I wanted to be prepared. Finding out what was going on in the co-op seemed a good first step.

As soon as I got home, I wanted to upend the box that Gwen had given me and just root through everything. But I knew it was best to sort things first. From what I had seen in Gwen's apartment, there were old photos and written documents. I could put the photos in one file, maybe sorted by date or subject, and sort through the written documents. I didn't know what I'd find, but I thought it best to get it in some order.

Of course that was easier said than done. I glanced at the backs of pictures to see if anyone had noted dates or the people in the photos. Few had any kind of identification. I found myself looking at them curiously, wondering if I would recognize anyone.

Some of the pictures were cute, showing kids in the playground or dressed up for a Halloween party. I glanced at each of them, trying to put them in order of date, based on the clothes and hairstyles of the people in the picture. It was easy to recognize the shoulder pads and big hair from the 1980s. Later pictures showed bangs flipped up and lots of leggings. Even if the files didn't help me understand what had happened to Les or what was going on in the co-op, I'd enjoy finding out about its history. This was going to be fun.

The piles of old meeting minutes were easy to put in order. Most of them had the date on them, although not all, I noticed. The minute taking at meetings was sometimes pretty casual, particularly for committee meetings.

There were other documents—lists of members from different years, newsletters, and other notes. I couldn't really see any pattern to them.

Near the bottom of the box I found something different.

It was a file folder with a single newspaper clipping, faded, yellowed and tattered. It was dated twenty years earlier. It showed pictures of two young girls. Another picture showed the co-op, the trees in front of it much smaller than they were today.

And a headline.

"Hope Fades for Finding Missing Girls Alive."

CHAPTER
Eleven

I read the story quickly. Two fifteen-year-old girls, Jessica Anderson and Amy Cole, had been missing for a month when the story was written. Amy had lived in the co-op, and Jessica, a school friend, had visited her that afternoon. The last place they had been seen was the co-op.

The pictures the newspaper had used were probably school photos. The two looked heartbreakingly happy. Jessica's face was covered in freckles. Her smile glinted with the silver of braces, and her long blond hair framed a face still chubby with baby fat. Amy looked like a sprite, with short dark curls and a heart-shaped face.

I shuffled through the remaining papers in the box but there were no other newspaper clippings. Some of the other papers seemed to be from the same time. I glanced through them quickly to see if there was more information about the missing girls but there was nothing.

I grabbed the phone on my desk to ask Gwen if I could pick up the other box she had. But I got her voicemail. It was too late for Ruth to be in the office, so I couldn't check there for more boxes.

I switched on my computer to see if I could learn anything else on the web. The search was as frustrating as the one through the papers in the box.

The newspaper's site yielded nothing.

I found a site that claimed to be a list of missing people and unsolved murders in Canada. But it seemed to be completely unofficial and run by a volunteer. The names of the two girls were not listed on the site.

Which could mean that they'd been found alive and safely returned home. They could have run away for some reason. Or they could have been murdered, with the case wrapped up and neatly solved. Or the guy who ran the site (I assumed it was a guy) might have simply missed this case.

I found a site that offered to sell me access to the archives of newspapers all over the world. A good idea, but not on my budget.

Oh, for the days when I had all the resources of a large daily newspaper at my fingertips.

Well, maybe I still did.

Glancing at my watch, I hoped I might be able to catch Dave in the newsroom.

"Hey, Bec, what's up," he said when I reached him. "I've only got a minute. I have to head out to the game soon."

"What's on tonight?" I asked.

"Geez, Rebecca," he laughed. "Hockey. You know, our national obsession? Canucks against Calgary? Don't you pay any attention to the sports pages?"

"Oh, sure," I answered. "Well, sometimes. I read your stuff, Dave. And I talk to Ben about what you're writing. All the time."

"Like my big feature in today's edition about the game tonight? I can tell that really grabbed your attention."

I laughed. "Okay, you got me. I didn't read it today. But seriously, Dave, you know I like your writing. You make hockey interesting even for someone who isn't a hockey nut. That's a pretty good skill."

And I did like hockey. Dave was a big fan, and I had sometimes gone with him to games. And I knew he hoped Ben could play when he was a little older. Dad quite often watched games on television. But I found I couldn't really get into watching games on our tiny television. And there was no way I could afford tickets to a game, not anymore.

"So, what's up, Bec," Dave was asking. "Are you buttering me up because you want something?"

Oops, busted. I quickly explained about the newspaper clipping I found and what I was looking for.

"So what's the story on this?" he asked. "You said the clipping was from twenty years ago, but there must be some reason you're asking about it now."

I told him why I was asking.

"Wait a minute. Is that building you live in the one where the guy died?" Les's death had received some media coverage, describing it only as "suspicious." I was surprised Dave hadn't realized it was our building. I thought Cara would have mentioned it.

"That's why I want to learn more about this disappearance. I doubt it's connected at all, but I was curious. Do you think you can help me?"

"Of course I'll help you, Bec. I don't have a lot of time before the game but I'll see what I can find out."

"I hope it's not too much trouble," I said. "I have no idea how much time it'd take to find this information. But it could be important."

"I'll let you know as soon as I find something out."

I started to read through the other papers, hoping I might have missed something about the girls' disappearance. I didn't see anything. But as I kept reading, I found myself getting drawn back in to the story of the co-op.

The meeting minutes seemed to show that co-op meetings had sometimes been as contentious as the one I attended but that other times the co-op members had pulled together to get things accomplished.

They had organized Christmas parties, with one of the older members dressing up as Santa Claus. They made sure that each of the children, particularly the ones from poorer families, got a gift. They had successfully dealt with city hall to get a traffic light installed at a nearby corner where there had been a lot of accidents. They had held work parties, much better attended than the one I went to, to clean up the garden or to install playground equipment.

Looking through the files, I began to see why Les had loved this co-op. There had been problems in the past, but the people who lived here had managed to work through them. They worked hard to make sure they were providing good, affordable housing. I had offered to take on the work of the co-op history for my own reasons, partly to help Gwen and partly to see if I could find anything related to Les' death. But I started to get excited about the project on its own merits. I hoped there was a way to help new members like me understand how and why the co-op had been built. To know what a debt we owed to the people who had started the co-op and kept it going.

Still, I was disappointed I couldn't find any more information on the missing girls. I had hoped there might be some hint in the minutes from that time. But maybe everyone then had known what was going on and were just trying to get on with the running of the co-op.

And the lack of organization in the files was frustrating. I sometimes found a series of minutes that ran consecutively for a while. But I couldn't see anything in them that was out of the ordinary. Then there were gaps where there didn't seem to be any minutes at all. Either they were missing, or the co-op was not meeting regularly. I hoped Gwen or Ruth could locate more files in the office. Maybe Ruth could help me with this project. She seemed more focused on the financial aspects of her job, but I thought she might like the idea of a tribute to Les.

I found a picture of him at a much younger age, with dark curls circling his face. He had been much older and balder when I knew him, but he still had a youthful air of enthusiasm and energy. In the photo, he was holding a certificate of thanks from the co-op, after working ten years as the co-op's manager. He was beaming, surrounded by co-op members. My eyes filled with tears.

I was so engrossed with the papers on my desk I jumped when the phone rang.

"Hi," Dave greeted me. "Just thought I'd call you before I left. I wasn't able to find what you were looking for yet. I'll try to get to it later."

I couldn't really blame him for my frustration. I know Dave took his work seriously and needed to be at the game. I tried Gwen's number again. Once again, there was no answer.

CHAPTER
Twelve

Les's memorial service took place on a Saturday. The day was sunny, but there was enough of an autumn chill in the air that I felt comfortable in my black suit.

I'd bought the suit about six years ago, before Ben was born. It was a classic cut that still worked. I paired the short, fitted jacket and slim skirt with a scoop-necked silver blouse and black heels.

I had originally bought the suit for work, but it was really too formal for the casual newsroom at the paper. And I'd soon become pregnant with Ben, so it hadn't gotten a lot of wear. The suit was perfect for some of my corporate clients and, of course, for funerals. I'd worn it to my mother's funeral too.

I hadn't known Les well, but I thought I should go to the memorial service.

"Sure," my father said, when I asked if he could look after Ben. "I guess most of the co-op will be going to the funeral, after he worked here for so long."

"I suppose so. I haven't met many of them, except at that awful meeting. But Mariana seems nice. Maybe I'll go next door and see if she's going."

She answered the door wearing a calf-length purple dress splashed with flowers in a darker shade. "Of course I'm going," she said in response to my question.

"I can use Dad's car today. Do you want a ride?"

When we met a few a minutes later outside our apartment doors, she was carrying another plate of cookies.

"Should I be bringing something?" I asked.

"Not at all. I just offered to help Ruthie out by bringing some food. I think she and her mother are doing most of the catering for the reception after the service."

That didn't sound like the sulky young woman I'd seen at the office. I hoped that Les would be given a good send-off.

As we were getting into the car in the parking garage, the elevator doors opened and Gwen hurried out.

The contrast between Gwen and Mariana couldn't have been greater. Whenever I had seen them before, they seemed to dress in similar styles, longer dresses and loose linen trousers in jewel colors. I thought that Mariana's dark purple dress was probably the most sombre thing in her closet. The dress emphasized her round figure, and her plump feet were crammed into low-heeled pumps that didn't give her any extra height. Her dark hair frizzed about her round face. But that face was smiling and I couldn't help smiling in return.

Gwen, in contrast, wore a tailored suit with a straight skirt. It was similar in style to mine but made mine look cheap. She towered over me in high black pumps.

"Are you going to Les's funeral?" I asked. "We were just leaving. Do you want a ride?"

She accepted with what looked like relief. "That would be very nice. I'm running a bit late."

I noticed she was carrying a large platter of something that looked like pastries. I helped Gwen settle the platter onto the back seat. She climbed in after it and gripped the platter firmly so that it wouldn't slide around. Mariana got into the front seat beside me and held her own plate of cookies on her lap. The car filled with smells of warm baking and the perfume the two women were wearing. I was becoming familiar with the sweet scent Mariana seemed to favor. Gwen's was a more sophisticated mix of rose and lavender, with a spicy note.

"Do you know if many people from the co-op will be coming to the funeral?" I asked.

"Well, everyone got a notice," Gwen answered. "I sent the email around myself because Ruth was taking some time off. And I posted the notice on the bulletin boards in the elevators and the laundry room. Jeremy phoned around to remind people. I hope people will come. Les worked for us a long time."

The church had an attached hall at the side for gatherings after the services. I parked in the lot near the hall.

"I'll just take these around to the hall kitchen," Gwen said as she got out of the car. "I could take yours too," she offered to Mariana. "I'll meet you inside."

The chapel was simply designed—lots of light wood and plain glass windows. The seats were fairly full, but Mariana and I found seats half way up the aisle. We saved a place for Gwen. As I looked around, I recognized quite a few people from the co-op.

"Looks like a good turnout," I said to Mariana. "Les would have been pleased."

"I don't see Aaron or Cara," she said, looking around. "I think they're both still upset about that last meeting."

"I just saw Kevin outside," Gwen said, sliding into the vacant seat beside me. "Aaron wasn't with him. But surely that last meeting wouldn't stop them from paying their respects at the funeral. I can't imagine they would be so petty. Les devoted himself to the co-op."

"I wonder if it's true that the police attend the funeral when they're investigating a murder?" Mariana asked, craning her neck. "I don't see those police officers. Did they tell you anything more about the death, Gwen?"

She shook her head. "I think they do consider it suspicious. I don't know if they think it was murder."

The police were still investigating. Gwen and I had been told that the coroner would be involved and that we would likely have to appear as witnesses if there was an inquest.

"I still think someone could have broken in, looking for something to steal," Gwen went on. "I can't think of any other explanation, if the police don't think it's an accident. It could have been one of the homeless people around the neighborhood."

"Speaking of homeless people," I said. "I had an odd encounter the day I first came to the co-op and I keep seeing the same person. Have you seen a woman . . . ?"

The sound of music interrupted me, and I didn't get a chance to ask about the homeless woman I had met. I recognized the opening strains of the protest song, *We Shall Overcome,* as Ruth came down the aisle. She was with a beautiful, dark-haired woman who looked so much like her I assumed it was her mother.

There was no coffin, just a large photo of Les at the front of the church, flanked by tall sprays of white and yellow flowers. Had Les's body been cremated? Or were the police still examining it? I wondered what kind of evidence they'd found about the death.

The service was short and simple. The minister, a tall, boxy woman in her late forties, spoke only briefly about Les. I learned he was originally from the United States but had been in Canada over forty years. I wondered if he had been one of the many young people who had fled to Canada to avoid the draft for the war in Vietnam. If so, he was older than I thought. My father had several friends who had come to Canada at that time. Les might have been close to retirement age. His death seemed even more cruel if that was the case. He should have been able to leave the co-op with a nice gift and plans for the future.

I gathered that Les hadn't been a particularly religious man. The minister's words about him were short and the chosen music was mostly folk songs or anthems from the civil rights movement, rather than hymns. But the solemn words of the service brought back memories of my mother's funeral and I felt tears gathering in my eyes. I tried to dry my eyes discretely with a tissue I found in my purse. Someone in the co-op had already been spreading rumors about my relationship with Les. I didn't want to add to them by sobbing through his funeral.

I was relieved when the service ended and we filed out of the church. Everyone had been invited to join the others for refreshments in the hall that adjoined the church.

Gwen slipped away from us as we left the church, whispering that she would meet us in the hall. Mariana and I looked around. Ruth and the woman I had guessed was her mother were surrounded by people. We could wait for a moment before paying our respects.

A long table had been set up with sandwiches and other food. At another table a group of women were pouring coffee and tea. "Let's get some coffee," Mariana suggested, moving over toward the table. I asked for tea and a smiling, gray-haired woman poured it into a beautiful china cup. I noticed she poured Mariana's coffee into another cup with a different pattern.

"What pretty cups," Mariana said, as the woman handed it to her.

"Well, we all had teacups we weren't using so we just donated them to the church to use for gatherings after the services," she replied. "It's so much nicer than using disposable cups, don't you think?"

"Oh, yes," Mariana said. "I remember my grandmother using a china service like this. I think she brought the tea service from England when she emigrated. She always set a beautiful table. It's lovely to use nice things and not just keep them in a cupboard, isn't it?"

Gwen joined us at that point, and I saw her give a questioning look to Mariana before asking for a cup of tea.

"How did you know Les?" I asked the woman at the tea table. No one else was lining up for tea or coffee, and the woman seemed willing to chat.

"Oh, I don't. Carol, of course, is a regular at the church," she said, waving her hand towards the woman I assumed was Ruth's mother. She was as tall as Ruth, with the same dark hair and oval face. "We wanted to help her and Ruth. They put together most of the food themselves but we helped where we could. They're such a nice family."

I thanked her for the tea, and we moved toward the center of the room. People were swarming around the food table but I wasn't really hungry.

"Hey, Gwen." Jeremy, the co-op's vice-president, had come up behind us. "I hear that Ruth put this whole thing together. Do you know if there was something going on between her and Les? I've heard all sorts of things. Some people are convinced she was in a relationship with him and other people think she was his daughter or his niece. Do you have any idea?"

"Perhaps she wanted to honor a co-worker who was kind to her," Gwen said sternly. "Excuse me. I see there's a bit of space around Ruth now. I really must go and give her my condolences." She headed across the room with Mariana. I was about to follow her when Jeremy stopped me.

"It's Rebecca, right? Sorry about that. She's right. I was being a complete ass."

I muttered some faint denial.

"No, really. It's just that I've only been on the board a little while. I'm still unsure about what we're supposed to be doing. If it was an accident, would the co-op be liable? That office was certainly a hazardous workplace. We kept talking to Les about cleaning it up."

I muttered something. I didn't have the faintest idea if the co-op could be held responsible for an office accident. But Jeremy just seemed to want an audience.

"Well, now we've lost our manager," he went on. "And there are all these rumors about him and Ruth. I don't know. If he hired a relative, we should have known that. And, if he was having an affair with his employee, then we should have done something about it. Either one would be wrong. But I don't really know what the board's responsibility is."

"You don't know if either of those things is true. So I wouldn't worry too much," I tried to reassure him. "Gwen seems to be a pretty competent woman. I'm sure she'll know what the board has to do. I guess the co-op will need to hire a new manager. But I don't think Les's funeral is the right place to discuss it."

"You're right. I'm being a jerk. Sorry about that. I'm not usually such an idiot." A dimple flashed in his cheek as he smiled. He really was very attractive. How much of a jerk he was had yet to be determined.

"Let's go over and say hello to Ruth," I suggested. Jeremy and I made our way over to the young woman. She had been surrounded by people earlier but now she was standing alone, looking a little lost.

"It's so nice to see so many people here to pay their respects to Les," I said, taking her hand. "I gather you organized it all."

"Well, Mom did. I helped, but I'm not really good at this sort of thing."

Up close, I got a chance to see how truly beautiful she was. Today her dark curls were piled up in a loose knot, with stray wisps framing her oval face. It was hard to imagine a romantic relationship between this willowy, beautiful young woman and the short, balding Les.

"There are lots of people from the co-op here," Jeremy said. "That's nice to see."

"Les really thought of the co-op as his home," Ruth said, looking around the room. "Most of the other people here are Mom's friends from the church. He didn't really have much of a life."

"He had you," I said. "You've obviously gone to a lot of trouble to arrange this service."

"Oh, sure," Ruth said. "We were close but he never really recovered after his wife died. Mom and I did what we could, but he just wasn't the same."

I looked at Jeremy and saw he had a puzzled expression on his face. He was still trying to figure out Ruth's relationship with Les.

Looking at him, Ruth frowned, then started to laugh.

"Oh, wait, you don't think . . . Oh, no, what have you heard? Oh, the co-op rumor mill! I don't think I'll ever get used to that. What are people saying? I suppose that I'm his mistress or his illegitimate daughter."

I think both Jeremy and I looked guilty.

"You know," Ruth went on, "Les was always so keen on the co-op that he didn't want to acknowledge that there were any problems, but . . ."

A new group of people came up to her then, wanting to talk to her. I wondered what she had been about to say.

CHAPTER
Thirteen

Jeremy shrugged as we moved away from the group around Ruth.

"Well, it doesn't sound like the rumors are true," he said. "She seemed to think the idea was pretty funny. And she had a pretty good idea about what those rumors would be. But we still don't know why Ruth was his emergency contact or why she organized the funeral."

"Friend? Co-worker?" I suggested. "It doesn't really matter unless there was something improper going on. And we don't know that there was. It's funny," I added. "Ruth always seemed a bit stunned when I talked to her in the office. But the funeral seems to be pretty well organized. I guess her mother did a lot of the work."

Jeremy was looking around the room. "It looks like people are starting to head out. I think I'm about ready too." He smiled at me and I felt myself responding in a way I hadn't in a long time. He was seriously good-looking.

"Hey, listen," he said. "Do you want to grab a coffee or something?"

I found that I really wanted to say yes. The idea of sitting down with a cup of coffee with an attractive man was very appealing.

"Oh, I'd like to. But I drove Mariana and Gwen here. I should see if they're ready to leave." He didn't suggest that we all go out for coffee. I hoped that meant he was interested in getting to know me and wasn't just interested in hashing out the co-op rumors or talking about plans to replace Les.

It really had been too long since I had even talked to a man I found attractive. I didn't want Jeremy to think I was brushing him off. Even if all he wanted was a friendly chat, I could use an ally in the co-op.

"But I'd love to get together with you. For coffee," I added hastily, hoping it all sounded like one sentence. "Are you free later this week?"

"I'd like that. I'll give you a call," he said. "Let's go find Mariana and Gwen."

The crowd was thinning out but, there were still quite a few people in the room. I saw Gwen's silver head for a moment and then lost sight of her when someone stepped in front of me. Mariana was short, and it was hard to see her in the crowd. Jeremy and I circled the room and eventually found Gwen, surrounded by a group of other co-op members.

"Well, I don't seem to be leaving right now after all," I said to Jeremy. "Looks like I have time for a coffee here."

We went to the refreshment table and then found two chairs at the edge of the room. Jeremy grinned at me.

"Not quite what I had in mind," he said. "But we are having coffee."

I smiled back. "How long have you lived in the co-op?"

"My son and I moved in two years ago after I got divorced but . . ."

Just then Gwen moved away from the group she'd been chatting with and headed towards us. I thought her feet might hurt in those high heels but she seemed untroubled by them.

"I just wanted to check if you thought we should be on our way," she said. "Have you seen Mariana?"

I noticed her over by one of the doors. I waved to her, and she walked over towards us.

"Whew," she said, pulling over a chair and slipping her shoes off. "It seems like I've been on my feet for hours."

"Imagine how poor Ruth must feel," Gwen agreed. "She's been talking to everyone. She must be exhausted."

"I saw you two had a chance to talk to her," Mariana said, nodding to Jeremy and me.

I hadn't seen Mariana when we were talking to Ruth but, as I said, she was hard to find in a crowd.

"I was wondering if you were ready to leave," I said. Mariana nodded, struggling to put her shoes back onto her swollen feet.

We were a subdued group as we said goodbye to Ruth and headed back to the co-op.

Gwen and Mariana both had to stop at the kitchen to pick up the plates they had brought. "I didn't even get a chance to taste the pastries and cookies you brought," I said. "They were gobbled up right away. They must have been delicious."

"I'll bring some over next time I make them," Mariana said with a sigh. "You know, Les was always very complimentary about my baking. I used to bring things down to the office sometimes. I'll really miss him."

Mariana offered the front seat to Gwen this time. "You need the leg room more than I do," she said, climbing into the back seat of the Toyota.

I glanced at the platter Gwen was holding on her lap. It was delicate china, with flowers painted around the rim and a cluster of blooms in the center.

"That looks valuable," I joked. "I'll have to make sure I drive carefully."

"Oh, it's mostly sentimental value," Gwen said. "It belonged to my grandmother."

"Oh, that's so nice that you both inherited china from your grandmothers," I said.

I thought Gwen frowned for a moment, but she answered quickly. "Yes, I like to use her things. They remind me of her."

I thought about the things I had that had belonged to my mother and how they reminded me of her. I felt the tears gathering in my eyes and quickly changed the subject.

"Les must have been a real force in the co-op," I said. "Jeremy was wondering what the board would do to replace him. But I guess today's a day to remember him, not to talk about his replacement."

"I don't even want to think about replacing him," Gwen said, her face wrinkled with sadness. "I don't know what the co-op's going to do."

"You know," I said. "The few times I met Ruth I admit I thought she seemed a bit clueless." Mariana giggled from the back seat. I glanced at her in the rear-view mirror. "I guess that sounds mean. Anyway, she seemed different today. She did a great job organizing the funeral. Maybe she could take on more responsibility."

"Well, it's worth thinking about," Gwen agreed. "It's something for the board to consider. I admit we've all thought she was a bit clueless too."

"At least she seems to be able to find things in that office," Mariana chimed in. "That's a plus." She smiled as she said it. Gwen and I returned weak grins. We were both thinking of the office covered with blood. I couldn't imagine Ruth would really want to work there again.

"We'll have to get someone in to clean the place up," Gwen said. "We can't expect Ruth to do it. Maybe the police can recommend a company that won't object to cleaning up blood stains."

We were silent for the rest of the ride home, lost in our thoughts about the death in our building. I doubted the co-op would ever feel the same.

I COULD HEAR VOICES as I put the key in the lock of my apartment door. I was surprised to find Sergeant D'Onofrio in the living room talking to my father. He rose when I came in, and I had to look up to talk to him. It was intimidating, but I felt a little jolt of something when I looked at those golden eyes of his. He was powerful, I thought, and not just physically.

As he looked down at me, I felt a little nervous. I'd always taught Ben that police were there to help us and he should call the police if he was in trouble. I should have felt good this man was trying to find out what had happened to Les. But I was suddenly worried about what he was going to say.

My father looked equally concerned.

"Sergeant D'Onofrio has been waiting for you, Becky," he said. "I told him I didn't think you'd be too long." As D'Onofrio glanced at my father, he added, "He says he needs to talk to you on your own, but I'll be just down the hall if you want me for anything. Ben's still napping, but he should be up soon."

"This shouldn't take long," D'Onofrio assured me as I looked towards Ben's room. "I just have a few more questions. On the night you found Mr. Walter in the office, did you notice a metal plaque? Did you happen to touch it?"

I thought back, trying to picture the office on that night.

"A plaque? No, I don't think so. I was focused on Les, and moving the boxes off him. I don't think I noticed much else in the room."

"So you don't remember moving a metal plate out of the way, maybe to help Mr. Walter? About this big?" He held his hands out, slightly less than a foot apart.

I thought about it. "No, I don't think so. But, as I said, that night was pretty much a blur."

He asked me a few more questions about what I had done that night, which I tried to answer.

"I understand you attended Mr. Walter's funeral today. It seems you appeared very upset during the service. Are you still saying you barely knew him?"

So the police did have someone at the funeral. I didn't think there had been time for them to have heard that through the co-op grapevine.

"Yes, that's what I'm saying. Are you still suggesting we had some kind of relationship?" I could feel my voice rising, but I knew he was just doing his job. "Look, to tell you the truth, I lost my mother last year, and funerals are still pretty rough to get through."

I thought I saw a look of sympathy on his face. But his next words were sharp. "It's always good to tell the truth to a police officer."

"It's good to tell the truth to anyone."

He asked me a few more questions before he left. Dad came out of his room as D'Onofrio was leaving, looking worried.

"How was the funeral, Becky?"

"About how you would expect a funeral to be. There were quite a few people from the co-op there. Ruth and her mother did a good job. But it was hard, Dad. I kept thinking about Mom."

"I think about her all the time, Becky. But, you know, she cared about you more than anything. She'd want us to be happy and for us both to get on with our lives. It's hard but I try to do it for her."

I leaned against him, tears in both our eyes. But I knew he was right.

"You know, Dad, I was wondering. Do you think we should consider moving? I mean, we don't know what happened to Les. Gwen thinks someone might have broken in. Do you think it's dangerous to live here?"

"Well, Becky. We don't know what happened to the manager. Maybe it was an accident. Or maybe it was something to do with him and what he was doing. We don't really know anything about the man. I can't imagine why anyone would want to kill him, but it could have been something in his past, or his relationships."

"But what if it wasn't? What if Gwen's right? What if it was someone who got into the building, trying to steal something? What if we're not safe here?"

"I don't know, Becky. This seems a pretty safe neighborhood. And the front door's kept locked. It'd be hard to get in, wouldn't it?"

"But it's not," I argued. "People prop the door open all the time, if they're bringing groceries in, or they're just taking the garbage out. They're not supposed to do that, but they do."

"Then maybe it's time for the co-op to follow the safety procedures they already have. I would think most people would be a bit more cautious now there's been a death in the building. And, you know, it might not have been murder. The police are treating it as a suspicious death, but they don't know quite what happened yet.

"Besides, it's been so much easier for me living here. It's made a real difference being able to get around on my own. I'm really glad you were able to find this place."

"But maybe I could find someplace similar. There are other co-ops around. Maybe we could get into one of them. I think I should see if we can move somewhere else."

"No!" I hadn't realized that Ben had woken up and been listening to our conversation. He came running into the living room, tears streaming down his face. "No, I don't want to move again. I like it here. I like having my own room like a big boy. I have friends here. We move too much!"

He was right. In his short life we had moved from the house I shared with his father to my Dad's townhouse, and now to the co-op. Each move had disrupted his life and changed his routines. And it was true he had made friends in the co-op. There were several little boys his age who he had met in the playground.

"It's all right, Ben," I reassured him. "Grandpa and I were just talking." Looking at my father, I shrugged. "It seems the men in my life have spoken. I guess we're not moving."

"I wouldn't worry, Becky," Dad said. "That D'Onofrio fellow seems like he knows what he's doing. I'm sure he'll figure it out."

He winked at me. "And if he doesn't, maybe you can solve the crime. You always were a big fan of Nancy Drew."

MUCH LATER, AFTER DINNER and Ben's bedtime, I had a chance to think about the questions D'Onofrio had asked. He was asking about a plaque. I didn't remember seeing anything like that the night Les had died.

But I did remember seeing something like that on the first day I visited the co-op. There had been a metal plaque celebrating the opening of the co-op. I had tripped over it and then moved it out of the way.

Was I a suspect? If that piece of metal had been involved in Les's death, were my fingerprints still on it?

CHAPTER
Fourteen

On Monday, I dropped Ben off at his pre-school. Dad was out, so I had the apartment to myself. I settled down at my desk to get some work done.

But I couldn't concentrate. I kept thinking about the questions D'Onofrio had asked about the plaque. I had assumed Les had been killed by the boxes falling on him. Could someone have hit Les with the plaque or some other weapon, and then toppled the boxes to make it look like an accident? Was it murder?

I would have to follow up with D'Onofrio, now that I'd remembered about the plaque.

As I picked up the phone to call him, I glanced out the window and saw the homeless woman pushing her cart down the street. I thought it was so sad that she treasured her odds and ends but had given away something that might have some value. I grabbed the pendant from the desk drawer. I had polished it and it looked quite lovely. The angel gleamed on the small oval pendant and the chain was clean. Surely she would want it back when she saw it. I grabbed my keys, slipped on some ballerina flats and headed outside.

But when I got to the front door, I couldn't see the woman on the street. Had she gone behind the co-op, looking for bottles in the garbage cans or recycling bins? Vancouver has a pretty good recycling program. But some people couldn't be bothered to return their bottles and cans for the small amount they could get for them. Local "binners" made money by retrieving the drink containers from garbage bins around the city.

I looked up and down the lane but didn't see the woman. The co-op's garbage bin blocked my view a bit, so I walked closer to it.

A china plate lay next to the bin, still smeared with a few streaks of something. The pretty ivory plate was rimmed in pale blue, with a scattering of flowers in pastels. It was similar to the china I had seen Gwen and Mariana use but the pattern seemed different.

What wasn't pretty was the very large black rat that scurried away as I came close to the garbage bin.

I shuddered at the sight of it.

Had someone been leaving food out for the homeless woman? Or were they feeding feral cats in the neighborhood? I'd even heard of people leaving food out for the raccoons that populated the neighborhood.

I didn't want to touch the plate if the rat had been eating from it. But I knew it wasn't responsible to just leave it in the lane, attracting more rats and other pests. I pulled a tissue from my pocket and used it to pick the plate up. I considered tossing the plate into the bin. But it was obviously worth something and probably belonged to someone in the co-op.

As I went back into the building, gingerly holding the plate with the tissue, I heard a sound from the office. I was surprised to see Ruth at her desk, working on her computer.

"I'm glad to see you're back," I said. "How are you doing?"

She looked up at me, her eyes a little unfocused, obviously still thinking about the work she had been doing.

"Oh, hi, Rebecca. To tell you the truth, I wasn't sure that I was coming back. But I wanted to finish the financial statements. And Gwen assured me she'd had the blood cleaned up."

I gulped as I remembered the way the office had looked the last time I had been here. Now it was tidy and clean. There were still lots of loose papers and files, but they were stacked neatly on one of the desks at the back of the room. The other desks were clear. And the large boxes that had lined the wall were gone. There didn't seem to be any signs of the blood that had covered the floor.

"It looks nice in here. They did a good job," I said.

Ruth shrugged. "I guess. I'm not sure I'll ever feel comfortable in here. But I feel like I owe it to Les to try to keep things together, at least until they hire a new manager. He helped me a lot."

I was dying to ask for more details about her relationship with Les. She had seemed kind of grumpy every time I was there, and not particularly good at her job. This dedication to helping the co-op didn't seem in character.

Seeing my face, she laughed. "Oh, yeah, I know this place. Once Gwen told the board Les had listed me as the contact on his personnel file, everyone started speculating about my relationship with him. Like I said at the funeral, I guess most people think I'm his illegitimate child or his mistress. Or both."

I smiled. As I had learned from Jeremy, the co-op rumor mill was very active on that topic. I was curious myself, but it didn't seem polite to pry.

"His wife was good friends with my mom. And we kept in touch after she died. So Les was almost like family. But that doesn't mean there was some kind of sneaky reason Les hired me.

"Don't they think I'm good at my job?" she asked suddenly. "Is that why everyone seems so suspicious about me and Les?"

I didn't know what to say. It was what people thought. I had thought that myself.

"Yeah, I can tell that's what they think," she went on, seeing the look on my face. "I know I'm not good with people. I couldn't be bothered with all that touchy-feely 'building community' stuff Les did. But I'm good with numbers. Les hired me as coordinator to help fix up the books and get the files in order. And I'm doing that. I've got the books totally straightened out, and I'm working on the filing system. Les knew he wasn't good at that. But he had the people skills. We made a pretty good team."

She sniffed.

"You wouldn't believe the files. Les just had stuff in piles, as you saw. But I'm finally getting everything in place." She smiled. "I feel like I almost know the co-op as well as Les did, after I've sorted through all those papers."

"I noticed that most of the boxes are gone," I said. "Did you file all that?"

"No, they're back in the storage room." She frowned. "At least some of them are. I think the police took some boxes. Or maybe the cleaners did? I hope the cleaners didn't get rid of them. I think a lot of that stuff can go, but I wanted to sort through it all. There were files going back to the beginning of the co-op. I'm sure there are some we should keep."

"Actually, I'm interested in some of the old files. I offered to help Gwen write a history of the co-op. But I've only looked through one box so far. Are there others I could take?"

"Sure," she said. "I can get them out of the storage room. But can it wait awhile? I want to look through them myself. Les was looking into something before he died. I know he was worried about something and was going through some of the files."

She sniffed again. "Do you have a tissue?"

I shook my head. I had picked up the plate using the only tissue I had. I realized I was still holding the plate.

She shrugged and wiped her nose with her hand. "I still get upset about Les. I'd known him since I was a little kid."

I held out the plate I had found in the alley. "Do you know if someone from the co-op is leaving food outside? I found this plate in the lane. I've seen a homeless woman around and wondered if someone was leaving food for her."

Ruth looked puzzled. "I've never heard of someone doing that. But, as I said, I don't pay much attention to what the people in the co-op are doing. Still, it seems pretty stupid to just leave a plate outside. Did you find it on the ground?"

I nodded.

"Maybe someone's feeding the feral cats that live around here. Or the raccoons? People think they're cute. But they really shouldn't. Raccoons are wild animals and the food could attract more of them. Or even coyotes. We sure don't want raccoons and coyotes hanging around the back where the kids play."

"It's already attracted a rat," I said. "That's bad enough."

"Yuck," Ruth said. "We sure don't need that. I'll ask Gwen about it. Maybe she'll know who it belongs to. It might be even be hers. I think she has china that looks like that. Or maybe Mariana. They're both always bringing food down to the office for us. It would be like them to feed a homeless person. But I don't think either of them would just leave a plate lying around in the lane. Leave it with me and I'll ask them."

"It's filthy," I said. "I'll just wash it off and bring it back. I think I hear someone coming to talk to you."

I thought I had heard footsteps approaching the office but the hallway was empty when I looked out. "Sorry, I guess I was hearing things," I said. "I'll be back later."

Back in my apartment, I filled the sink with soapy water and slid the plate in. Not wanting to take any chances, I added a splash of bleach. I left the plate to soak and went to the bathroom to wash my hands carefully. Seeing the rat had really creeped me out.

Looking at my watch, I realized it was time to pick Ben up at his preschool. I hadn't made much progress on the work I had planned for today. I'd have to get some work done once Ben was in bed.

Dad had taken the car so I needed to hurry to get to the preschool in time. When we got home, I found my father and Mariana in the front room.

"I ran into Mariana at the community center," he told me. "I was just leaving the pool when I saw her coming out of the library. So I offered her a ride home."

"I would have walked back if I knew he was going to offer me a glass of scotch when we got here," Mariana said, swirling some ice cubes in one of the crystal tumblers my mother had given to Dave and me as a wedding gift. "I could have burned off some calories in advance."

"Surely there can't be many calories in a glass of scotch," my father said.

I almost laughed out loud. Before he developed arthritis my father had been very active. He and my mother had spent a lot of time walking, cross-country skiing, and swimming. With his long, lean frame, he had never worried much about his weight. And he still spent as much time swimming and walking as he could.

My mother had been very petite and I don't remember her ever talking about dieting.

I didn't think Dad realized that Mariana probably expected him to make some kind of polite remark that she didn't need to lose weight. But he surprised me.

"I probably shouldn't say so, but you look pretty good."

Mariana's laugh tinkled like the ice cubes in her glass. "Well, that's very flattering, Angus, but I have to make sure the calories in don't exceed the calories out. We have to think of those things at our age, don't we?"

"Speaking of calories," I interrupted. The sight of my father flirting was a little unnerving. "I'm about to make dinner. Would you like to join us, Mariana? It's only spaghetti, I'm afraid. We tend to eat meals that appeal to a four-year-old, at a four-year-old's dinnertime. But there should be plenty."

"Yes, we'd love to have you, Mariana," my father urged. "I'm sure a sophisticated woman like you usually dines much later, at a more sophisticated place. But I have to say my daughter makes a pretty good plate of spaghetti."

"Mom makes meatballs!" Ben added. "She says she learned how to make them from my Grandma, so they're extra special."

"Well, if you're serving extra-special meatballs, I don't see how I can resist the invitation," Mariana said, smiling at him.

So, with dinner and getting Ben to bed, it was late by the time I realized I had forgotten to ask Mariana if the plate was one of hers, or if she knew who it belonged to.

And I had meant to return the plate to the office.

I decided it was too late. Ruth would surely have left the office by now. It could wait until later, I decided.

CHAPTER
Fifteen

I was pleased to see an email from Dave the next morning, with a newspaper article attached. Dave wasn't the most reliable person, so I was glad to see he had actually followed up on my request for articles on the girls who had gone missing from the co-op.

I clicked eagerly on the attachment. "HAVE YOU SEEN THESE GIRLS?" was the headline from the *Province*, the morning tabloid newspaper.

HAVE YOU SEEN THESE GIRLS?
Jessica Anderson and Amy Cole, both 15, have been missing since yesterday afternoon. Anyone with information is asked to contact the police.

And that was it. I looked back at Dave's message, hoping I'd missed another attachment. This was obviously the very earliest article, when the girls had first disappeared. But I already knew they had disappeared. I wanted to know what had happened to them. I was staring at my computer screen in frustration when my phone rang.

"Did you get that article I sent you?" I heard Dave asking.

"Is that all you could find?" I asked, trying not to sound critical.

"So far. It's old, so I couldn't find the files online. I had to ask the staff at the library. They should be able to find more, but it'll have to wait until next week."

"Next week?"

"Yeah, they'll be back on Tuesday. They're off for the long weekend."

"Long weekend?" I asked.

"Yes, Rebecca," Dave said. "I know you don't work regular hours any more, but I thought you'd remember Thanksgiving. I'm covering a game tomorrow, but I'm off for a couple of days after I file my story. I'll see what I can find out for you next week."

Damn. Not only was I going to have to wait to find out if the paper had more information on the disappearance in the co-op, but I'd forgotten Thanksgiving!

There were usually lots of reminders—flyers advertising turkeys on sale, craft projects from Ben's preschool. And it was an important family holiday. I'd been distracted by what was going on in the co-op. But maybe there was another reason I hadn't considered the holiday.

I thought back to last year. Mom had been in the final stages of her cancer, in palliative care. Dave was being uncharacteristically helpful and had taken Ben for the weekend. I was pretty sure he hadn't cooked a turkey, but Ben seemed to have had a good time.

And Dad and I had not been the least bit interested in celebrating the holiday. Mom had always made a pretty big deal of holidays, cooking dinner for the family and inviting friends over. She usually made a point of inviting people who didn't have close family and who wouldn't have a celebratory dinner otherwise.

Last year Dad and I had just grabbed something to eat and headed for the palliative care center to spend time with Mom. We hadn't thought we had much to celebrate.

But this year we had a new home. And I still had my father and my son. They deserved a good holiday. And we were making some new co-op friends. Mom would have wanted me to carry on the tradition. I shuffled the papers into file folders.

I had a turkey to buy. I hoped I hadn't left it too late.

I had time to stop at the store before picking Ben up, especially if I could use the car. I wasn't sure how Dad would feel about a Thanksgiving celebration. Each of the holidays without my mother had been hard on us. I was really dreading Christmas, but knew I had to make it special for Ben.

I found my father reading in the living room.

"Hey, Dad. I was just talking to Dave, and he reminded me that it's Thanksgiving this weekend. Are you up for Thanksgiving dinner? I thought I'd pick up a turkey."

He considered for a minute. "That'd be nice. But isn't our family a little small for a whole turkey these days?"

"I thought I might invite some of the people from the co-op. I met this young couple at the co-op meeting. I don't think they have any family nearby. And Gwen, the president, seems pretty upset about Les and everything else going on in the co-op. She might enjoy dinner, if she doesn't already have plans."

Dad perked up. "I think Mariana next door is on her own. She mentioned that her son plans to move back to Vancouver but not yet. And it doesn't sound like she has anyone else."

Interesting. Was Dad just being neighborly or was he showing interest in Mariana? Either way, it was a good idea.

"Great. Well, I'll get some stuff before I pick up Ben. Okay, if I take the car, or will you need it?"

He smiled. "That's fine. I'm not planning on going anywhere. And it sounds like you'll need the car if you're buying everything for a big Thanksgiving dinner."

Fortunately the store still had turkeys for sale, and I managed to find one I thought would work for our gathering. I picked up potatoes, cranberries and a range of vegetables. I remembered a recipe for pumpkin cheesecake I'd read in the newspaper and used my phone to check the paper's website for the recipe. I wasn't much of a baker but it sounded easy enough. With the ingredients for that added to the cart, I thought I was ready for Thanksgiving.

I probably should have invited people first, I thought. Then I'd know how much food to buy. But Mom had always approached the holidays with such a casual, welcoming attitude, preparing a feast and inviting a crowd. I hoped I could learn from her example.

Ben ran to greet me when I arrived at his pre-school. He was clutching sheets of paper coated with bright paint. He handed me one with round splotches of bright orange paint dotted all over it. "A pumpkin patch!" I exclaimed. "Beautiful."

Ben grinned. "I made that one for Grandpa. And this one's for Daddy. I told the teacher you all had to have one."

Dave's picture featured round brown splotches, which I guessed were turkeys. "And this one's for you, Mommy."

Mine showed a brick-colored rectangle covered at random with other squares and rectangles. Stick people were lined up in front of it, along with a round object that looked like a cat. It was the same size as the people. The painting was done with a four-year-old's style but the subject was unmistakable.

"It's the co-op," Ben said. "This is me, and you and Grandpa. And Maui," he added, pointing to the round spot I had guessed was a cat. "And these are all our friends in the co-op."

"It's beautiful," I said, hugging him. "Thank you so much, baby." I was glad I was planning a Thanksgiving dinner. Despite the problems in the co-op, my little boy was happy there. And I was giving thanks for that.

I was unloading my groceries from the car, finding a light bag Ben could carry, when Jeremy pulled into the parking lot. He pulled into his spot and walked back to our car with a lithe grace I couldn't help admiring.

"Need a hand?" he asked.

I almost shook my head and then glanced at the piles of bags in the trunk. I clearly needed help, unless I was going to make multiple trips. "Might as well take advantage of another man with strong arms," I said. "Thanks for the offer."

Oh, my gawd, had I actually said that? Take advantage of . . .

I gestured to Ben. "I mean, I already have one man with strong arms but another would be great."

Jeremy appeared not to notice my embarrassment, but I did think I saw a small grin on his face as he bent over the trunk to gather the bags. "Glad to be taken advantage of."

My face was red as we headed for the elevator, but Ben chatted happily. Jeremy helped me carry everything into the kitchen and even lifted the heavy turkey into the fridge.

"That's quite the beast," he commented. "Are you having a lot of family over?"

I laughed. "No, there's just us. It was the smallest one I could find. I think I might have left the shopping a bit late. But my mother always had a tradition of inviting lots of friends for holiday dinners, especially people who had nowhere else to go. We haven't done much in the way of celebration since she died. But I thought I'd put something together . . . maybe invite a few people from the co-op." I looked at him. "Say, Jeremy, do you have plans?"

He smiled. I found myself momentarily distracted by how white and even his teeth were, and how his short red beard framed his mouth.

"Nope," he answered. "I do have my son this weekend. But, I'm sorry to say, I haven't even thought about a turkey. It's a bit much for just the two of us."

"Then why don't you both join us? I'm sure Ben would enjoy having another kid around. As for the dinner, I won't promise it will be anywhere near as good as my mom's but I'll do my best."

We agreed on Sunday at 5:30. After he left, I grabbed the phone and the list of co-op members. I hoped a few other people were free.

CHAPTER
Sixteen

It would be awkward if it was just Jeremy and our family. He'd think the invitation was more than the friendly gesture I'd intended.

But was that really all I intended? It had been so long since I'd paid any attention to a man. But he was very good looking and I thought I liked him. Maybe I did want to get to know him as more than a neighbor. And maybe he wanted that too. This would be a chance to find out.

"I've already phoned Mariana," Dad called from the living room. So he'd taken the initiative to invite her, I thought. That made it seem like more than a casual invitation too. "But I wasn't sure what time. I said you'd call her about that."

Mariana answered right away when I called her about the time. "Yes, Rebecca, Angus did say you'd call. Five thirty on Sunday? Perfect. Now what can I bring?"

"You don't have to bring anything," I assured her.

"Nonsense. Hosting a holiday dinner is hard work. At least let me bring a salad."

I agreed that would be very nice and went on to my next call.

"No, I don't have plans," Gwen answered when I called. "Thanksgiving's such a family event, isn't it, and I don't have any family close by. What a lovely idea to invite people from the co-op. That's very thoughtful, Rebecca. I'd like to bring something to help out. How about dessert?"

"Well, I thought I'd try that pumpkin cheesecake recipe that was in the paper this week."

"Ooooh, that sounds scrumptious," Gwen said. "But you know, not everyone likes pumpkin. I've got a chocolate pecan pie recipe that's very popular, particularly with boys. I think your Ben would like that, don't you. That way people could have a choice."

I almost laughed out loud. My mother was always making two or three desserts for her dinner party, just in case someone wanted something else. "You really can't have too many desserts," she would say.

"You're right," I agreed. "I think Ben would much prefer chocolate pecan pie. And maybe my dad would too. That's very kind of you, Gwen.

"By the way, I've started to sort through the box you gave me. I wondered if I could come down and pick up the other one."

"Oh, Rebecca, it's so good of you to be working on this. But I'm just heading out the door. I'm going out to a movie with a friend, and she's going to be picking me up any minute. I don't want to be late. Why don't I bring the other box up to you on Sunday?"

I was dying to go through the other box. But I couldn't really pressure her. "Sure that'd be fine. And I guess I'll have to talk to Ruth about going through the other boxes."

"She's off for the weekend," Gwen said. "And she should probably take a few extra days too. She's got holidays due her and heaven knows she probably needs a break, poor thing. I think she's helping her mother clear out Les's apartment. That must be hard. But she said she had things to do, so I think she'll be back on Tuesday. I'm sure she can help you when she gets back."

I was really being frustrated in my research about the co-op. But I knew I'd probably be too busy getting dinner ready to do much until after Sunday. And I still had people to invite.

Anna was next on the list.

"Oh, that'd be so cool, Rebecca. This'll be our first Thanksgiving with a baby, so we wanted to do something special. But we don't have any family nearby and cooking a turkey seemed like so much trouble for just the three of us. My mom always has so many leftovers, even with a big family. Can you imagine how much turkey we'd have if I made one for just us? "

I imagined the cost of the bird would have been a consideration too. Anna and John didn't look like they had much money. And, with a new baby, their finances must have been stretched.

"I really wished we could have gone home for the weekend," she went on. "But you know, it just wasn't possible. I miss my family so much. It's so nice of you to invite us, Rebecca. Having dinner with some of the co-op members will be almost like having a family around. I'm really looking forward to it."

I looked through the list but couldn't see anyone else I knew well enough to invite to Thanksgiving dinner. Besides, there was a limit how many people we could fit in our co-op apartment.

"Everyone said yes," I called out to my father. "I think this was a good idea. Most of them would've been alone on the holiday and they seemed really happy to come. And nearly everyone wanted to bring something. So it will be more like a potluck."

"That sounds good," Dad said, moving from the living room to the kitchen where I'd been phoning. "Who's coming?"

I quickly listed off everyone I'd invited. "Jeremy and his son, Mariana, Gwen, Anna and her family . . . that's 10, including us. Seems like a good size for a Thanksgiving dinner. Although, I don't imagine baby Jordan will be eating much turkey."

"And Daddy," Ben said, running down the hall into the kitchen. "Mommy, you forgot to count Daddy."

Ben was laughing. "Ten, and Daddy makes one more. That's twelve," he said proudly. Ben had learned how to count at pre-school, and we practiced at home, but he was still a little fuzzy at anything over ten.

"Eleven," I corrected automatically, then turned to look at him. "But, Ben, you know Daddy doesn't live with us anymore. That's why I didn't count him."

"But he's still part of our family, right, Mommy," Ben insisted. "Remember, Mommy, that's what you said. He doesn't live with us but he's still my daddy."

"Yes," I agreed. Ben had been pretty small when Dave and I separated, but he obviously listened to the things we had told him at that time.

"Yes," Ben echoed with enthusiasm. "So, he should come. Mommy, you said you didn't want people to be alone on Thanksgiving. I'm not staying with Daddy this weekend, so he'll be alone if he doesn't come here. I don't want Daddy to be alone, Mommy."

Ben was right. No one should be alone on Thanksgiving. Knowing Dave, I very much doubted he would be. It would be a little awkward having my ex-husband at dinner along with my new co-op friends, particularly if my friendship with Jeremy started to go anywhere. But he probably already had plans.

"Okay, Ben, Daddy might have to work or he might be busy. But you can ask him. Why don't you give him a call?"

Ben grabbed the phone and pushed the speed dial number for his father. I could hear him chattering to his father as I planned the menu for the Thanksgiving dinner and started preparations for tonight's meal.

"Sure, Daddy. You can talk to her," Ben said, before handing me the phone. "He's coming but he wants to ask if he can bring someone called Carrie."

What? I took the phone from Ben.

"Hey, Bec, that's so great of you to ask me for dinner. Ben seems very excited about it all. He said he has a picture to give me."

"Yes, he did some painting in pre-school. But he mentioned you wanted to bring someone named Carrie?"

Dave laughed. "No, Cara. You remember. She lives in your building. I've been seeing her. We were going to spend the weekend together, but I'm sure she'd jump at the chance of a turkey dinner. Her daughter's away this weekend with her ex."

I was speechless. I very much doubted Cara would want to spend an evening with her boyfriend's ex-wife and other co-op members. She probably had something much swankier in mind. But I guess she fell into the category of people who didn't have family around for the holidays."

"Because I guess I can't come if I can't bring her. And, you know, Ben seemed so excited about it."

I thought that Ben would likely be confused by seeing his father with someone else. And not happy. I figured he still hoped we would get back together. But he probably should learn that this wasn't going to happen. And, knowing Dave, Ben was going to have to get used to seeing his father with other women.

"Sure, if she wants to come, that's fine," I agreed.

So now my ex-husband was bringing a date to my Thanksgiving dinner. This was going to be some meal.

And I laughed as I realized that Ben had been right. There had been ten people planned for dinner. And Daddy coming was going to make twelve.

CHAPTER
Seventeen

I got up early on Sunday to start preparing for the evening meal. I'd made the pumpkin cheesecake the night before, and it was chilling in the refrigerator. Time to get started on the turkey.

I used my mother's stuffing recipe. While the pumpkin cheesecake was a bit of a departure from the pumpkin pie my mother used to make, familiar dishes seemed right on this holiday. Her recipe called for cubes of bread, seasoned with celery and onions, with lots of sage. Just the smell of it reminded me of her, and I blinked a few tears out of my eyes as I saw her handwriting on the recipe she had written out for me after I'd been married. I'd actually never used this recipe. Dave and I always seemed to spend the holidays with his parents or mine.

Time to grow up, I told myself firmly and started cutting a loaf of bread into cubes.

The scent of onions and sage was already making the kitchen smell great. I was having trouble mixing the stuffing in the largest bowl I had, but I was enjoying working on this. Preparing the turkey was another thing altogether. According to the recipe, I had to remove the neck and giblets from the cavity. That meant sticking my arm into the cold, damp center of the bird. Gross. I was surprised my fastidious mother had been willing to do such a thing.

Maybe my father had helped, I thought brightly. Too late now, but I'd try to remember that for Christmas. I suppose I would have to cook another turkey then.

My mother had noted that I should keep the neck and add it to the turkey bones to make broth. I'd never tried that but we might be able to get a few cheap, healthy meals out of some turkey soup. I obediently wrapped the neck and stored it in the refrigerator for later.

Placing the stuffing in the cavity was another messy task. The turkey was large, cold and wet, and it tended to almost slip off the plate as I spooned the stuffing inside. I pushed the stuffing further back until the bird was full, cringing at the slippery feeling on my hands.

I used skewers to close the gap and keep the stuffing in. I placed the turkey on the rack of the roasting pan, being careful not to drop it.

I lifted the heavy pan and placed it in the center of the oven.

Which was stone cold.

Had I forgotten to turn it on for preheating? Nope, the dial was set for 325.

I checked simple things. Yes, the stove was plugged in and the top burners worked. There didn't seem to be a problem with a blown fuse. The oven element didn't seem to be loose.

I grabbed my laptop and googled "electric oven won't work." The sites I found suggested that the oven could be accidentally set in self-clean mode. I wish I had a self-cleaning oven, but I was pretty sure this one required scrubbing to clean. It also suggested that the self-timer could be on.

Everything else, from a problem with the thermostat to a burnt-out element or a broken wire seemed to imply I should call a repair service. Which was probably not going to happen on a holiday. At least not in time for me to cook a turkey for the twelve people I was having for dinner this evening.

Dad sometimes liked fiddling with gadgets and electrical appliances, but the arthritis in his hands made it hard for him to do much handyman work. And I was hopeless at that sort of thing.

But I remembered Mariana saying the apartments in the co-op were all similar. Her stove was probably the same as mine. And she was used to doing a lot of cooking and baking. Maybe she'd had a similar problem and knew how to fix it. Or knew something about the stove I wasn't getting. I glanced at the clock. It was early for a Sunday but I hoped not too early. I headed next door and knocked on Mariana's door.

"No, I don't know what the problem could be," she said. "But I could come next door and take a look at it." She glanced down at the jeans and sweatshirt she was wearing. They weren't the elegant outfits I was used to seeing her in. Her clothes, while perhaps a little snug, looked appropriate for a casual morning at home, but I thought she usually dressed up for my father and was uncomfortable being seen in these clothes.

"I just thought you might see something I'm doing wrong," I said. "You have the same stove as me, right? But I don't want to bother you if you're busy."

"No, that's fine. I think all the co-op stoves are the same. I'm not sure if I can help, but I'll come and look at it."

Mariana followed me next door but, as she predicted, she didn't know what was wrong. As far as she could tell, I hadn't set the automatic timer on accidentally. And she confirmed that the stove didn't clean itself.

"But, I'll tell you what," she said. "I'm right next door and my oven works. Why don't we bring the turkey over to my place?"

The beauty of living in a co-op, I thought, as Mariana headed back to heat up her oven and I prepared to carry the heavy roasting pan next door. We might not have top-of-the-line appliances but we had neighbors who could help out in an emergency. That was something to give thanks for.

Mariana agreed to keep an eye on the turkey but asked to borrow a turkey baster. "My goodness, it's been a while since I cooked a turkey," she said. "But there's not much to it. You've done all the hard work."

With that in hand, I settled down to preparing the rest of the dinner. Cranberry sauce was a snap. I poured the fresh cranberries into a saucepan with some sugar and water and listened as the berries popped in the boiling liquid. So easy. I had never understood why people would buy canned cranberry sauce. The sauce just needed to cool. My mother had always used a pretty glass bowl to serve the sauce. It showed off the ruby color to perfection.

Peeling enough potatoes for twelve people was a bit of chore, especially as I was more accustomed to cooking for three. But I finally had them ready to cook, along with a selection of fresh vegetables.

Apart from the potential disaster of the broken oven, everything was going smoothly.

Both Ben and my father had been napping for a while. Dad's arthritis tired him out a lot, and it was good for him to rest before having a bunch of people over. But now I could hear that they were both awake.

"Can you guys help me with the table?" I called. Ben came running, and Dad followed more slowly. Unfortunately, today seemed to be one of his bad days. He was walking, but his steps were slow, and he leaned heavily on his walker. I could tell from his face that he was in pain.

"Oh, Dad, I shouldn't have asked for help if you aren't feeling well. Ben and I can manage."

"I'm still man enough to wrestle a dining room table into submission," he said. "Don't worry about me, Becky. I'm just a bit stiff after lying down."

I could tell he was in a lot of pain but he was willing to help, which was a good sign. Dad was usually good natured but the pain sometimes made him a little testy. He helped me add leaves to our dining room table. It was an ingenious design, a table my mother had inherited from her own mother. It folded small enough to seat just two people but had enough leaves to stretch it to seat ten. I added the small table I usually had outside on the deck to the end of the dining table. It was a bit lower than the main table but I hoped it would do for the two boys. With the whole thing stretched across our combined living/dining room, there should be space for everyone to sit and still have room to move around.

I placed a couple of my mother's pretty tablecloths on the tables and used her good china. A vase of chrysanthemums in the center, and we were ready.

I had just enough time to change into a dress, a comfortable knit in a warm brown shade, and slip on my brown patent ballet flats. I was about to head next door and check on the turkey when my guests started to arrive.

Anna and John were the first, with baby Jordan in a carrier. "I brought some rolls," Anna announced. "I made them myself. I used to bake all the time with my mother, but I haven't tried it since we moved out here. I hope they're all right." She handed me a basket of whole-wheat rolls, still warm from the oven.

"Well, if they taste as good as they smell, they'll be wonderful," I assured her.

I introduced my father to the young couple. Ben came running down the hall but skidded to a sudden stop when he saw Jordan.

"Mom," he said in disbelief, "you told me a boy was coming. That's not a boy. That's a baby."

"There's a bigger boy coming," I assured him, as there was another knock on the door of our apartment.

This time it was a bigger boy. Jeremy's son, Aiden, had the red hair Jeremy must have had as a boy. He was about seven or eight, with a wide gap where his front teeth had been. Although Ben had met some of the kids from the co-op in the playground behind the building, the two boys hadn't met. I remembered Jeremy saying his son lived with his mother for part of the time.

Ben was suddenly shy with this stranger and huddled close to me.

Jeremy was holding a casserole. "I made a sweet potato casserole," he said. "We can't have Thanksgiving without sweet potato casserole. Isn't that right, Aiden?"

Ben looked dubious. "Is it as good as pizza?" he asked, pizza being the best thing he could imagine.

Aiden laughed. "No way! But Dad puts marshmallows on top, so you can just eat those if you don't like the sweet potatoes. That's almost like eating dessert."

"Aha!" Jeremy yelped, putting down the casserole and reaching over to tickle his son. "You eat your vegetables, young man, and don't be spreading your bad habits to impressionable kids."

Both Aiden and Ben dissolved into giggles.

"Do you like cats?" Ben asked suddenly. "I have a kitten," he added as Aiden nodded. "Do you want to play with Maui? He's in my room." The two boys ran down the hall to Ben's room.

Anna watched them leave. "It's hard to believe Jordan will be that big one day."

"Sooner than you think," Jeremy and I said at the same time.

"They grow up faster than you want them to," I added. "Your Jordan will be moving around and getting into things before you know it." I smiled at the chubby baby asleep in his carrier and oblivious to everyone around him.

Jeremy picked up the casserole he had momentarily placed on the floor. "Let me get this out of the way," he said. "It's still warm, but I should probably heat it up in the microwave for a few minutes just before we eat. And I just need to go back to my place for a minute. I bought some wine but couldn't carry everything at once."

Gwen was with him when he came back, and he was carrying a large box.

"I ran into Jeremy in the hall," she explained. "He said he was heading back to his place, but I was bringing up that box of stuff I promised you, and he offered to carry it."

"Where do you want this?" Jeremy asked.

"Could I have it in my bedroom?" I asked. "I mean, I have an office in my room." I showed him a spot next to the desk, hoping I wasn't blushing. "Thanks," I said. Gwen had followed us into the room, and I turned to her. "That looks heavier than the other one you gave me."

"It is heavy, so I was glad to run into Jeremy." She placed a file folder on top of the box and took a firmer grip on the pie plate she was holding. The smell of warm chocolate wafted toward me. "I shouldn't even have tried to carry everything. I'll just go put this down."

"Gwen told me you were helping her with a history of the co-op," Jeremy said. "That's nice of you. Gwen's got a lot on her plate right now. Now, I'll just go get that wine."

I went back to the living room, where Gwen had already introduced herself to my father and was chatting with Anna and John.

Jeremy was back a minute later and handed me a carrier bag with two bottles of white wine.

"Hey, that's the same wine I bought," I said. "But I only bought one bottle, so thanks. It was recommended as the perfect accompaniment for turkey in a column I read in the paper." It had been the cheapest of the wines recommended by the expert who wrote the wine column in the local paper. But the description had sounded good.

"Ah, so that's why great minds think alike. I read the same column."

Dave and Cara arrived next. I'd somehow thought that Dave would buzz our apartment from the intercom but of course he would go to Cara's first. I was expecting it, but I still felt a bit of a pang when I saw him at my door with another woman.

"Daddy!" Ben yelled, running out of his room where he'd been playing with Aiden. "Come see the picture I made for you."

"Sure, my man," Dave said, "just let me get rid of my coat." He gave me a questioning look.

"I think the closet is pretty full," I said. "Could you just put it on my bed." Dave did and then followed Ben into his room.

I was left in the hallway with Cara, who looked a little annoyed at being abandoned by her date.

"We brought some wine," she said, handing me a bottle of red. "Dave knows it's my favorite." I suspected the wine was more expensive than the one Jeremy and I had chosen. I ushered Cara into the living area where the other guests were gathered.

She was wearing knee-high boots with spiky heels. I winced a little as her heels tapped on the wooden floors in our apartment. The floors were fir, commonly used in older buildings in Vancouver but soft and easily damaged. I wondered why she had chosen to wear boots when she wasn't even leaving the building. Probably because they went with the black dress she was wearing. The dress was short, with a deep cowl neck, so the boots provided some balance to the look.

I shrugged. I needed to check on the turkey and to get Mariana over here with the rest of the guests. I excused myself and went next door.

The warm smell of roasting turkey greeted me as Mariana opened her door. She had changed into a knit dress in a dark wine color.

"Hi, Rebecca. I think it's looking pretty good, and it's certainly smelling wonderful," she said.

"Everyone's arriving next door," I said. "Can you come over and join us? This should be about done."

"I checked the meat thermometer a few minutes ago and it's almost at the right temperature. I think it needs a few more minutes, but we can probably leave it alone for that time." She smiled. "I think we could hear the smoke detector from your place if it went off. Just let me get that salad."

Mariana pulled a large glass bowl filled with greens from her refrigerator and we went back to my place. As we entered the door, I could see my father talking to Dave in the hallway.

"I know Rebecca said it was all right," my dad was saying, "but I think you have a hell of a nerve bringing that woman into my daughter's home."

CHAPTER
Eighteen

Both men had red faces.

"Dad, it's okay," I interrupted. "Dave and I are divorced, and we're both going to be seeing other people. But he's Ben's father, so we're going to see him at family functions some times. It's no big deal."

I could see Mariana looking curiously at the two men.

"Mariana, I think you met my ex-husband, Dave. Ben invited him to dinner. And he's seeing Cara now, so she's here too. Come on in. Everyone's in the living room."

Dad muttered something, but the two men followed us into the living room. I hoped things would go smoothly during dinner. I know my father was concerned about me. The divorce had only been finalized recently, but Dave and I had been separated for over a year. And the marriage had been in trouble for some time before that, probably from the time I got pregnant with Ben.

I had thought that Dave and I were a good pair, his strengths complimenting my weaknesses and vice versa. He was fun to be with and that exuberance was what made me fall in love with him. But he hadn't seemed to understand that a woman who was eight months pregnant might not want to stay at a party until 3:00 am. That the parents of a newborn couldn't just drop everything and head out for dinner on Saturday night on the spur of the moment. That buying a big-screen television maybe should have waited until after we'd bought everything we needed for the nursery.

At this point, far from being upset that Dave no longer loved me, I was starting to be amazed we had gotten together in the first place.

But I didn't have time to think about that. I had a dinner to get on the table.

The next few minutes were a flurry of activity. But everyone pitched together to help. Anna placed the rolls she'd baked at one end of the table and made sure the butter dish was near them. Mariana's salad was next to it. Jeremy reheated his casserole in the microwave. Even though his hands were troubling him, Dad opened the wine Jeremy had brought. Even Dave got into the act and mashed the potatoes I'd cooked.

Mariana went next door and returned to say she thought the turkey was done. "But I realize it's rather heavy," she said. "When we decided to cook it at my place, I hadn't thought about how we were going to carry a blazing hot pan of turkey over. Do you think we should carve it over there?"

"I'll get it," Jeremy said, grabbing the pair of oven mitts he had used to bring over his casserole. "I lifted that sucker yesterday when it was raw, so I'm sure I can handle it now." He followed Mariana next door.

Dave looked over at me. "Bec, are you seeing that guy?"

"Jeremy?" I said, glancing up from the broccoli I was spooning into a serving dish. "Oh, well, we've just met through the co-op. But he's nice. And he has been very helpful with the turkey."

Jeremy and Mariana came back then, with him bearing a perfectly roasted bird.

"Oh, Mariana, it looks beautiful," I exclaimed. "Thanks so much for cooking it."

"It didn't take much to baste it from time to time and keep an eye on the meat thermometer. You did all the hard work."

"Well, it would have been raw if it wasn't for you. We wouldn't have had much of a dinner."

Mariana shrugged off my thanks. But she looked pleased.

Dad opened the case of the knife he always used to carve the turkey at our family dinners. Then he looked at his swollen knuckles. "You know, I hate to say it, but I don't think my hands are up to this job anymore." I saw Dave make a slight move toward him. "What do you say, Jeremy?" Dad continued. "You seem to have a history of helping out with this turkey. Do you think you're up to carving it?"

I smiled slightly as Dave turned back to mashing the potatoes. Things were over between us. But I couldn't help feeling just a little bit of pleasure at seeing how red his face was. And not just from the effort of mashing potatoes over a hot stove. Maybe he was finally starting to realize that while he was moving on from our relationship, maybe I was too.

Gwen helped me make the gravy, and then we were ready to move everything to the table. It had been a bit of a challenge to get everything ready at the same time, and to keep things warm without a working oven. But the table looked great, laden with the platter of golden turkey and vegetables in an array of colors.

Ben and Aiden had glasses of milk in the cranberry-red glasses Mom had used on special occasions. Dad moved around the table, offering the adults either a mix of cranberry juice and sparkling water or the white wine Jeremy had brought.

"I'd really prefer red wine," Cara said when he reached her seat. "Could I have some of the wine Dave brought? It's my favorite." She smiled at him in a way I was sure usually got her what she wanted.

"Certainly," Dad said. "Dave, why don't you get your friend a glass of the wine she wants?"

"Sure," Dave said. "I'll have some red too." He filled both their glasses and placed the expensive bottle on the table in front of him.

"Would anyone else prefer red?" Dad asked pointedly, his voice sweet but with a mischievous look on his face. Gwen tried to stifle a giggle but failed. Both Dave and Cara flushed almost as red as the wine.

"Um, sure," Dave said. "Red wine, anyone?"

"I'm good," Jeremy said. The rest of us declined as well.

I could see Dad's point. Both Dave and Cara had been a little rude. But I needed to pull this dinner party back together before my father's sniping at Dave ruined the party for everyone.

"Dad, why don't you sit down and have some of this turkey?" I passed him the platter and soon we were all handing dishes around and filling our plates.

"This is so nice," Mariana said. "I was hoping my son and grandson could be here this year. But flights are so expensive, aren't they? My son called earlier today. Maybe they'll come at Christmas. I always think it's important for family to be together at the holidays." Her face was wistful.

Cara didn't say anything, but there was an odd look on her face. Perhaps she was missing family too.

Anna and John chimed in about how their families usually spent Thanksgiving. "You're right about being with family for the holidays," Anna said. "I really miss them. But I'm so glad we get to have dinner with all of you. When Jordan is older, we can tell him how he spent his first Thanksgiving in the co-op. Oh, that reminds me, I wanted to take some pictures. I want to put them in Jordan's baby album." She pulled a small camera out of her bag and moved around the table, capturing shots of the guests and the food.

Dave and Cara had been quiet after Dad's rebuke, but they obligingly posed for Anna. Her bubbly enthusiasm gradually relaxed any tensions left in the room.

Jeremy's son, Aiden, lifted a drumstick and held it up like a scepter. "Take a picture of me eating this *huge* drumstick!"

Ben grabbed the end of the other drumstick. "Take a picture of me eating this one!"

"Take a picture of me eating Aiden's drumstick," Jeremy said, pretending to nibble on the other side. "I think it's big enough for two." Aiden shrieked and tried to move away from his father. Gwen and Mariana started laughing.

I blessed them all for helping to defuse the tension. I was starting to think that maybe Les's vision of the co-op as one big, happy family might not be so far-fetched.

So I turned to Cara, hoping to establish some sort of relationship with her. If Dave was serious about her, we would no doubt be spending more time together, and there was no need to be uncivil. "So, Cara," I asked. "What do you do at the *Sun*?"

"Why do you keep talking to me about the *Sun*?" she snapped. "I don't even read the stupid thing. It's got nothing but bad news. It's all so boring." I could see Dave starting to frown. "I mean, except for Dave's articles." She smiled at him. "They're always interesting. And I get to go to some games with him. He's promised he can introduce me to some of the Canucks. I love hockey."

I wondered if Dave would come to regret introducing his girlfriend to a rich, handsome hockey player. But that was none of my business.

"I'm sorry," I said. "I don't know where I got the idea you worked at the paper." I could see Dave flushing at the memory of his story about needing to spend time with a "colleague" at work, instead of with his son. "So, where do you work?"

She named a restaurant known for hiring only young, attractive staff. Cara wasn't as tall as most of the staff they hired but she had the other attributes. "That's where I met Dave."

Dave jumped in so quickly I wondered what he thought she was going to say. Maybe *when* they had met. Like maybe while he was still married to me?

"So, Bec, that project you were working on for the co-op . . . Did you find out any more about . . . ?"

Baby Jordan screamed.

CHAPTER
Nineteen

Gwen was right. That kid could be loud.

I hadn't noticed, but Maui had crept down the hall during our dinner, no doubt attracted by the smell of turkey. Then he must have been curious about the strange small person asleep on the couch in the living room. Because, when we all turned to look, Maui had been up on the couch sniffing at Jordan.

The movement, or the tickling kitten whiskers, must have awakened the baby. His shriek wasn't really one of fear, more of surprise. But Maui was likely already a little alarmed by all the noise in his home and the shriek from this strange new creature terrified him.

He leapt back, knocking the small side table. The potted cyclamen I'd placed on the table wobbled and fell to the wooden floor. The lovely green ceramic pot shattered into dozens of pieces. Jordan shrieked even louder. Maui raced back down the hall to the safety of Ben's room. Ben jumped up, knocking his chair over in the process, and ran down the hall after his kitten. Anna hurried over to comfort her baby. And I got up to clean up the mess of the broken pot and to see if I could salvage the cyclamen.

Anna was cuddling her screaming baby with all the attention of a brand-new mother. John was hovering nearby, patting the baby's back. Jordan's cries were piercing.

"Is there somewhere I can go to feed him?" Anna asked. "And see if he needs changing? Or I could just take him home."

"You haven't even had dessert yet," I said. "I'm sure you can get him settled in time to have some pie." I almost suggested she could just feed him there. Surely everyone had either nursed a baby or seen a woman breastfeeding. But she seemed shy, so I showed her into my room, where I had a comfortable armchair. John followed us, looking worried. I was sure the baby would benefit from a quiet place. Besides, if he needed changing, it would be good to do it far away from the dining area. Ben hadn't been in diapers for a while, but I still remembered how bad it could be.

I left Anna and John in my bedroom and went to Ben's room. He was lying on the floor, trying to persuade Maui to come out from under the bed.

"Come on, Ben. He'll come out when everyone's gone and it's quiet. Come finish your dinner."

"But he's scared," Ben said. "I don't want to leave him."

I crouched down beside Ben and peered under the bed. The kitten was huddled against the wall, shivering a little. I wiggled my fingers and crooned at him, but he didn't budge. Ben started to crawl under the bed, reaching out for his kitten but Maui skittered into the far corner. Ben started to cry. "He's afraid of me. Maui doesn't like me any more."

"I've got an idea." I gave Ben a hug.

I went to the kitchen and grabbed two of the dishes I used for Maui's food. I added a few pieces of turkey to one of them, tearing the meat into small pieces. Then I grabbed the bag of dry kitten food and headed back to Ben's room.

Maui usually came running when he heard me putting food in his dish. I put both the saucers on the floor and crouched down beside Ben again. I could see the kitten's nose twitching at the smell of the turkey, but he wasn't moving.

The familiar sound of the bag of kitten food crinkling and the dry pellets rattling into his dish did the trick. Maui crept cautiously forward until he could reach the dishes. He sniffed at the turkey, tried a piece and then gobbled the rest down. Then he started on his dry food. Ben stroked his kitten as he ate and Maui started to purr.

"See, he's fine. Now it's time to finish your own dinner."

I reheated our dishes quickly in the microwave. "Finish your dinner," I told Ben. "It's almost time for pie."

Anna and John were still in my room with Jordan but everyone else had finished eating.

"I'll just go and see if I can help," Mariana said, heading to my room. "My lullabies have a pretty good track record of getting babies to sleep."

Anna and John came back to the dining room, and I stood up to reheat their meals but Dad interrupted me. "Let me do that, Becky. You finish your dinner."

Anna was looking a little tearful. "It was nice of Mariana to look after Jordan," she was saying. "But it makes me wish his own grandmothers were here. He's growing so fast. I hope they'll come for Christmas."

"Well, if they don't, maybe we should plan a co-op Christmas dinner for people who are alone," Gwen said. "This was such a good idea, Rebecca."

Dad returned with warm plates for Anna and John. "I'll start getting the pie and cheesecake ready."

Gwen got up to help him, and they were happily slicing pies when Mariana returned with a sleeping Jordan. Mariana gave a worried glance at my father and Gwen, but she smiled at Anna and placed Jordan back in his carrier.

"Still got the touch," she bragged. "I used to sing my son to sleep every night. I hope I'll get more of a chance to do that with my grandson before he gets much bigger. Did I tell you my son is planning on moving back here?"

I thought I saw Cara flinch a little, but I couldn't imagine why.

The rest of the evening went smoothly. Both desserts were a hit. Aiden announced he wanted both the chocolate pie and the pumpkin cheesecake. He glanced at his father to see if he would object to his son eating too much sweet stuff.

"Excellent idea," was all Jeremy said. "I think I'll have some of both too."

Then Ben copied them, insisting he wanted some of both desserts too.

"Honey, you said you don't like pumpkin," I reminded him.

"But it's Thanksgiving," he answered, as if that explained everything. Which I guess it did.

It was late by the time we'd cleaned up and everyone had left. I glanced briefly at the box of co-op material Jeremy had left on my desk. I was anxious to go through it, but I was too tired to start. The papers I had placed in neat piles were now a little messed up. Maybe someone had accidently brushed them going past my desk. But I was too tired to worry about that. I went to bed.

CHAPTER
Twenty

After the excitement of a big dinner, Ben and Dad both slept in the next morning. So I had time to go through the second box Gwen had given me.

I lifted the file folder Gwen had placed on top of the box, then remembered the material I had gone through before had been messed up. I had arranged some material in folders and others in neat piles, but now some loose papers were lying on the desk.

Ben sometimes went to my desk to find paper to draw on. There'd been an incident when he was much smaller when he'd crayoned on the reports I was summarizing for a client. I'd had to talk to him about which paper he could use and he'd been pretty good about only taking blank paper since then.

I picked up the loose papers and glanced through them, hoping that it would be easy to place them back in the right piles. One of them was a scribbled note.

"This is none of your business," it said in shaky block letters. "Stay out of it."

I suddenly felt very cold.

I told myself the note could have been mixed up in the papers before. I might have just missed it.

Or it might have fallen out of the new file folder Gwen had brought. I wondered if the note had been sent as a warning to Les. Was it related to his death? As I put the papers back in the file folders, I realized the newspaper clipping about the missing girls wasn't in the file where I'd put it.

And I knew for sure the note had been left for me.

I thought about who had been in my room. Who had had a chance to find out what I was looking into?

Just about everyone had been in my room at some point. Anna, John, and Mariana had all been in the room with baby Jordan. Jeremy and Gwen had dropped off the second box. Dave had left his coat in my room, and Cara had followed him in when he went to retrieve it before they left.

But surely none of those people—the people I was starting to consider friends—would have a reason to leave me a threatening note.

I sat there for a moment, shivering even though warm morning light was pouring into the room.

Then I stood up. The only way I could see to deal with this was to find out more about what was going on in this building.

I tore open the box Gwen had given me last night.

I hoped to find something more about the missing girls. But the new box contained nothing more than sets of minutes and old photographs.

Many of the pictures had nothing to indicate when they were taken or who the people were. They were the same kind of photos I'd seen before—members at meetings, with a large cake celebrating a co-op anniversary, summer picnics outside, and parties held in the common room.

I smiled at one picture showing a group of young people in front of a basketball hoop that must have been newly installed.

I looked closer and saw that one of the children looked like Amy Cole, one of the missing girls. She was standing beside a hulking teenage boy. This picture was one of the few with names noted on the back. Yes, that was Amy in the picture and the boy beside her was listed as Eddie Cole. Her brother, I assumed.

A small blond girl was named Cara. The last name was different, but she might have changed her name when she married. I looked closely at the picture. The triangular face and small stature were familiar. I was sure it was Cara. The hair, though fair, was not the almost white blond her hair was now. "Unusual for hair to get blonder as you grow up," I muttered to myself. So Cara had grown up in the co-op.

My attention was caught by a redheaded teenager who looked very much like Jeremy's son Aiden.

I quickly checked the names on the back of that picture, finding that it was, indeed, Jeremy.

But I was sure Jeremy had told me he had moved into the co-op when his marriage broke up. Was I mistaken? Or had he lied?

I felt tears in my eyes. Frustration, I told myself. But I could feel my heart beating too quickly as I tried to ignore the fact that one of my neighbors had left me a threatening note and the man I was starting to think I was interested in had possibly lied to me.

I brushed the tears away and tried to cope the way I dealt with everything, by trying to understand it, to find out what was going on. It was what made me a good reporter, I told myself. It was what made me strong.

I put my feelings aside and looked through all the papers, putting the minutes in order of date and trying to sort the photos by subject. I didn't find any more pictures of Jeremy. And I didn't find anything more about the missing girls. Although I was impatient, I knew I was going to have to wait to see if Dave could find out anything more from the newspaper's archives. That would have to wait until tomorrow at least.

And the co-op office was closed today for the Thanksgiving holiday. I would have to be content with what I had.

CHAPTER
Twenty-One

I was surprised when Dave called a few minutes later and asked if he could take Ben for the day. This wasn't his weekend to have him, and I had expected him to be spending time with Cara.

"There's this new movie out I think Ben would like. I thought I'd take him to see it, then have dinner out somewhere."

I'd read about the movie he'd suggested. It was supposed to be suitable for kids but with jokes that adults would appreciate too. The animation was supposed to be stunning. I had thought about taking Ben to it myself, but the cost of movies meant we didn't go as often as we wanted to.

I had planned on taking Ben to the playground. But I wasn't going to stop him from spending time with his father. Dave had missed several of his weekends with Ben lately and I knew my son missed his dad.

"Sure, that'd be fine." Ben was awake by then, so I arranged a time for Dave to pick him up and then passed the phone to Ben so he could talk to his father.

As I expected, Ben was excited about the idea of seeing the movie and spending time with his dad. He was jumping around in his bedroom. I thought a little time spent outdoors would both calm him down and give him the exercise he wouldn't get at a movie theatre, or the burger or pizza place his father would no doubt take him to later.

Clouds were starting to blow in, but it wasn't raining yet. I could see a few children in the play area at the back of the co-op.

When we got down there, Ben was thrilled to see Aiden. He ran over, eagerly chatting about the movie he was going to see.

Jeremy stood up from the bench where he'd been sitting at the edge of the playground. Thinking about the note I'd found, and the picture of Jeremy in the co-op so long ago, I hesitated before joining him. But his smile was so welcoming, I thought my nervousness was ridiculous. Jeremy had been so friendly. He couldn't be responsible for the note. And I must have misunderstood what he'd said about moving into the co-op after his divorce.

I walked over to join him.

"Dinner was great last night," he said. "Thanks again for organizing it."

His gorgeous smile was welcoming. I still felt nervous, wondering if I should ask him about the picture I'd found. But I hesitated. If someone was trying to warn me not to investigate, then announcing I was still looking into things would be stupid.

"It was nice, wasn't it?" I said, trying to sound casual. "And everyone helped too. So it really wasn't much work at all. Thanks for bringing the wine, and the casserole. I'm pretty sure Ben ate some of the sweet potatoes as well as the marshmallows. He was always so easy to feed when he was a baby. I never had much of a problem getting him to try new things. But now he's turned fussy. And he's usually such an easy-going kid."

Jeremy didn't seem to notice anything amiss in my manner. "I think Aiden went through a picky stage at about the same age," he said. "Fortunately he's going through a growth spurt right now, so he pretty much eats everything. Not that he doesn't have favorite foods, though. I think he'd live on hamburgers if I let him."

I laughed. I really thought I could like this guy. It was crazy to think he had anything to do with the note. "With Ben, it's pizza,"

I said. "He thinks pizza is just about the best thing on earth. Spaghetti is almost as good, but broccoli or salad, not so much."

"I think I felt the same about vegetables when I was his age. I remember my mom making me stay at the table until I ate at least some of my peas. I used to really envy this kid I knew who had a dog. One little slip from the plate to the floor and the vegetables were gone."

I thought that part of Ben's problem was that his dad didn't make him eat balanced meals when they spent time together. But I wasn't going to share that with Jeremy.

"I guess I just need to keep giving him healthy food and hope he eats at least some of it," I said. "I look forward to him growing out of the picky stage."

"Cheer up," Jeremy said. "Once he reaches puberty, you won't be able to keep food in the house. I remember when I was that age and my mom complaining about how much groceries cost every week. I guess I'll have to start saving up for when Aiden's that age."

I looked at my little boy, laughing as he tried to use the teeter-totter with the much bigger Aiden. He kept rising to the top and shrieking with protesting laughter until Aiden pushed off and let him down again. It was hard to imagine him as a gangly teenager, eating mounds of food and growing quickly. I hoped his dad and I would be able to cope with the teenage hormones.

Jeremy had given me the perfect opening to ask if he had lived in the co-op as a teenager. But then he went on.

"So," he said. "I gather you used to work at the *Sun*."

"Yeah, I was a reporter for a few years. I liked it. It was always exciting. Now I'm doing contract work, mostly writing and editing for corporate clients but also some articles for magazines and newspapers."

"That's a coincidence," Jeremy said. "I'm self-employed too. I do graphic design—mostly ad or newsletter layout, or designing logos and packaging. But I get to do some illustrations. And I paint when I have the time. I like the freedom of being self-employed, but it's been a bit tough finding work in the current economy."

"Tell me about it! But working from home makes it easier to spend time with Ben when I need to. And moving into the co-op has really helped us. We were spending so much to rent the condo we lived in. And the stairs were really hard for my father. The co-op was really a life-saver for us."

"Yes, it's been a good place to live. And to raise kids in. Aiden likes the co-op a lot. And of course . . ."

Again there was a chance to ask him about the picture. But we were interrupted by shouts from the two boys. They had moved to the swing set and were yelling at us to watch how high they could go.

"Of course," Jeremy went on, "Les was a bit concerned because Aiden spent a lot of this summer with his grandparents in Ontario, his mother's family. You know we've had a bit of trouble with over-housing in the co-op? Some of the children of the older members have grown up and moved out. So the members are living alone in two or three bedroom apartments. And they don't want to move, but the co-op is trying to encourage them to downsize to a smaller apartment. So Les was a little concerned when Aiden wasn't around for a couple of months. It's up to the board to set a good example. Anyway, Aiden is back at school now, and he lives with me every second week. So I guess I can keep my two bedrooms."

I sighed. "Yes, I heard about that policy. Apparently one of my neighbors wanted my apartment for her daughter and grandchild, even though there are only two of them. She seems to hold me personally responsible for the fact that they didn't get into the co-op."

"Ah, yes. Naomi. I think we've all heard her on that subject. It's too bad but don't worry about it. I think everyone understands why your family got that unit."

We lingered there for a while, chatting. I kept thinking I could ask if he had grown up in the co-op, or at least had known some of the children. But somehow I couldn't think of how to frame the question without making it sound like an accusation.

Some intrepid reporter, I chided myself. I suspected that some of my fears were of endangering what was a new friendship and might be more. And I looked at his engaging smile and thought he couldn't possibly have anything to do with the note or Les's death.

And then I told myself that it wasn't the first time a man had lied to me. But thinking of Dave reminded me it was getting close to the time he had arranged to pick Ben up.

I stood up, calling to Ben.

"It was nice talking to you," Jeremy said. "We should do this again some time."

My head was a mess of conflicting thoughts as we headed back to the apartment. But I found myself smiling. Jeremy was fun to talk to. And maybe our friendship would develop into something more. In any case, it was good to know he was a graphic artist. I'd have to look at his portfolio. I quite often collaborated with artists on the layout of some of my projects. Maybe some of his clients could use a good writer. We might be able to forge a useful work alliance, if nothing else.

If he wasn't a murderer.

CHAPTER
Twenty-Two

I eyed Ben's clothes when we got back to the apartment. He'd been running around the playground with Aiden, but he seemed clean enough to go out again without changing. I threw a change of clothes into a bag for him. I didn't think Dave would have a full set of clothes for Ben at his apartment. A chance encounter with a mud puddle or an upset tummy could be a disaster as far as a four-year-old was concerned. Better safe than sorry. I added one of his favorite books, an apple, and a granola bar too.

Dave arrived on time, and there was the usual bustle of getting Ben's jacket and saying goodbye. Dad had been napping while we were at the playground, but he came out to give Ben a goodbye hug.

I sat down at my desk again and started to make notes for an outline of the co-op project. I hadn't come across any information from the very early days, but I knew I wanted to start with the origins of the co-op. I had heard that cooperative housing in Canada started in 1968, with numbers growing rapidly throughout the 1970s and 1980s. The baby boomers, the large generation of people my father's age born after the World War II, were growing up and starting families, creating a need for more housing, particularly in the large urban areas. Lobbying from co-operative organizations to a supportive federal government led to funding programs to help create affordable homes.

I hoped I could find some materials from the very early days when the co-op was just starting. Or perhaps Gwen could let me know which members had been in the co-op since the beginning. I knew I could get some basic historical material about the start of housing co-ops in general from the local cooperative housing association. But I really wanted some personal stories from early members. I thought that would make the history a lot more engaging.

I knew that my own story—a single mom in desperate need of a rental home I could afford—was likely repeated over and over throughout the years. But the co-op had also sheltered new Canadians arriving in the country as refugees, women and their children leaving abusive relationships, and people with HIV/AIDS during the dreadful years when the disease swept through Vancouver's gay community. Seniors and disabled people needing accessible housing had also found a haven here.

I hoped telling some of the individual stories of how people came to live here would be more interesting than a simple accounting of how the co-op started.

I was sorry again that Les was gone. I'm sure he could have told me the sort of personal stories I was looking for.

I hoped I could find others willing to share their stories of the early days.

When Dad came back, he had Mariana with him. "Hi, Becky," he called. "I ran into Mariana in the hall. We're just going to have a drink. Do you want one?" He was heading for the kitchen and the bottle of his single malt scotch. I'd given it to him for his birthday, and he usually limited it to special treats. This was the second time he'd offered it to Mariana.

"No thanks, Dad. I'm in the middle of some work." I wanted to give the pair some privacy. Although my father was devoted to Ben and spent a lot of time with me, I knew he had been lonely since my mother died. It gave me a bit of a pang to see him show an interest in another woman, but I thought it was for the best. I liked Mariana, and it was nice to have her around. We would always miss my mom, but we needed to get over the grief and move on with our lives. I knew my mom had wanted, more than anything, for us to be happy.

"We're thinking of going out to dinner later," Dad said. "Just one of the Italian places up the street. Do you want to come?"

Dad's invitation seemed genuine, but the way he phrased it, *we're* thinking of going out to dinner, do *you* want to come, was certainly quite different from *let's* all go out to dinner. I thought I got the picture.

"No thanks, Dad. Dave should be bringing Ben back soon. I'd better wait for him. And I've got lots of work to do, anyway. Now's a good chance to do it, with Ben out with Dave." I thought I'd got as far as I could with the co-op history for now but I did have some more work for clients I needed to do. And I could spend time on some proposals for a few other potential clients I hoped I might do some work for. "We have plenty of leftovers, so I can just grab something to eat when I get hungry."

I did manage to get a lot of work done before Dave brought Ben back. I hugged my son and sent him to get ready for bed.

"So, I've been working on that co-op history," I couldn't resist saying to Dave as he turned to leave. "I think it will be pretty interesting. But remember you're going to ask the librarians if they have any more information about that story I asked you about."

"Yeah, sure," he replied. "I don't know how fast they can find anything. You know it's not really a priority. In fact, they're doing it as a favor to me. It's not really the kind of thing they're supposed to do."

I knew from experience how charming Dave could be when he wanted to be. I could imagine him turning that charm on the staff who worked in the newspaper archives. I supposed I should be glad he was able to help me out.

"I told Cara what you were working on," he went on. "She remembers the two girls and that something happened to them. But she was pretty young at the time. She says she remembers the kids talking about it and everyone being scared. She thinks the parents were trying to shield the kids a bit and not talking about it, so she doesn't remember it very well. But you might want to talk to her about it."

I was pretty sure Cara wouldn't really want to talk to me. Helping me out wasn't likely a big priority for her. But I might try, if I couldn't find information another way.

Later, after Ben was in bed, I made myself a sandwich with leftover turkey. I was feeling a little sorry for myself.

I wished Dave hadn't talked to Cara about what I was working on. And I hoped she hadn't told too many other people in the co-op about it.

CHAPTER
Twenty-Three

I waited impatiently the next morning, trying to concentrate on my paid work and not fretting about whether Dave would be able to find out anything more about the two missing girls.

But he called earlier than I expected. "The librarians were able to find some stuff," he said. "Apparently it was easier than they thought it would be. They said this was a big story at the time. There was lots of coverage. Then it all sort of faded away.

"I'm going to email you some stories. I wonder if I should tell someone at the City Desk," he went on. "If there's a tie between the current death and what happened back then, that would certainly be news."

"Maybe . . . look, Dave, could you hold off on telling them for a while? I don't know if it's anything, but I was the one who started this. And I'm on the scene. Do you think the paper would be interested in something from me, if I pitched it to them? I mean, I used to be a pretty good reporter. And I could use the money, if I could get an assignment. Or maybe a job? I tried to get rehired a while ago but they said they weren't hiring."

"Well, Bec, I don't know," he said. "I don't think the paper is hiring. But it could be a great story. I can see that, even if I'm totally into this sports beat. The paper usually wants staff to cover stuff but they might buy something if it was a really great story and you've got a personal angle. You might be able to pitch it to them if you could figure something out. That'd be cool. Anyway, I'll send you the stuff I found. But you keep me posted, okay?

If there's a story here and they find out I've been keeping it under wraps, I could be in trouble, you know. We're all supposed to be loyal to the cause."

I agreed I'd let him know as soon as I found out anything.

In the meantime, I needed to look at the material the newspaper's librarians had found.

I opened my email and waited for the message to download. There were articles from both of Vancouver's daily papers. The first article was from two days after the girls had disappeared.

NO SIGN OF MISSING TEENAGERS

Police are still searching for Jessica Anderson and Amy Cole. The two girls, who both attend Vancouver's Britannia Secondary School, were in classes Tuesday. According to classmates, the pair planned to go to Cole's home after school to work on a school project.

Les Walter, the manager of Waterview housing co-operative, where Cole lived, said he saw the two returning from school about 3:30 P.M. yesterday afternoon. He didn't notice them leave again. Marian Cole, Amy's mother, said the two girls left a few hours later, heading for Jessica's house.

Neither has been seen since.

There were the usual contact details for anyone with further information. But I'd stopped reading.

I don't know why the last name hadn't tipped me off. I'd been focusing on the past. But I was now pretty sure that Amy was Mariana's daughter. They had got the first name wrong—sloppy reporting, I thought—but it must have been her.

I hadn't yet read the other articles Dave had forwarded to me, but I was pretty sure they were going to be bad news. Mariana had talked about her son, but she'd never mentioned a daughter. My heart clenched. I knew how I'd feel at even the idea of something happening to Ben. I couldn't imagine losing him.

My heart went out to Mariana. I knew I could probably just ask her what had happened. But I was reluctant to bring her more pain. I was sure I could find other ways to satisfy what was mere curiosity at this point.

I read quickly through the other stories Dave had sent me. One could only hint at the desperation of the girls' families.

FAMILIES PLEAD FOR INFORMATION ON MISSING GIRLS

The families of missing teens Jessica Anderson and Amy Cole pleaded today for anyone with any information on their whereabouts to come forward. Elizabeth Anderson and her husband, Donald, said Jessica, their only child, had never run away before.

"But if that's what happened, if Jessie felt she had to leave for some reason, then we want to assure her that she can come home. We love you, Jessie, and we'll welcome you home, no matter what.

"And if someone has taken her or knows anything about where she is, I beg you to let her come home safely."

Marian Cole, Amy's mother, said she always thought her daughter was safe in her own neighborhood. "It's hard to think about this happening. A daughter comes home from school and then vanishes. I just want her to come back."

The girls were last seen at Waterview housing cooperative, where Amy lives.

I scanned the photos of the desperate parents. Despite the worry that wrinkled their faces, Elizabeth and Donald Anderson were a handsome couple in their forties, prosperous-looking and well groomed. Jessica had obviously inherited her mother's blond good looks.

The photo of Marian Cole made me wonder if I'd been wrong in thinking it was Mariana. The picture showed a heavy-set, almost obese woman with big hair and too much makeup. She was dressed in a beaded sweatshirt, leggings and high heels. I squinted at the photo on my screen. Enlarging it just made it look more grainy.

Maybe I was wrong about it being Mariana. Maybe it was a former co-op member with a similar name. Mariana was plump, but this woman was much heavier. I hoped I was wrong and that it wasn't our friendly neighbor who had suffered the horrible tragedy of a missing child.

I read through the other articles quickly, desperate to find out more. Then I wished I hadn't. "BODY OF MISSING TEEN FOUND," the headline screamed. Jessica's body had been found in some bushes in New Brighton Park, near the waterfront. She had been strangled.

I read the final article, written some time later. It summarized what I'd already read about the disappearance of the girls and the discovery of Jessica's body. The police had not found Jessica's killer. And Amy had never been seen again.

That was all the information I had from Dave, and it didn't really resolve anything. I remembered that there were other boxes of files in the office, and I wanted to ask Ruth if I could look through them.

Glancing at my watch I realized the office was likely closed for the day. It was time to start dinner. I decided that looking through the boxes could wait until tomorrow. It was a decision I'd regret.

CHAPTER
Twenty-Four

The next day, as I was about to head down to the office, I remembered the plate I had found. I went back to the kitchen and picked it up to give to Ruth in the office. I hoped she would be able to find out who it belonged to, both because it looked like something the owner would want back and because the co-op would want to stop people leaving food out in the alley.

At that time of day, the office should have been open. But I found the door locked and another co-op member waiting at the door when I got there.

It was Aaron, the man I'd battled with over the motor home. He was banging on the closed door and muttering under his breath. He stopped and glared at me as I approached.

I wondered if he was going to go into another tirade about me. But someone else was the target of his anger today.

"I don't know how I'm supposed to pay my housing charge if the co-op can't keep the office open."

I must have looked puzzled because he went on.

"Housing charges. That's what we call rent in the co-op. If you're such a great new co-op member, you ought to know that. It's supposed to make us feel special, I guess. That Les was always on about how we were co-owners, not tenants. We still had to pay on time though, else we'd be in trouble.

"That Ruth called me yesterday to remind me I needed to give her more post-dated checks. That's how I pay. I usually give them enough checks for the year. But I guess I was running out of checks when I paid in January. She called to say the last one was for October and I needed to give her some more. At least, that's what she *said*. You can't really trust anyone these days."

I paid my own rent through a direct transfer from my bank account to the co-op's, which seemed the easiest way. But it appeared that some people still used checks.

"But I can't pay if there's no one to give it to," Aaron went on. "I don't know what kind of a place we're running here."

"Yes, well, a death does tend to disrupt things a little," I said. "You'd think Les could have been a bit more considerate and waited to die until after you'd paid your 'housing charges.'"

I regretted the words before they were out of my mouth. I was alone in the co-op lobby with a large and very angry man. A man I'd already had run ins with over his stupid motor home. My mother had often told me I needed to think more about being smart and not just smart-mouthed.

I could see his face getting redder. Was he just a bully who yelled or could he actually be violent?

"Just who do you think you are?" he screamed. "You come in here and all of a sudden I have to move my motor home so you can park your little car. I've lived here for twenty years and you just got here, but your car takes priority. Why is that, huh?"

I took a step back but I tried to keep my voice calm. "Look, I have one parking spot, just like everyone else. It's not special treatment. I don't know why you think that."

"Oh, yeah, Naomi told me all about you. And other people too. I guess you and Les had some kind of *special* relationship that got you *special* treatment. That's so unfair. But I guess you won't be getting any *special* treatment now, will you?" He was yelling and almost spitting out the word "special."

"Aaron, I only want to park my car in the parking spot I'm paying for. That's not unreasonable. And I understand people were complaining about the motor home long before I moved in."

"Yeah, that Les. No one else. Now he's gone, I guess I don't have a problem do I? Unless you keep causing trouble."

He shook his fist in my face. I backed up a little. Would he actually hit me? He followed me, waving his arms and shouting.

Was Aaron actually saying he had something to do with Les's death? Over a parking spot for a motor home?

I was relieved to see a door open down the hall. Gwen poked her head out of her apartment.

"Oh, hi Rebecca, Aaron. Is everything all right? I thought I heard yelling."

"No, everything is *not* all right," Aaron replied, his face getting red again. The man was surely a heart attack waiting to happen. "I'm just trying to pay my housing charges. The co-op comes down on me hard enough if I'm a few days late. You're quick enough to charge me a late fee if I don't pay on time. Is it too much to expect the office to be open during office hours?"

"Well, Aaron . . ." Gwen began. She was obviously going to make some comment about the difficulty of keeping the office open when the key staff person had died. But she seemed to think better of the comment. She was more diplomatic than I was.

"I'm sorry, Aaron," she went on. "You can certainly pay your housing charge. I thought Ruth was coming in today. Is the door locked?"

"Locked," Aaron said. "And I banged on the door but no one answered. The office is supposed to be open nine to five." Aaron's face was red, and he was breathing loudly. "I don't know why I live in the stupid place anyway. You guys have no idea how to manage a building."

I was astonished that Gwen could remain so calm listening to Aaron's tirade. She was obviously used to his behavior.

"Just let me get my keys and I'll let us into the office. I can take your check, and Ruth can deal with it when she comes in." Gwen hurried into her unit and came out jangling a heavy set of keys.

"I do hope Ruth is coming in today," she added. "She did a great job last week sorting things out. She told me she'd found some quite interesting files about the co-op in the early days. I didn't even know we still had some of that stuff. I asked her to let you look through it for the co-op history. She stayed quite late though, so maybe she just decided to come in later today."

The keys on the ring clanked as she unlocked the office door and pulled it open.

"That's odd," she said. "The lights are on." She walked quickly into the office, followed by Aaron. Then I heard her scream.

Aaron's huge body was blocking the doorway but he was backing out quickly. He was making gagging sounds and I smelled the sour odor of vomit. I looked after him, puzzled, as he rushed outside. Then I heard Gwen scream again, louder this time, and I rushed into the office.

The smell of vomit was overpowering. I was used to cleaning up after Ben when he was sick but this smell was putrid. There was a small puddle of vomit on the floor near the door, where it looked like Aaron had thrown up. But surely that couldn't account for the horrible smell.

For a moment I couldn't see Gwen. Then I saw her crouched down on the floor by one of the desks. There was something on the floor beside her. As she stood up, I realized that it was Ruth. She was surrounded by pools of vomit, and she was frighteningly still.

Gwen's face was pale. "Call an ambulance," she said, her voice shaky. "But I don't think it will do any good. She might have a pulse but I can't find it."

CHAPTER
Twenty-Five

I picked up the office phone and called 911. Then I went outside to direct the paramedics when they arrived.

I found Aaron sitting on the front lawn, his head between his legs. He had been copiously sick in one of the flowerbeds by the front door. The smell was unpleasant, but the fresh breeze wafted most of it away.

"I've got a sensitive stomach," Aaron said, turning his head to look up at me. "I couldn't stand the smell. And I saw Ruth . . . what happened to her?"

Well, at least his stomach was sensitive.

"I don't know. I've called an ambulance."

The ambulance arrived with wailing sirens. The hallway filled with residents attracted by the noise, and we all watched anxiously as Ruth was loaded into the back of the ambulance. I hoped they had been in time to save her. But somehow I didn't think that was likely.

I saw the homeless woman slip into the open door of the building and join the crowd. She was looking around, gazing into the faces of the people in the crowd as if she expected to see someone she knew. No, as if she *hoped* to see someone she knew.

But she kept edging through the crowd, heading towards the open office door.

I saw she was focused on the china plate I had dropped just outside the office door when I heard Gwen scream. Miraculously, it seemed unbroken. I headed over to the woman as she swooped down and grabbed the plate, tucking it inside her overcoat and clutching it to her body.

She looked over at me as I edged closer to her.

"It's mine," she said defiantly. "My life was taken. I just want it back."

The woman seemed more disturbed than I thought.

"I found that plate out back," I said. "Has someone been leaving food for you?"

"Ha," she laughed. "Tried. Took my life and then tried to take my life. But couldn't. I saw. I saw you. You found the plate. I was watching."

Her voice croaked as if she didn't use it much. I was a little nervous at the idea that the woman had been watching me.

"I was looking for you," I said. "That pendant you gave me might be valuable." Her face wrinkled with a worried look. "Remember you gave me that pendant?" I went on. "I think it's real silver. I thought you might want it back."

"Noooo," she croaked, grabbing my arm with her dirty hand. I shuddered to think of the filthy garbage cans she might have been rooting through. "No, you need it. I told you bad things happen. I told you. You need it."

She started tugging my arm, urging me out of the hallway. I was surrounded by co-op members still gossiping in the hallway but I felt afraid. I tried to pull my arm away.

She peered at me with blue eyes that suddenly looked totally sane. "Please come with me," she said in a clear voice that sounded completely different from the one she had used a moment ago. "Please. I just want to show you something."

I was so shocked I allowed her to pull me to the door. Outside, she let go of my arm but gestured to me to follow her.

She led me to the back of the co-op. Her shopping cart was waiting beside the co-op's garbage bin. She rummaged around among her stuff and pulled out another china plate that matched the one she had picked up in the hallway. This one was still smeared with dirt and the remains of something sticky.

"See," she said. "My life was taken and now they want to take my life."

I had been misled by a moment of seeming lucidity. This woman was clearly crazy, and now I was alone with her in the back alley.

"I've got to go back," I said. "I'll bring you out your pendant. You could get some money for it."

"No, wait," she said. She used her cultured, sane voice again. "I need to show you something else."

She pulled me towards one of the shrubs that lined the fence in the co-op's back yard. Reaching in, she parted the stems and gestured to something on the ground. It was a large black rat, very dead. Flies were already buzzing around it. I shuddered.

"Thank you for showing me that. We'll have to get rid of it and clean up. *Is* someone leaving food for you? Do you know who it is? I should tell them to stop, if it's attracting rats. But I could give you some money for food, or take you to a shelter. There are places where you can get help."

"No," she said, shaking her head. Her eyes had a wild look again and she grabbed my arm. "No, *your* rat."

"My rat?" She nodded, as if I was supposed to know what she was talking about. "*My* rat. You mean the rat I saw before? When I found the plate?"

She nodded again, her forehead was wrinkled, as if she was concentrating hard. She grabbed my arm again and looked into my eyes.

"Your rat." She pulled out the plate that she had kept clasped to her body under her coat. "Your rat. His plate. He ate." She smiled. "Sounds like a poem. But he died."

I frowned. "Are you saying he ate from the plate and then died? That someone poisoned him."

She nodded.

"But you know . . ." I broke off. "I'm sorry. I don't know your name. I'm Rebecca."

She looked at me. "E . . . er, Betty. My name is Betty." She held out her filthy hand in a gracious manner. I cringed a little inside but took her hand and shook it.

"You know, Betty, there are all sorts of things that could kill a rat. People do put out poison but he could have been hit by a car or just died of old age."

"He ate from this plate and he died. She ate from the other plate and she died." She clutched my arm again. "You watch out. I told you. Bad things happen."

She tucked the plate into her shopping cart and pushed it away down the lane.

"Wait," I called after her. "Don't you want your pendant back? I told you I think it's worth something."

She shook her head firmly. "Keep it. You need it more than me. You live here."

She moved away faster than I would have thought possible for a woman her age. I went back to the co-op, pondering what she had said.

Had someone been putting poisoned food out to kill the rat? If so, it was a dangerous thing to do. Vancouver, being a port city, did have a rat population. The resident coyotes and other urban predators usually kept them under control, but people did sometimes put out rat poison. It was supposed to be in containers that only rodents could access, though, to avoid poisoning pets, birds, and other animals.

If someone in the co-op was doing their own do-it-yourself pest control, we had to put a stop to that.

Betty seemed to be implying that someone had been trying to kill her too. She clearly had mental health issues, and it could be paranoia talking, but there was something very odd about leaving china plates around in the lane.

I walked back into the co-op to find Sergeant D'Onofrio in the front hall with Gwen.

"Oh, there you are," Gwen said. "I was just telling the officer about finding Ruth."

"I heard there had been another incident in your office," he said. "Your building seems to have a pretty shaky safety record when it comes to your staff. What's going on here? You found her?"

"Gwen and I. And Aaron. But I don't know what happened."

"She was unconscious. And she'd been sick," Gwen offered. "The office was locked. She could have been in there all night for all I know. Poor little thing."

I smiled at the expression Gwen had used. She was tall, but Ruth had still towered over her. But I knew what she meant. Ruth was very young.

Is *very young*, I reminded myself. I didn't know for sure she was dead. But I had seen her. I was sure.

"First Les dies and then this happens to Ruth," she went on. "I really don't know what's going on."

"You know," I said. "There's this homeless woman that hangs around here. She just showed me a dead rat in the back lane. She seemed to think that the rat had been poisoned. And

I'm not sure, she wasn't really clear, but she might have been saying that Ruth was poisoned too."

Gwen gasped in surprise, but D'Onofrio looked thoughtful. "Well, it's certainly strange that things keep happening to your staff. We're still investigating Mr. Walter's death, and we're thinking he was murdered. And now this happens. I'm going to ask you to keep the office closed until I find out what happened. Don't touch anything."

"But there's vomit everywhere. Ruth must have vomited a lot, and then Aaron threw up when we found her. We should clean up."

D'Onofrio's phone rang then, and he moved away to take the call. His face was grim when he hung up. "We checked with the hospital. She didn't make it. The autopsy will show for sure, but the emergency room doctor thinks she may have been poisoned.

"Don't touch anything," D'Onofrio repeated. "You better show me this rat."

CHAPTER
Twenty-Six

I led the sergeant around the back of the building, pointing out the bushes where the rat lay.

He pushed the branches aside and glanced at it. "I see," he said. "Well, a dead rat in an alley is not really surprising, but I suppose it might be related. I'll get one of the technicians to pick it up, and we'll test it. Who did you say showed it to you?"

There was no sign of Betty, but I imagined she might be leery of authority figures. "It's this woman I've seen around the co-op. I think she's homeless, at least she's always pushing a shopping cart around the neighborhood. She told me someone had poisoned the rat and that they had poisoned Ruth too.

"At least, I think that's what she was saying. She wasn't really clear, you know. I think she has mental health problems, so who knows if she's just imagining things."

"We'll look into it. What did you say her name was?"

"Betty," I answered. "She said Betty, but I thought for a moment she was going to say something else."

"Okay, we'll try to track her down."

He gave me a serious look, and I found myself staring back into those golden eyes.

"You know," he said. "One of your neighbors pointed out that all the trouble with the co-op staff started after you moved in. Do you have any explanation for that?"

I sighed. "I know I seem to have gotten on the wrong side of a few people, but I can assure you at least some of my neighbors like me," I answered quickly.

I thought I saw a flicker of amusement in his eyes. "I'm sure," he replied.

"And I know Les's death and now Ruth's happened after I moved in. But I had nothing to do with either of them." I took a deep breath. "You know, you asked me at one point about a plaque and whether I'd touched something like that. I guess I should have told you earlier, but I do remember touching something like that . . . not on the day I found Les though," I went on quickly, seeing he was about to speak, "but earlier, before I moved into the co-op. I tripped over a metal plate in the office, and I moved it. I don't know if it's the same thing you were talking about."

"Sounds like it," D'Onofrio said. "You're right, you really should have told me this earlier. That's why I gave you my card, in case you had anything to add to what you told me."

"I'm sorry." I stopped. I didn't really have any excuse for not telling him. "I know I should have called you. But that happened months ago. I don't know how long fingerprints last. I probably touched a bunch of things that day. And I suppose I also touched all sorts of things in the office when we were trying to save Les. It's all a bit of a blur."

"Yes, well, our forensics people did find your fingerprints on a bunch of things in the office. Including the plaque we think he was hit with. But I'm told they weren't in the right position to have struck that kind of blow. And they were covered up by a number of other marks, so they seem to agree with your story that they were made earlier. "

I sighed with relief. "You know . . ." I began. "You know there was another murder in this building, years ago. A teenage girl. At least, I don't know if she was murdered in the co-op. Her body wasn't found here. But apparently this is where she was last seen."

D'Onofrio frowned. "Yes, we did a search on other events in the building, and the background of some of the people who live here. So we know about it. Are you saying it's related?"

"I don't know. I don't see why it would be. It was a long time ago. But I've been working on a history of the co-op, and I just found out about it through old newspaper clippings in a bunch of papers. And Ruth had mentioned that Les has been looking through the old co-op files and had been worried about something. I wanted to find out if whatever was troubling Les was related to his death. But then I found this note, a warning."

"A warning?"

"It said, 'This is none of your business. Stay out of it.' But the thing is I didn't see it the first time I went through the papers. But I might have just missed it. I wondered if someone had been threatening Les."

I didn't add the other possibility, but it was clear to D'Onofrio. "Or someone was warning you," he said. "You're not trying to play some amateur sleuth, are you? Miss Marple? Or Nancy Drew? I guess you're a little young for Miss Marple."

I laughed, in spite of his serious look. "Well, I'm a bit old to be a teenage detective, so Nancy Drew isn't really appropriate either. And I'm not trying to do your job. But I used to be a reporter, and I guess I can't help being curious. And trying to find out what happened."

"Well, you better give me this note you found. And I wouldn't advise trying to do my job," D'Onofrio said. "Believe it or not, I'm actually quite good at it. And I wouldn't want you to get involved. People are dying. You could be in danger."

I knew that, in the mystery novels my mother had been so fond of, cops are always warning the amateur sleuths to stay out of the investigation. Maybe it was just wishful thinking but I thought I heard a more personal concern in D'Onofrio's voice when he added, "I wouldn't want anything to happen to you."

CHAPTER
Twenty-Seven

Ruth's funeral was eerily similar to Les's. The same church, same minister. I drove Gwen and Mariana to the service and found many of the same people there. Gwen and I were wearing the same dark suits. I was sure we would find many of the same women serving tea at the reception after the service.

But the differences were heartbreaking. Where Ruth had been with her mother at Les's funeral, today her mother, Carol, walked to the front of the church escorted by a middle-aged woman who seemed to be almost holding her up. Carol's face was haggard. I could almost see Ruth's tall, slim ghost following her mother to the front of the church.

There were more people attending this funeral. Some younger people, likely friends of Ruth, sat together. They whispered quietly, their faces streaked with tears. They looked uncomfortable, unfamiliar with the funeral service.

I hadn't seen Aaron at Les's service, but he was here for Ruth's. I saw his bulky frame a few rows in front of us. His partner, Kevin, sat beside him. I caught sight of D'Onofrio as he slipped into the back of the church just as the service started. He nodded at me, with what might have been a smile on his face. I smiled back and then turned around quickly as the music started.

I had hoped to get through the service without breaking down the way I had at Les's funeral. But I thought of the way Ruth had moved around after the service for Les, organizing things and greeting people in a friendly manner. Then I remembered finding her body in the vomit-covered office. It was hard enough losing my mother, but I couldn't imagine the grief Carol must feel at losing her daughter. Tears filled my eyes, and I tried to wipe them away. Gwen patted my hand. Mariana reached over and placed her arm around my shoulders. They were comforting gestures, but they reminded me again that my mother was gone. I could feel the tears spilling over and running down my cheeks.

"Do you want to leave?" Mariana whispered to me.

I shook my head. "No, I'm okay," I whispered back. "I just can't stop thinking about poor Ruth. And Carol. I can't imagine what Carol must be going through."

I suddenly remembered that she had lost her daughter too, if she was really Amy's mother. But she didn't say anything. She simply patted my arm in a motherly way, and we turned our attention back to the service. I would have to try to be more tactful. I wouldn't want to bring up painful memories for Mariana.

The reception after the service was more crowded than Les's had been. There were the same sandwiches, the same women from the church serving tea. But it was livelier and noisier. The young people were shocked and grief-stricken. They cried as they hugged each other. But their natural exuberance soon took over and they started to chat together, sending text messages to friends who were not there and reading them to each other.

"Could you excuse me for just a minute?" Gwen said. "I just want to check if they need any help in the kitchen." She hurried off to the other end of the hall.

I turned to Mariana. She was wearing a black suit today, very different from the flowered purple dress she had worn to Les's service. The color was a bit too harsh for her complexion and the fabric stretched tightly against her hips. The purple had been more flattering on her but maybe she had decided it was too bright for a funeral. Or maybe it was just at the cleaners or in the wash. Or maybe she just wanted to wear something different.

"You both brought baking again," I said. "Do you think I should have brought something?"

She shrugged. "There seems to be plenty of food, although with all these young people it might go fast. It's too late to worry about more now. And I hope we won't be going to many more funerals. Gwen and I both like to cook. She's always bringing cakes or cookies to the co-op meetings."

"Yes," I answered. "Ruth mentioned that Gwen quite often brought stuff for the office staff to eat. In fact, I think she had brought something the last time I talked to Ruth."

I spoke without thinking but Mariana's gasp made we realize what I had just said.

"Did you mention that to the police?" she asked.

"No, of course not. I'd forgotten until just now." I could feel myself growing cold. "But I don't even know for sure if Gwen gave her anything the day she died."

"But she could have. It's worth finding out," Mariana insisted.

"Even if she did, there couldn't have been anything wrong with food that Gwen brought. That's ridiculous."

"She wouldn't do anything intentionally, I'm sure. But people get food poisoning all the time, in restaurants or wherever. You're always hearing about food recalls. I'm sure there are lots of things that could go wrong when you're buying ingredients or cooking."

"That's a comforting thought!"

"I still think you should mention it to that handsome young police officer. He might be around. I saw him at the service."

Gwen bustled up then, dusting off her hands.

"Everything seems to be under control in there. I don't know why I even asked. Those women from the church do these kinds of things all the time. They must be experts by now. I did put out another plate of the pastries I brought. The other ones were all gone."

She stopped talking and looked at us.

"What's wrong?" she asked.

"Gwen," I asked. "Did you bring any food to Ruth on the last day she was in the office, the day before we found her?"

"Yes, of course." She looked at Mariana. "You know I like to bring treats to meetings, and quite often I brought something to the staff. On that day I knew she was working very hard, trying to do her job and Les's. I knew it would be hard for her. I left some muffins for her in the office, with a little note to thank her. I stopped in later to ask if I could make her something for lunch but she said she had enough."

She smiled at us tentatively. "Why are you asking?"

"Gwen," I asked. "Is there any chance there was something in the muffins that made Ruth sick?"

"What? No, of course not. Do you think she died because of my muffins? There was nothing wrong with them. I ate some myself for breakfast. They were lovely." She was talking faster and I could tell she was very upset.

"Unless she had allergies. Let me think. Did I use nuts in those muffins? No, I'm sure not. So many people have allergies."

I patted her arm. "No, I'm sure it's not your fault. But perhaps you should mention it to Sergeant D'Onofrio. They're probably trying to sort out what Ruth ate that day. But just to rule it out."

"I'll find him right now. I saw him earlier. I'll see if he's still here."

She hurried away.

"Hi, fellow co-op members." Jeremy had come up behind us. "What's up?"

"I believe Rebecca just accused Gwen of killing Ruth," Mariana said. "Excuse me. I think I'll go find her and see if she's all right."

Jeremy was looking at me with a curious look on his face. "What's she talking about?"

"It appears Gwen baked some muffins for Ruth the morning before she died."

"What? But that's just Gwen. She's always baking things. If I ate all the stuff she brings to the board meetings, I'd weigh 300 pounds. But no way she'd hurt Ruth."

Aaron loomed up behind us. Kevin hovered behind him.

"So now you're telling people that Gwen had something to do with Ruth's death. And you told that police officer that I got to the office before you."

"You did get to the office before me, Aaron." I tried to keep my voice calm.

"That's not how I remember it." His voice was getting louder. "It seems you're just looking around for anyone to blame. First me, then Gwen. But everyone knows we never had any problems before you moved in!"

He was yelling by then. His face was red and veins were standing out on his neck and forehead. People were turning to stare at us. I backed a step away from him.

Kevin was patting Aaron's arm and trying to calm him down.

"Now, now, Aaron," he was saying. "I know you're upset but it's not Rebecca's fault."

Jeremy joined him in trying to calm Aaron down.

"Let's go outside," Jeremy said. "I bet you're dying for a cigarette, aren't you."

Jeremy and Kevin urged Aaron outside. People in the crowd stared at me for a moment, and then they started to chat to each other again.

I saw Mariana coming towards me, and I walked over to meet her.

"Gwen's upset. We couldn't find that police officer," she said. "She wants to phone him and tell him about the muffins but she doesn't want to do it from here."

"Oh, sure," I said. "I'll just go get the car."

She looked me in the eye. "No, Rebecca, she's really upset. I think it's better if I just take her home in a taxi. She just wondered if you could bring her platter back to the co-op. It's on the table with the last of the pastries on it. She has her name written on a piece of tape on the bottom."

"Yes, of course I'll bring it. But I could just get it now and put the pastries on another plate. I could drive you both home right now."

"Rebecca, I don't think she wants to see you right now. She'll get over it. I know you didn't really mean to make it sound like she killed Ruth, but that's what she thought you were saying."

"But you—"

I broke off as she patted my shoulder. "It'll be fine. But I should get back to her and get her home. I'll talk to you later."

I stood alone in the middle of the room, cursing myself. I usually thought of myself as sensitive and considerate of other people. But I certainly hadn't handled that well.

I thought back to our conversation. I'd been certain that Mariana had first brought up the idea. And I'd thought she was suggesting that we tell D'Onofrio about it. But that was silly. She did mention food poisoning in general. She'd certainly been concerned about Gwen. Another example of me just charging in, trying to find something out without thinking it through. Fools rushing in.

I seemed to be working on ruining my relationship with the few people in the co-op I'd hoped were becoming my friends. And there certainly were enough people in the co-op who were ready to dislike me. I didn't need more.

I thought about leaving. But I still hadn't paid my respects to Ruth's mother, Carol. I hoped she hadn't noticed the commotions I'd caused with Aaron and Gwen.

I found Carol standing with the same woman she'd been with in the church.

I took her hand. "I'm so sorry for your loss," I said, knowing the conventional words couldn't begin to help. I thought about Ben and tried to imagine how I would feel if anything happened to him. I didn't really even want to think about it. How could this woman cope with the loss of her daughter?

I wasn't sure Carol would remember me from Les's funeral, but she turned to the woman who stood beside her. "Would you mind fetching me a cup of tea?" she asked.

"Of course," she said. "I should have thought of that. You must be dying for one."

As she headed to the side of the room where the women from the church were serving coffee and tea, Carol took my arm and led me over to some chairs.

"Do you mind if we sit down a moment?" she asked. "I've been standing for hours and I'm not really used to these shoes. You're from that co-op, aren't you," she went on. "What's going on at that place?" She looked at me with some urgency.

"I don't really know. The police are looking into it. I know Ruth said that Les had been worried about something before he died. But, maybe both deaths were just accidents. The boxes fell on Les, and Ruth might have had food poisoning from something she ate."

"They think it was mushrooms," Carol said. "Apparently there are lots of them growing this time of year. They said people often mistake the poisonous ones for the edible wild mushrooms." Her face was gray.

"Lots of people get sick," she went on, "but they usually don't die. Ruth had a weak heart—a birth defect. She'd had surgery when she was a baby, and we thought she was fine. But the doctors said her heart just wasn't able to handle it when she started vomiting so violently."

"Were they hallucinogenic?" I asked. "Or might she have thought they were?" Ruth was, after all, barely out of her teens and young people did often experiment with drugs. Then I mentally kicked myself for being tactless again. The last thing I wanted to suggest to a bereaved mother was that her daughter's death was her own fault.

"No, apparently not. Just some local poisonous toadstool thing," she replied. "Anyway, Ruth might have tried drugs with her friends at a party. I'm not the kind of naïve mother who thinks their kids would never try drugs. But at work, at the office? Doesn't sound likely, does it? And she wasn't the kind of person who went out picking wild mushrooms under the trees. She was a typical city kid—thought food came from Safeway, if she had to think beyond believing it just turned up magically in the fridge.

"Besides, it's a bit of a coincidence, wouldn't you think?" she said, looking at me sceptically. "Two deaths in the same office?"

I realized how ridiculous I sounded, clinging to hope that my nice new home had not just been the site of two murders.

"Yes," I agreed. "There's something going on. But I don't know what."

"Les loved that place," she said, smiling. "They didn't pay him a lot, but he was always talking about what a great community it was and how proud he was to be working at a place that was making a difference in people's lives."

"Yes," I said, smiling back at her. "I've heard Les talking about the co-op. And I was certainly very happy to find a home there. My father and son love it there. It really made a difference to our family, so I know why Les was so proud of the co-op. But now . . ."

"It was good for Ruthie too," she said. "Oh, I probably shouldn't say that now, but she was happy working there. You may have noticed that Ruth's social skills weren't that great. When she was younger, I thought she was just shy, but recently she was diagnosed with mild autism. Perhaps Asperger's syndrome. She was getting tested, and we were looking at ways to help her cope better. But she's really good with numbers, and she's proud of being able to help Les sort out the books and the office."

She stopped suddenly. "I can't stop talking about her as if she was still here. Isn't that silly? I wonder when it will sink in.

"Anyway, about the co-op . . . they were both happy there. But you're right, there was something bothering Les before he died. Something about someone who lived there or who used to live there. I never paid much attention."

The woman who had been with Carol was coming back, carrying a teacup and a plate of small sandwiches. Carol hurried to finish what she was saying.

"Ruth used to laugh at him and say that there were problems with all the people in the co-op, that Les just couldn't see it. But after he died, she started to think about what he had said.

When she went back to the co-op, she planned to look through the files to see if she could figure out what had been bothering him."

"Did she?" I asked. "Did she know what was wrong?"

"I never found out what it was," Carol said. "But I think she was figuring it out. My girl was never very good at understanding what makes people tick. But when she wanted to figure something out, she went at it without stopping. I talked to her the day she died. She called to tell me she was planning on working late. She said she had an idea about what was worrying Les. She told me not to bother with dinner for her. Someone had left her some food, so she wasn't hungry."

"Did she say who had brought the food?" I asked. We knew Gwen had brought muffins earlier but someone else could have stopped by too.

She shook her head.

"Unfortunately not. The police asked that too.

"But you see," Carol finished as the other woman approached us with the tea and sandwiches. "You might be clinging to the idea there were a couple of bad accidents in the co-op. But I know they were both murdered."

I moved away from her, pondering what she had said. What was going on in the co-op? And would it all end now that both of the staff were dead? Or were we all in danger?

I was so deep in thought I almost walked straight past Jeremy.

"Hey," he said. "I don't make a practice of trying to pick up girls at funerals. But do you want to go grab a coffee now? It looks like your excuses have already left."

I smiled at him. He was making an effort to lighten the mood and make me forget the confrontations with Gwen, Mariana, and Aaron. Despite my misgivings about him, it was just what I needed.

"I think that's a great idea," I told him. "Just let me get Gwen's platter. I promised I'd bring it back for her."

The platter was no longer on the table so I hurried into the kitchen. I found it already washed and waiting on the counter. I checked for the small piece of tape on the bottom of the platter with the name Arsenault written on it. It was a lovely piece—creamy china with gold trim, a dark blue band, and delicate swirls of dark blue flowers and green leaves. It looked very old and very precious. I held it gently. I remembered she had said she inherited some china from her grandmother. I knew she must treasure this piece, both for its beauty and for the family connections.

"I'm glad I found this," I told Jeremy.

"Oh, yes." Jeremy said. "I recognize that. She uses it a lot when she brings food for potlucks."

"I wish she hadn't just left it here then. She must have been very upset when she left."

"Yes, she said she just wanted to get away. She thought people must be watching her and thinking she killed Ruth."

"Well, I'll have to be really careful with it." The plate slipped a little in my hand. It had been warm in the kitchen and my hand was sweaty. "Oops." I said, taking a firmer grip on the platter. "I'd better be more careful. Gwen would probably kill me if anything happened to it."

"An unfortunate choice of words, under the circumstances," Jeremy said. It took me a moment to realize he was joking.

Jeremy had brought his car too, so we agreed to meet at one of the Italian coffee shops near the co-op. He was already at a window table when I arrived. He smiled at me as I walked in. His chestnut hair gleamed in the sunlight coming through the window. He didn't have the very pale skin some redheads had. He had taken off his jacket and rolled up the sleeves of his shirt. His arms still had a golden tan, and the hairs on his arms shone with more gold.

What had he said when he asked if I wanted to go out for coffee? Something about picking girls up at the funeral? So was he interested in more than having a friendly coffee with me? I should have liked the idea. But I remembered that he had possibly lied to me about growing up in the co-op. I wondered if I should confront him about it.

We gave our order—a latte for me and a long espresso for him. He leaned across the table in our sunny corner.

"So, how's the co-op history project going?" he asked. "There should be lots of material for it but, knowing Les, it won't be in any logical order."

"I've only been through a couple of boxes," I told him. "There should be lots more. I think the police have finally finished going through the office and Gwen was going to get someone in to clean it up." I grimaced. "But I don't think I'm quite ready to go back in the office. I keep thinking of finding Les and Ruth." I shuddered at the memory.

"There should be other boxes in the storage room," Jeremy said. "You could go through those first. I've got keys to that room, so I can let you in. And, when you're ready to tackle the office, I could go with you. Make sure you're safe."

"Thanks for the offer. I want to finish it soon. Gwen didn't say if she had any particular deadline for this project but I do want to get it done for her."

"Yeah, I think it's worthwhile to document some of the stuff that happened in the co-op. I know I didn't have much of a clue about what happened in the meetings when I was a kid, but it was still a pretty cool place to grow up."

I was silent for too long. "I was sure you told me you moved into the co-op with Aiden after your divorce," I said.

"Oh, yeah, sure. I did," he said. "But I guess I wasn't clear. My parents moved into the co-op when I was really little. We moved out just after I turned fourteen. Dad got a job teaching at a community college up north, and we moved away. They're still up there, but they're thinking of moving back down to Vancouver now that Dad's retired. I think they'd like to spend more time with Aiden.

"Anyway, I came back down to Vancouver when I went to art school, and I stayed. And when I got divorced, I was looking around for a new place to live. Things in Vancouver were getting really expensive then, although not as bad as they are now. So I called the co-op. They had a vacancy, and I think Les spoke up for me with the board. He'd known me since I was little, and I think he liked me. Anyway, we moved in, and the rest is history."

I couldn't believe the wave of relief that washed over me. Jeremy hadn't lied to me after all.

"Dave told me Cara grew up in the co-op too," I said.

"Yep, same story. She's a bit younger than I am, but I remember her as a little kid. I think her parents moved in just before she was born. In fact, I don't think she ever moved out. She got married quite young and was able to move into another unit in the co-op. Her daughter's lived there since she was born too. Cara's mom died a few years ago, but until then she was able to help out with Cara's daughter quite a lot. They were very close. And a real co-op family."

I wondered if that was why Cara had looked upset when Mariana was talking about her son and grandson coming back to the co-op to live. Cara must be missing her own mother as much as I was missing mine. I couldn't seem to get along with Cara, but I could sympathize with her all the same.

"Say, that might make an interesting anecdote for the co-op history, don't you think?" Jeremy went on. "How the co-op sometimes has been home for generations of families. Could be interesting. You could interview me and Cara—Eddie if he comes back." I must have looked puzzled because he explained, "Eddie Cole—Mariana's son. He grew up here too. She keeps saying he's going to move back."

He frowned a little. "I guess he's coming back soon. Les was concerned Mariana's been in a three-bedroom apartment for a number of years on her own. He was suggesting she move to a smaller apartment. But if Eddie's coming back that won't be a problem."

I had been suspicious of him before, wondering if he was lying about living in the co-op, or if he might have left the threatening note. But he had been so open just now, I decided to venture a question.

"Did Eddie have a sister?" I asked.

"Yeah, sure, Amy. Stepsister really, her dad married Mariana when Amy was quite little and adopted Eddie. I guess Mariana adopted Amy too. Then he had a heart attack and died. That was really sad. I know Amy had a hard time with that. Her mom had died of cancer when she was small and then her dad goes when she wasn't even a teenager."

It was hard to lose a parent at any age, I thought. But I pressed on, anxious to satisfy my curiosity. "I found something about Amy when I started researching the co-op history. I actually found some newspaper clippings about a murder."

He looked solemn. "Yeah, Jessie. She was Amy's friend. I knew her a little bit. But all that happened after my family moved up north. We heard about it, of course. It was all over the news. But I didn't really know what was going on. And it's not exactly the kind of thing I could talk to Mariana about."

"I wasn't sure if she was Mariana's daughter," I said. "I saw a newspaper clipping of the parents when the girls went missing, but the woman in the picture didn't look at all like Mariana. In fact, the paper kept referring to her as Marian."

"Well, I always called her Mrs. Cole. But, yes, Amy was Mariana's daughter. And Mariana did look different then. She was quite heavy, I remember, but I think she tried to lose some weight, or at least eat better, after her husband had that heart attack. Too late for him, but maybe it helped her a bit. She had a heart attack herself a few years ago. That's when she finally quit smoking and lost some more weight. She looks a lot better now and dresses differently too. I think when Gwen moved in, Mariana liked the kind of clothes she wore and started dressing a bit like her."

I had noticed that Mariana and Gwen quite often dressed in a similar style. "Maybe they just shop at the same stores. I know my mother used to complain that it was sometimes hard to find clothes she thought were appropriate. Even I find that sometimes. A lot of the stuff in the stores seems designed for teenagers."

"Maybe," Jeremy said. "But I think Mariana did change after Gwen moved in. Before that she dressed a bit trashy. Too much makeup and skirts that were too short."

"I didn't think men had such an eye for fashion," I teased.

"Hey, I do call myself an artist," Jeremy said. "And I do notice women, or at least some women."

His smile was very attractive. But I suddenly noticed the time and realized I needed to get back home.

"Thanks for suggesting this," I said to him. "I guess we both needed cheering up after the funeral. Not that this has really been a cheerful topic."

"I'm not sure you want to rake up all the stuff with Jessie for the co-op history," Jeremy cautioned me. "She didn't live in the co-op. And Amy's disappearance was sad for her family and friends, but it was a long time ago."

"But don't you wonder what happened to her? She was one of your friends," I said.

"Not really," he replied. "We lived in the same place. I'd sometimes play basketball or something with her brother when we were little. But I really spent more time with my friends from school. But, if you want to find out more about Amy and Jessie, you could ask Cara. She was a few years younger than they were but they'd sometimes hang with each other."

Everyone was urging me to talk to Cara. I might have to.

We agreed to get together again, and I went back to the co-op.

I was a bit nervous about seeing Gwen again, but I wanted to return her platter right away.

Her eyes were red when she answered my knock on her door. But I was relieved to see she smiled at me in greeting.

"Oh, Gwen, are you all right?"

"I'm fine, Rebecca," she answered. "I was just so upset about everything. First Les, now Ruth. Now we don't have any staff. And I just know no one else will want to work here, at least until we find out what happened to them. I guess we can get by with the board doing the work for a while but not for long. I just don't know what to do."

She started to cry again, and I moved into the doorway to give her a hug, somewhat hampered by the platter I still held.

She laughed at my awkwardness. "I'd better take that. Thanks for bringing it back. I don't have much to remind me of my grandmother. I probably shouldn't use it as much as I do. I shouldn't have left it at the funeral, but when Mariana said she was ready to leave, I just wanted to get out of there."

I thought of the china plate I had found by the dumpster, the one that Betty had taken. It was a different pattern from the platter, but I wondered if they belonged to Gwen too. But after the incident this afternoon I wasn't about to ask her.

And I wanted to ask her if she had spoken to Sergeant D'Onofrio. But I wasn't going to bring up that topic either.

I found Mariana with my father again when I got home. They were sipping his single malt scotch. I would need to get him another bottle soon. Maybe that could be his Christmas present, although I might have to get him several bottles if I could afford it.

"Hi, Becky," my father said. "Mariana said she brought Gwen home early, but we both expected you home quite a while ago."

This was the downside of living with my father. He tended to want to know where I was going and when I was coming back. Fair enough when he was looking after Ben for me. But Ben was with his own father this weekend. My dad sometimes made me feel like I was still sixteen.

"Did the reception go on for so long?" Mariana asked.

"No, I left a little after you did. I stopped for coffee with Jeremy."

"That red-haired guy who was here for Thanksgiving?" my father asked. "Well, it's nice that you're making friends in the co-op, Rebecca. But surely you could have driven Mariana home first."

She really must be starting to mean something to him, if he was getting protective of her.

"Now, Angus," Mariana chided him. "Gwen just needed to go home early. She's been very upset lately. She's worried about the co-op and what we're going to do about staff. I'm not sure anybody's going to want to work here until the police find out what happened to Les and Ruth. It was no problem to come home in a cab."

"It was kind of Mariana to bring Gwen home," I said. "I just talked to her, and she's still very upset. I was glad I stayed though. I had a chance to tell Ruth's mother how sorry we all were."

"The poor woman. She must be devastated," Mariana said. "I'm glad you stayed to talk to her. She was always surrounded with people while we were there. Did she say whether the police have any more information about what happened to Ruth?"

"Well, they know that she was poisoned," I said. "Mushrooms apparently, although she had a bad heart too or she might have lived. But they don't know anything more than that. Or, at least she didn't say. Well, she wouldn't would she? She doesn't really know me. And I certainly didn't ask. I'd already made my share of untactful remarks by then." I tried to smile.

"Speaking of untactful remarks," I asked, "do you know if Gwen did talk to Sergeant D'Onofrio about the muffins she brought to Ruth? I guess if they suspect poison mushrooms, it's not really relevant, but I think she should tell them just in case."

"Yes, well, she said she was going to call him when she got home," Mariana said. "I assume she did."

I wasn't about to share Carol's belief that both Les and Ruth had been murdered. And that their deaths were related to something in the co-op.

"Well," I said, "I'll leave you two to your scotch. I've got some work to do."

"And maybe lots to think about?" Mariana smiled at me. "I wouldn't describe Jeremy's hair as plain red, Angus. I think it's a very handsome chestnut color, as handsome as he is himself." Then she winked at me.

I smiled. But somehow when she said the word handsome, the image in my head wasn't of Jeremy. It was D'Onofrio, smiling at me at the funeral.

CHAPTER
Twenty-Nine

I decided to try my luck with the newspaper the next day. They had run small pieces on both Les and Ruth's death but only on inside pages. I knew D'Onofrio's involvement meant the police were treating both deaths as suspicious, but no one except Carol had publicly uttered the word "murder."

I had sent a short email to the City Editor, proposing a freelance article. Now I followed that up with a phone call.

"Yeah, Rebecca, good to hear from you. How's it goin'?" was his gruff reply when he heard my voice. "Got your email," he went on. "Any other time I might be interested. But, hey, we're facing another round of layoffs. Advertising revenue is down apparently. We're hoping it'll pick up soon, now that it's close to Christmas. But I sure don't have much of a freelance budget, and I don't think I could commission you to write anything without the union going after my head."

I tried to sound confident as I outlined the possible connection to the death twenty years ago.

"You mean kids are in danger? That might be an angle. I thought it was just the staff who died? And no one's said anything about murder."

I backed off a little. "I'm not sure the two things are related," I said. "And the police are just saying the deaths are suspicious right now. They haven't gone any further, but—"

"Well, I might be able to sell a personal angle," he interrupted me. "Sort of a 'My life in the co-op of death: residents live in fear' kind of thing. Let me think about that. I'll get back to you."

He hung up before I was able to protest that wasn't at all the angle I was aiming for. Enough co-op members seemed to resent me already. I didn't want to add to the number by portraying their home as a death trap.

I guess, in my eagerness to get an assignment and work my way back into the paper, I'd acted too soon. At least Dave didn't have to worry about telling the paper about a story they might find interesting.

But I needed to find out if there really was a connection between the deaths.

I remembered Jeremy said he had keys to the office and the storage area. Maybe I could start searching through more boxes of materials. Even if I didn't find out any more about the deaths in the co-op, I'd at least be further ahead on the co-op history. But I only got voicemail when I dialed his number. And the same when I tried to reach Gwen.

I had just put the phone down in frustration when it startled me by ringing.

"Is this Rebecca Butler?" a hesitant voice greeted me. "It's Carol, Ruth's mother."

Her voice choked a little. "I've found some papers in Ruth's room. I think they belong to the co-op. I thought I should let someone know. I mean, if she brought work home, it's probably important, right." She took a long, shuddering breath. "I'm sorry. I just thought I should start clearing out her room, maybe giving away some of her things other people could use. But I guess I'm just not ready."

"No, of course not," I agreed. "It is a hard job." I remembered trying to sort through my mother's things after she died.

Dad had wanted to do the same thing, hoping someone else might get some use and enjoyment out of things she would no longer need. But neither of us could face it for months.

She rushed on. "Anyway, I found these papers, and I thought the co-op would want them back. But when I called the co-op office, of course there was no one there. And Ruthie's voice was still on the voicemail . . ." She started to sob openly, then checked herself.

"I remembered your name from the funeral. I wondered if you wanted to come and pick them up. Or I could send them by courier I guess."

The papers Ruth had been working on before she died? That she had thought important enough to take home? It might have been nothing, of course. Maybe just some bookkeeping she needed to catch up on.

But I was going to find out. "Of course, I can come and get them," I said. "When would it be convenient for me to pick them up?"

Her address wasn't too far away, but I checked with my father to see if I could use his car. Carol hadn't said how much material there was, but it would certainly be faster to use the car. And I was impatient.

She greeted me at the door of a neat bungalow a few blocks east of Commercial Drive. The house wasn't as old as some of the Victorian and Edwardian houses in this neighborhood, and lacked the gingerbread trim and stained glass some of those houses had, but it had a cozy charm. It dated perhaps from the late 1920s or early 1930s. The house was nestled in a pretty garden, with a winding path to the front door. A location on a hill gave it a stunning view of the North Shore mountains. The rainstorm we'd had a few days earlier had turned to snow at that elevation, and the mountains were covered with a light dusting of white that shone in the sunlight.

Carol's eyes were red but she smiled at me. "Thanks for coming," she said. "I hadn't noticed when I talked to you but there appear to be three boxes of stuff. You'd think I'd have noticed that Ruth was bringing masses of work home."

She frowned. "You know, maybe Les had them. Ruth and I cleaned up his apartment after he died, and I think she brought some stuff home from there. I think she did say something about things missing from the office and wondering if Les had them. But she didn't tell me she'd found anything. I thought maybe she was bringing home a few things to remember him by—he was always good to her when she was little—or maybe just some household stuff she thought she could use when she got her own place."

Her eyes filled with tears. "She was planning on moving out, you know, talking about getting her own apartment, now that she was working. I was worried about her, but girls have to grow up. Of course, she won't now."

I hugged her as she sobbed on my shoulder. "Could I make you some tea?" I asked. I knew tea wouldn't soften her grief, but that's what people did. "Or I could call someone to stay with you. A friend? Someone from your church?'

"No, I'll be all right, thank you. I just have to get used to her not being around. Let me show you the boxes. I can help you carry them to your car. You do have a car, don't you? The boxes are quite heavy."

I assured her I did. I was glad I had brought the car. I couldn't imagine trying to walk home carrying even one awkward cardboard box. Even taking the bus would be difficult. And carrying all three would have been impossible.

I thought about Carol as I drove home. Both Les and Ruth had been part of the co-op. Surely, there was something we could do to help her. I thought I could drop off a casserole and a salad for her, so she could eat well without worrying about cooking. And maybe Mariana and Gwen could make something for her. Then I remembered that Ruth had likely been poisoned in the co-op. Maybe food wasn't a good idea.

Carol had mentioned something about Ruth's weak heart, and a suspicion of autism. Perhaps we could make a donation in Les and Ruth's name to the heart and stroke foundation or a group that worked to help autistic kids. Maybe we could donate to an organization that developed affordable housing, either in Canada or the developing world. Or maybe we could hold some sort of memorial in the co-op, or even rename the building after them. I'd have to talk to Gwen and Jeremy about it. Maybe the board could come up with an appropriate tribute. I could certainly mention them in the history of the co-op I was working on. That would be one way to recognize their contributions.

Although I could have used help carrying the heavy boxes, I was glad no one was around when I pulled into the parking garage. I really didn't want anyone in the co-op to know I had found some more information, at least until I had a chance to go through it. I realized that I might have brought back nothing more than the receipts needed for the financial statements for last month. Or even last year. The boxes might contain nothing of interest at all. But I could feel a growing excitement.

I managed to carry all three boxes to my apartment without running into anyone. As I was carrying the last box home, I thought I heard a door open. I thought it was from Naomi's side of the hall, but I wasn't sure. I looked over my shoulder, but all the doors in the hall were closed.

I shrugged and carried the last box to my bedroom office. I tore them open eagerly. The first was a disappointment. As I'd feared, it was filled with invoices and copies of cancelled checks from this month and the two previous months. Obviously Ruth had been working on the current quarter's financial statements for the next board meeting.

I was thrilled when I opened the next box. It was from the year Amy and Jessie had disappeared. But it seemed to contain nothing more than the usual meeting minutes and old pictures I had come to expect. There was a brief mention in one of the board minutes after the girls had disappeared, wondering if the co-op could do something to help the families. But I couldn't find any further mention after the date that Jessica's body had been found.

I looked at the boxes in bemusement. Was this how other organizations handled their filing? There might have been extra copies of the minutes in neat binders in the office but somehow, remembering what the office always looked like, I doubted it. Maybe that was something I could do after I'd sorted the materials for the co-op history. Or maybe the new staff person could organize the files. I knew the board had advertised the position but there had been few applicants. I could guess why.

It was in the last box that I found the only interesting information. It was a piece of paper in Les's handwriting attached to a complaint form on the co-op's letterhead. The ink was faded, but I gathered that Cara's mother had filed a complaint to the co-op against Eddie Cole under the co-op by-laws, and was asking that Mariana and Eddie be evicted.

I shuffled through the rest of the papers but couldn't find anything else about the complaint. There was nothing in the board minutes to show that the complaint had ever been dealt with, let alone resolved. I knew from experience that conflicts could arise among co-op members. But an eviction was a serious action.

Maybe it had been nothing. Mariana was still living in the co-op, and Eddie was planning to move back. But I was still curious.

Dave and Jeremy had both suggested I talk to Cara about the co-op history. I had been reluctant, but now it seemed like a good idea. I had no idea if she would be home. I knew she worked different shifts at the restaurant. But I thought it might be easier to just turn up at her door, rather than call and get put off.

I checked the co-op members' list to confirm her unit number and took the elevator down to her floor. Cara looked a little nervous when she answered her door, but I tried to look friendly.

"Hi, Cara," I said, smiling. "Do you mind if I talk to you for a few minutes?"

"Um, sure," she said, hesitantly. "Do you want to come in?"

Her unit was similar to mine but smaller. I could see only two bedroom doors leading off the hall and the living/dining area was smaller than in my unit. She didn't have the light our apartment got on the top floor. I was beginning to see why some co-op members resented the fact that we had moved into that unit.

I knew the co-op kept an internal waiting list of members wanting to move to a larger, smaller, or more desirable unit. But I also knew Les would have made sure a unit adapted for people in wheelchairs would have gone to someone who needed it.

"Is this about Dave?" Cara asked nervously. "You know he told me his marriage was over when we first met. I had no idea you were still together."

Aha, so Dave *had* started dating Cara while we were still married.

"No, nothing like that," I assured her. "Water under the bridge. Although you might want to consider that if you're serious about a relationship with him. If he cheated on me, well . . .

"But no, it's about the co-op. Both Dave and Jeremy told me you grew up here. I thought it might be interesting to talk to you about growing up in the co-op, and what it's like to raise your own family here as an adult."

"Oh, sure. Well, I've never lived anywhere but the co-op, so I don't really have anything to compare it to. But it was a nice place to live as a kid. I mean, you must know that with your son. All the kids in the playground have a great time together. I know you've been going through some of the files from the co-op, but I think I have some old pictures in my mom's things you might be interested in. I could get them out for you to look at."

She was smiling at the memories. "We did have some great times here," she said. "We always had a big Christmas party and Santa came. I was always so excited. I remember one year when I was really little and all I wanted was a tricycle. And then Santa came to the co-op party and brought me this brand-new pink trike, with sparkly streamers on the handles. I was so thrilled I was almost afraid to ride it in case I damaged it or got it dirty.

"I didn't realize until years later that Santa was really Les dressed up in a costume. And my mom told me that year my family had hardly any money. My dad had been really sick and wasn't working. And the co-op and some of the members chipped in to get me the tricycle I had my heart set on. Because I kept saying that Santa was going to bring me a trike for Christmas, and they didn't want me to be disappointed.

"That was really sweet, wasn't it? I haven't thought about that Christmas in years. I guess that's a good story to put in the co-op's history, isn't it?"

"That's exactly the kind of story I'm looking for. But I guess things aren't always perfect around here. I heard that your family had filed a complaint against Eddie Cole and were asking for Mariana and Eddie to be evicted. I guess there are stories of conflict to go along with the wonderful times, aren't there?"

I'd asked the question out of overwhelming curiosity. But I was shocked by Cara's reaction. She went dead white, and I thought for a moment she was going to faint. She started to shudder as she looked at me.

"Oh, Eddie Cole. Mariana keeps saying he's coming home. But he won't if I have anything to do with it. When Mariana started saying she couldn't move to a smaller unit because Eddie and her grandson were coming home, I told Les he better tell her to move. Because Eddie Cole is moving back to this housing co-op over my dead body."

CHAPTER
Thirty

She was still shaking but her small chin was set in determination. "I thought about moving out myself, when Mariana first started talking about Eddie coming back. I've got my daughter to protect. But I've lived here all my life, and I don't want to be driven out by the likes of him. There are other kids in the co-op and other people who would be in danger if he moved back.

"So I talked to Les, and he said the board could probably keep Eddie out if we could show that his behavior would be detrimental to the co-op. Even though he'd be living with Mariana and she's lived here for years. Les was going to look up the old complaint, so he'd have some documentation.

"What was that complaint about?" I pressed her. I could tell she was very upset, and I was being unpardonably rude, but I couldn't resist my curiosity.

"From the time I was about eleven Eddie Cole kept trying to touch me," she said. "At first I thought it was just accidental. You know, bumping into me when we were all playing basketball and touching my breast by accident. But then it became clear he was deliberately groping me whenever he got the chance. I tried to avoid him, but he caught me alone in the hall one time and tried to drag me into the stairwell of the fire escape. He pushed me down and was trying to pull my shorts off. I don't want to think about what he would have done if one of the neighbors hadn't come out of her apartment and heard us.

"Eddie tried to pretend we were just goofing around, but the neighbor could see how upset I was. I ran away, but she must have said something to my mother because Mom asked me if Eddie was bothering me. That's when I told her. I think I would have been too scared to say anything otherwise."

I was horrified. "Mariana always speaks so warmly about her son. But he sounds like a bully, at the very least."

Cara shuddered again. The memory was still very painful after all these years. "I know he used to beat up some of the kids in the co-op. And I think he used to hurt some of the co-op pets. Eddie Cole was much more than a bully," she said.

"But did your family pursue the complaint? I couldn't find anything more about it in the files. And Mariana's still here."

"No. That was right around the time my dad got really sick. He'd been sick off and on all my life but he really started going downhill right then. It was just before he died. So my mom didn't really have the energy to pursue the complaint. I'm sure she would have if Eddie had still been around. But right after that he got arrested for the first time, and he was in a juvenile detention center, so I didn't have to worry about him."

"Arrested for the *first* time?" I asked. "He's been arrested more than once?"

"Eddie's a career criminal," Cara said. "He started dealing drugs to other kids in high school, and that's mainly what his arrests have been for—drug trafficking. I haven't kept track of all his convictions—so long as I know he's in jail, that's all I care about—but I believe he's been charged with assault and armed robbery. I think the sentence he's serving right now is for manslaughter. I don't know why it wasn't murder. He beat this guy to death with a metal pipe. But it was another drug dealer, and I think his lawyer persuaded the judge that it was a fight that got out of control.

"I know he had some kind of alibi but I'm absolutely convinced Eddie murdered Jessie Anderson."

"But Amy also disappeared," I protested. "Surely he wouldn't kill his own sister."

"Amy Cole was his stepsister. Her dad married Mariana and adopted Eddie when he was little, and Amy was even younger. But I don't think it would have mattered if she *was* his real sister. I don't have any proof, but I'd bet Amy was the first girl he molested.

"Besides, what do you mean 'kill his sister'? Amy's not dead. She's in Toronto."

I looked at her, stunned. "Amy's not dead? But the newspaper said she disappeared the same time as Jessie."

"Sure she did. And for a while we all thought she might be dead. Our parents wouldn't really talk to us about what had happened. I remember we were all kind of scared, and we thought Amy had been killed too. But eventually she got in touch with one of her friends here, and then we all found out she was okay."

"But Mariana never mentions her. She talks about her son all the time but never mentions Amy."

"Well, Amy was her stepdaughter. Mariana and Amy's dad got together when Amy was little so Mariana raised her. But we all know the wicked stepmother stories. My daughter hates my ex's new girlfriend. And your Ben's quite ready to correct anyone who thinks I'm his mother when I go out with him and Dave."

I winced a little. I wasn't worried about Dave being in a new relationship, but I sure didn't like the idea of my little boy being part of a new family. I was secretly pleased to hear he didn't want anyone thinking Cara was his mommy.

"Poor Mariana," I said. I knew from my own teenage years that being the mother of a teenage girl wasn't always easy. "Raising a teenage stepdaughter alone must have been hard."

"I don't think they were a happy family even before Amy's dad died," Cara said. "And there were all those problems with Eddie. I don't think Amy kept in touch with Mariana after she left. But I bet she had good reasons for running away, even before what happened to Jessie."

"You don't think she had anything to do with that?" I asked. "I know you said you thought Eddie had killed Jessie. But there have been several cases lately of teenage girls committing murders. Jealousy's sometimes a motive. Or it can be bullying gone way too far. Did anyone think Amy was guilty? I mean, she did run away."

"She could have been a witness, if Eddie was guilty. Or she could have been afraid it would happen to her. Look," Cara said. "I told you what I thought. Maybe the police know more. They didn't arrest Amy, or Eddie for that matter. Or you could talk to Mariana."

"It's not exactly the kind of thing you ask your neighbor . . . oh, by the way, do you think your son or daughter committed a murder?"

"Well, you don't seem to mind bugging me about it," Cara said in exasperation. "And I don't know anything."

"I'm sorry. I didn't mean to bother you. I just wondered if it had something to do with what happened to Les and Ruth. I don't want to think we might all be in danger, especially if Eddie is guilty and he's moving back here."

"I told you, Eddie will move back here over my dead body."

"Maybe a poor choice of words, under the circumstances," I said.

"Maybe, but I'll make sure he won't come back. Somehow."

"Look, Cara, two people are already dead. I don't know if it's related to what happened to Jessica, but I think both Les and

189

Ruth were looking into your family's old complaint against Eddie before they died. If you know anything, you should tell the police."

"I don't know anything more than what I told you. But I will tell that Sergeant D'Onofrio, if you think it might help. But, if you want more information, why don't you just talk to Amy."

I looked at her in surprise. "You know how to get in touch with Amy?"

"Not personally. But I think the friend I mentioned, the one who told us she had just run away, is in touch with her. I could ask her if Amy would talk to you."

"Do you think Amy would be willing?"

"Who knows? I don't want to talk to you and I am, aren't I? You can be damn persistent. I'll ask anyway. I'll let you know. Now leave me alone, won't you?"

CHAPTER
Thirty-One

I guess I had worn out my welcome, even if Cara hadn't exactly welcomed me in the first place. I hoped she would really try to get in touch with Amy. I wasn't sure what Amy would be able to tell me, but I wanted to talk to her.

Dad and Ben were both napping when I got back from Cara's. I sat down at my desk and started to make some notes about what Cara had told me. I loved Ben and Dad, but it was nice to have some quiet to get down to work.

It was too quiet, I realized suddenly. Maui usually napped when Ben did, but the kitten woke up easily and he usually came to greet me when I came home. I was just going to check Ben's room when I heard him getting up.

"Mommy, where's Maui?" Ben asked. He was dragging his plush cat as he came into my room. "I woke up, and he wasn't in my bed."

Good question. Where was the kitten?

"Maybe he's hiding," Ben said, as he ran into his room, looking around and calling his kitten's name. "Maybe he wants to play hide and seek." He crouched down beside the bed and looked under it, remembering when the kitten had been hiding on Thanksgiving.

"Not here," he said and ran down the hall to the living room, calling out for the kitten.

Dad heard Ben shouting and got up too. "What's up?"

"I can't find Maui," Ben explained. His lip was trembling.

The apartment wasn't that big. The kitten must be somewhere.

I called him.

But no little cat came prancing out to greet me.

I checked the laundry hamper. Maui liked to curl up on top of the clothes in there. He had learned to push the lid of the wicker hamper askew, opening it just enough that he could crawl in and sleep on the laundry inside. The first time he'd done it, I hadn't realized the cat was inside and I'd automatically pushed the lid closed, only to be summoned later by the indignant cries of the kitten, who had woken up to find himself trapped in the dim light of the closed hamper. He'd been clawing at the wicker and mewing in the imperious way that had given him his name.

The kitten wasn't in the laundry hamper. He wasn't on any of the cushions that ran along the back of the couch next to the window in the living room. He liked to perch there and watch the birds fluttering in the maple trees out front, the squirrels scampering along the telephone lines, and people walking past. But he wasn't there now.

The kitten wasn't in the kitchen either. I checked to see if he was eating the dry kitten food in his dish. I called him again, my voice a little tighter now, and shook the bag of kitten food, hoping he'd come running the way he usually did. But he didn't.

I checked under each of our beds, I looked on and under chairs. I looked in the closets—the front hall, each of the bedroom closets—thinking he might have found a hiding place.

I kept calling his name, hoping the kitten would answer. I finally went back to the kitchen and opened one of the pop-top cans of kitten food. The sound of a can opening was almost guaranteed to bring a kitten running.

But no kitten came.

I was getting horribly afraid that our little gray-striped kitty had somehow managed to get outside the apartment. But surely he couldn't have gotten further than the hallway. And wouldn't I have seen him when I came in?

I looked out in the hallway. There wasn't anything there that he could hide behind. I called him just in case, but there was no answer. Could he have found his way into one of the other apartments?

Ben was crying in earnest now. He wanted to come with me to look for the kitten, but I persuaded him to stay with Dad. "You keep looking around in here," I told him. "That's probably where he is. There are lots more hiding places to look. Have you tried under my bed? You can look for him and call my phone when you find him, okay?" Ben ran into my room to look for the kitten and I went out into the hallway.

I knocked anxiously on Mariana's door.

"Your kitten is missing?" she said when she answered the door. "Oh, dear. No I'm sure he couldn't have come in here but just let me check."

I followed her into the apartment, calling Maui's name. Mariana checked a few obvious places a kitten might be hiding.

"I can't imagine how he could have made it in here," she said. "I don't think I had the door open all day. Could he have climbed out on the balcony? If a window was open?"

I rushed out to Mariana's balcony, looking across at our own. There was no kitten on our balcony. I glanced down five stories to the ground below. Could he somehow have managed to get out there? Could he have fallen?

Even if he hadn't fallen and hurt himself, Maui wasn't a cat used to being outside. He was not quite three months old—still a baby—and we'd kept him protected in our home.

I thanked Mariana and headed to the other side, to Naomi's apartment.

She frowned when she saw me at her door. But I thought I saw a flicker of sympathy when I explained I was looking for our kitten.

"No, I haven't seen him," she said. "I don't think he could have come in here."

I explained what Mariana had said about the balcony. "Yes, I guess it's quite possible for a cat to jump from one balcony to another. You can check my balcony if you want. Come in."

I was pleased with this sign of rapprochement from my neighbor. I checked her balcony and called Maui's name for good measure. But he wasn't there.

"Thank you so much," I said. "Please let me know if you hear anything."

"I don't think I'd miss him if he meowed," she said. "I can hear him through the walls sometimes. He's quite loud, isn't he?"

"I'm sorry if the noise has bothered you," I told her. "We try to be quiet, but it's not always easy with a little kid and a cat."

She shrugged. "It's an old building. The walls aren't as soundproof as we'd like. I do hope you find your kitten."

I knocked at the other apartments on our floor but didn't find anyone home. It was beginning to look as if our kitten had somehow made it into the elevator and off our floor.

I took the elevator to the ground floor and peered out the front door. The first thing I saw was the rusty motor home in front of the co-op, and Aaron and his partner working on it.

Aaron had been belligerent every time I saw him. I wasn't sure I wanted to face him. But I needed to find the kitten.

There was a lot of shrubbery in front of the co-op, with lots of spaces for a kitten to hide.

I poked around the bushes in the front, calling Maui's name. His gray stripes would make him hard to see in the shadows.

"You want to go to Maui, I don't think hollering about it is the way to get there," Aaron said snidely. I almost ignored him but I needed to find Maui.

"Our kitten's missing. Have you seen him? A little gray tiger cat, about three months old?"

Aaron just scowled at me, but his partner, Kevin, stopped what he was doing. He had been perched on the bumper of the motor home, reaching up to rake the fallen leaves off the roof.

"We haven't seen a thing, but we've only been out here for about half an hour."

"Getting this thing ready to move," Aaron growled. "Don't know where we're going to put it. My son wants to use it on some property he's buying in the Gulf Islands, but he hasn't closed the deal yet. Still, I can't have it in the co-op. People who just moved in don't like it."

Kevin looked at him in exasperation. "Aaron, her cat's missing. Think about that and get over the motor home. You may not like her, but you like cats." Turning to me, he said. "We'll let you know if we see him."

I decided to go back inside to check the apartment one more time and to pick up a bag of his dry kitten food. The crinkling sound the bag made was usually very enticing to our kitten.

But, as I picked up the bag in our kitchen and gave the bag a shake, there was still no answer.

Ben was still looking in every possible hiding place in the apartment, but Dad looked worried. "I was having a bit of a nap," he said. "But I don't see how he could have got out. I've been looking for him everywhere I can think of, but I don't think he's here."

"Dad, I'm sure I'll find him. I don't see how he could get out either."

I headed out the front door again, calling Maui's name. I looked around the front yard of the co-op without success and went around the back. Kids were still playing in the playground, but none I recognized.

I looked up at our balcony high above us. I shuddered. I didn't think Maui could have made it out on our balcony, but I was sure he'd be hurt if he had fallen.

But there was no sign of Maui in the co-op's back yard.

I headed for the underground parking garage. The area was brightly lit with bluish fluorescent lights, and I could see it was deserted.

"Maui," I called, peering under cars and shaking my bag of cat food. The bicycle storage area, screened off by chain link panels, looked promising. I shone the small pocket flashlight attached to my key ring to search in there.

But after a few minutes it became clear he wasn't in the parking garage. I'd checked all the places a kitten could hide.

I hadn't spent much time checking out the condos around the corner from the co-op, but I supposed the kitten could have gone there.

The street in front of the co-op was lined with mature maple trees, but this street was planted with young cherry trees. The City of Vancouver had planted flowering trees along most of the city streets. Starting as early as January some years, the city's trees covered themselves in froths of pink and white blossoms as the plum, cherry and dogwood trees bloomed in succession throughout the spring. When they were done, the petals littered the ground under the trees in layers inches deep, covering the cars parked underneath them with pink confetti.

Right now the trees were covered in handsome claret-colored leaves, only a few scattered on the grass underneath them.

As I bent down to peer under the cars parked along the street, I heard Kevin calling my name. I dashed back around the corner.

"Rebecca, we found your cat," Kevin said. "But, honey, I'm afraid he's hurt."

CHAPTER
Thirty-Two

"I think his leg is broken," Kevin continued.

My eyes went immediately to Maui. Aaron was crouched on the curb, holding him.

"We just heard him meowing," Kevin was saying. "He was lying there under a car. I guess he must have heard you calling him, after all.

"Aaron got a sheet of cardboard from the motor home and managed to slide it under him so he could move him without hurting him more. Then he got a towel to keep him warm."

Aaron was gently stroking the kitten's tiny striped head but his angry expression was clear.

"He was probably hit by a car," he said, his voice outraged. "They must have known they hit him, but they just left him there. How could someone do that to a kitten? He was just lying there, poor little guy."

The kitten recognized my voice and looked up at me, eyes unfocused with pain.

"I'd better get him to the vet's as quickly as possible," I said. "Just let me get his carrier. Thanks so much for taking care of him."

Ben ran to the door when I got back to the apartment. "I couldn't find Maui, Mommy? Did you find him?"

I was so glad I'd been able to find the kitten. "Yeah, I found him. But you know what, Benjy-bear? Maui has to go to the hospital. Remember when Grandpa went to the hospital? He was hurt, and they made him all better. That's what they're going to do for Maui too." I hoped that was true. I didn't know how badly the kitten was hurt.

Ben looked at me quizzically. "Did you call the ambleeanse for Maui?"

I laughed. "No, Maui's going to a different hospital and Mommy's going to drive him."

"Is he scared?" Ben asked. "Does he want me there?" He was starting to cry again.

I thought a crying Ben was the last thing the little cat needed. "He's a little scared, but the vet will take good care of him. You stay with Grandpa, and I'll bring Maui home when he's better."

Aaron gently helped me nestle Maui in his cat carrier. We were able to slide the cardboard into the carrier without jostling the kitten too much.

"I thought it was better to keep him stable, to give his leg some support and in case he had other injuries."

"What a good idea," I told him gratefully. "Thank you so much for finding him and for looking after him so well." He looked a little embarrassed by my thanks.

"Yeah, well, you're a pain, but I can't hold that against a poor little cat."

Kevin smiled. "He's good with animals. They all seem to like him. I think he should have been a vet."

I thanked them again and headed to the parking garage to get Dad's car. Maui's vet, a clinic that specialized in feline veterinary medicine, was already closed, but their recorded message directed me to a twenty-four-hour emergency clinic. I phoned them to say I was on my way, and they were ready when I walked into the clinic waiting area.

Maui and I were quickly taken into an examination room, and I laid the kitten, still wrapped in Aaron's dark-green towel, on the examining table. The vet was a small woman about my age, with long black hair, a perfect oval face and huge dark eyes with the longest eyelashes I had ever seen. She looked far too beautiful and exotic for the clinic, with its harsh overhead lighting and stainless steel fittings. But she was obviously skilled and perfectly at home here. Her small, brown hands were gentle as she examined the kitten, but he still snarled and hissed when she touched his leg. She gently probed the rest of his little body, then carried him away for X-rays. He was still hissing as he went.

I went back to the reception area and chatted with the receptionist as I waited.

The animal emergency clinic was quiet. I seemed to be the only person there, aside from the staff. I could hear Maui yowling from the X-ray room, and there was the occasional woof or meow in response from other animals in the back.

The vet came back to confirm that Maui's leg was broken in two places but that he didn't seem to have any other serious injuries, just some bruising. "It's quite a bad break," she told me. "We should operate and put a pin in temporarily. He's young enough that he should heal quite well."

She quoted me a fee that almost made me gasp out loud but I handed over my credit card without a word. The cost was more than I made in a good couple of months, but I knew I could pay that bill eventually. Maybe Dave would help, if I asked him. I didn't have a lot of money, but I knew there were plenty of people who were worse off than I was. I wondered how they coped with vet bills and other costs of having a pet.

The vet told me they would do Maui's surgery soon but would want to keep him at least overnight for observation.

"There's not much point in you waiting around here. He'll be sedated for quite a while. We can call you when we've finished the surgery to let you know how he is, if you'd like. And you can probably take him home tomorrow or the day after."

I thanked the vet and the receptionist and steered my car back toward the co-op. Dad and Ben came out to the hall to meet me. When Dad saw that I didn't have the carrier with me, his face fell. Ben had tears in his eyes, and I could see he was going to ask where his kitten was.

"Maui's going to be fine," I reassured them both. "He does have a broken leg, and they're doing surgery right now. But they think he'll be fine."

"Oh, I'm so glad," Dad said. "But I just can't figure out how he got outside."

It was a struggle to get Ben to eat his dinner. He was upset and worried about the kitten. I was very relieved when the clinic called after a couple of hours with a report that Maui had come through his surgery and was recovering from his sedation.

Ben was glad to hear the news, but then he wanted his kitten home right away. "Maui always sleeps with me. He'll be lonely."

I didn't quite know how to explain anesthetic to a four-year-old.

"They still need to look after Maui at the hospital," I tried. "Remember when Grandpa had to stay overnight? But then he came home, and he was really glad to see you. And you were glad to see him."

I tried to change the subject. "I bet Maui's sleeping right now. If you go to sleep, time will pass quickly, and Maui will be home before you know it. Let's get you a bath and then into bed."

Ben protested a little. He was tired and upset.

"Maui won't want to see a dirty boy when he comes home," I told him. "And when we go get Maui, you don't want him to think you're too stinky."

Ben laughed. "Maui will think I'm stinky!" he chortled. "Maui likes stinky things. His food is stinky!"

"Well, you sure don't want Maui to think you're his stinky dinner and try to eat you up."

Ben giggled at that and got into his bath happily enough. I watched him playing with the bright plastic boats that filled the bath, making sure he was clean. I wrapped him in one of the large fluffy white towels my mother had bought and then helped him put on his pajamas.

He cried a little as I tucked him into bed. "I miss Maui, Mommy, and I know Maui misses me," he said.

"Maui will be sleeping and you should too," I told him. "He'll need you to take care of him when he comes home, and you don't want to be too tired to do that."

I noticed a scrap of paper on the floor. I picked it up as I kissed Ben good night and turned off his bedroom light.

I glanced at the paper as I left his room. It was a receipt from a women's clothing store. I had shopped there when I was still working full time but I couldn't afford to buy clothes there anymore. I thought that was where some of Gwen's clothes came from. Maybe it had fallen out of her purse or pocket when she was here at Thanksgiving.

I doubted she would need it, but I thought I should ask her. I shrugged and put the receipt down on my desk to remind me.

CHAPTER
Thirty-Three

When the phone rang the next morning, my father answered it. I heard him laughing in a way he hadn't done since Mom died. An old friend I guessed, but I turned out to be wrong. I heard him wheeling his chair down the hall.

"That was Mariana," he said. "She said she'd been worrying all night about whether you found Maui. You might have let her know." He looked at me reproachfully.

"You're right, Dad, but I was a little busy taking him to the vet's."

I thought about pointing out he might have called her but was glad I hadn't when he said, "I didn't know you'd talked to her about it."

That made me realize I also had talked to Naomi when I'd been looking for the kitten, and I hadn't let her know I'd found him. I knew she didn't like me, but she had been helpful about the missing cat. Kevin and Aaron had helped even more, and I made a mental note to thank them for that too.

I decided to pop next door to let Naomi know that I'd found Maui.

Her worried look when she saw me made me glad I had come over.

"I just wanted to let you know I found our kitten yesterday. Thank you for checking your apartment for him."

"Oh, I'm glad," she said. "I haven't heard him meowing, and I was afraid you hadn't found him."

Just how thin were the walls in this building? I usually didn't hear anything from Mariana or Naomi on either side but they were single women living alone and must be pretty quiet usually. I knew I'd have to try to remember to keep Ben and Maui from making too much noise.

I explained about the broken leg. "But the vet assured me he would be fine. He should be coming home soon."

"I'm glad," she said. Then she looked down at the ground. "You know, Rebecca, I guess I've been a little unfair to you." She blushed. "There's a two-bedroom opening up pretty soon, and I think my daughter's going to get it. She told me Les had mentioned a possible vacancy before you moved in. It's not right next door but it's close enough, and she thinks it's better for her. It's smaller than your apartment, so it's cheaper.

"She was horrified when I told her I hadn't been speaking to you," she went on. "She said 'Gawd, Mom, what if I move in and someone refuses to even talk to me because I got the apartment they wanted for someone in their family? Think how I'd feel.'"

She blushed. "I know Les was usually pretty fair about allocating apartments to people who needed them. I didn't realize your father uses a wheelchair so often. The first time I saw him he was walking."

"He uses his walker as much as he can," I said. "And he tries to exercise so he can stay mobile as long as possible. But his arthritis is getting worse, and he probably won't be able to walk at all some day. This co-op unit has been great for us. We couldn't have stayed in the place we were living. It's made such a difference for Dad. And my little boy loves it here."

"Well, my granddaughter likes it here too." She smiled. "It'll be so much easier for us if she can live here. My daughter needs a place she can afford. And I can help look after her little girl without taking the bus across town. That's partly why I was so mad at you the first day I saw you. I'd just come back from my daughter's place, and the bus was so crowded, I had to stand all the way. I was so tired and cranky. But I know I shouldn't have taken it out on you. It was really Mariana I was mad at. She's been living in that big three-bedroom unit for years on her own and getting away with it."

"But she says her son and grandson are coming home to live with her," I explained. I was worried about what Cara had told me about Mariana's son. But Mariana had been a friendly face in the co-op from the start.

"Oh, yeah," Naomi spat out. "I heard her son was living with her off and on for a while, but that was a long time ago. And now she keeps saying he's coming home. But he never does. I understand she did that before. She had someone else living with her for a while. Her sister, I think. But she moved out after a few months, and Mariana kept saying she was coming back. But she never did. Then she did emergency foster care for a while." Naomi sighed. "That's a very worthwhile thing to do. I know there's a real need. But she only had a couple of kids for a few nights. And she kept telling the co-op she needed the rooms for foster kids. But she never had any more kids stay with her.

"I think you saw at the meeting how some people can bend the rules by getting people to sympathize with them. I wasn't here at the time, but I think something happened to Mariana's daughter a long time ago. So people feel sorry for her. But somehow or other Mariana Cole has managed to live by herself in a three-bedroom apartment, at low rent, for almost twenty years."

I couldn't help trying to find out if she knew more. The reporter in me was a dreadful snoop some times. "I've heard a little bit about Mariana's daughter. Do people talk about her much?"

"No, not really" she said. "I only know someone said something bad happened to her so we should be nice to Mariana. I wasn't really paying attention. You can see why I was so mad Les was making such a big deal about my daughter moving in to an apartment that was too big," she went on. "But I know it wasn't your fault."

It wasn't exactly an apology. And Naomi seemed to have turned her fury from me to Mariana. I could easily understand how the co-op members would have sympathized with Mariana at the time of Amy's disappearance. She'd been widowed, her daughter had disappeared and perhaps died, and she had a troubled son. It would be hard to imagine a sympathetic housing co-op forcing a bereaved woman to move. It had been a long time since Amy had left but still . . .

"I don't know all the details," I said, "but I've been doing some work on the co-op's history, and I know Mariana went through some very rough times."

I was hoping for some sympathy but Naomi just shrugged. "Lots of people go through rough times. Most of them just try to get through the bad stuff and move on. The co-op tries to help people out as much as possible. But I think some people just take advantage."

I remembered how Cara had managed to get the co-op to allow her to have another pet, even though it was against the rules, just by crying. And how Aaron had blustered and threatened the membership into submission. But surely this was quite a different situation.

"I know Gwen and the board do their best to be fair," Naomi went on. "And Les too. It was so sad he died. He was a nice man."

Naomi had turned even redder. "You know, it wasn't Les who said you slept with him to get the apartment. It was Aaron

206

who was telling people that, and I knew he was just saying it because he was mad about the motor home. I'm sorry about all that."

I thanked her. "I'm glad your daughter might be moving in. And I promise you I'll try to make her feel welcome if she does. I hope we can put all this behind us and be good neighbors." I didn't like the idea of Naomi feuding with Mariana, but I was glad she didn't seem to be gunning for me anymore. And Naomi's daughter certainly sounded like someone I might like and could be friends with.

I smiled at her. "And I'll do my best to keep the kitten quiet when he comes home. I didn't realize you could hear him."

I went back to my apartment feeling a bit better about the co-op.

I planned to thank Aaron and Kevin next, but I was interrupted by a call from the veterinary clinic telling me that I could pick up Maui.

The kitten was asleep in one of the wire cages that lined the clinic walls when Ben and I entered, but he lifted his head when he heard our voices and gave us a slightly unfocused stare.

"Is he still sedated?" I asked.

"Not from the anesthetic, but we've been giving him some medication for pain. He'll be a little groggy for a while," the vet told me. She handed me some liquid medication. "He should have this three times a day for the next two days. I'll just show you how to give it to him."

The vet wielded the small dropper with expertise, and Maui was swallowing the yellow drops before he realized it. I had my doubts I would be able to do a comparable job, but I was willing to try.

"He needs to be kept as quiet as possible and not move around too much." She sent me home with a large kennel, big enough to contain Maui's cat bed, his litter box, and food dishes. "You can take him out and let him sit on your lap if he needs a cuddle, but he should be kept quiet the rest of the time."

I managed to fit Maui's cat carrier and the large kennel, in pieces, in the back of the car.

Back home, I reassembled the kennel in Ben's room and placed the litter box at the back. I folded a towel for the kitten's bed and lifted him gently onto it.

Ben, who had been watching and softly petting his kitten while I assembled the kennel, grinned.

"Maui's in a cage like a lion," he said.

I wondered where Ben had got the idea of lions in cages. I hadn't taken him to the zoo, although maybe his father had. Or was it from a cartoon or something else he'd seen on television? I felt guilty immediately. Was he watching too much TV? Should I be spending more time with him?

I'd much rather my son had an image of lions roaming free on the African veldt.

"Well, he won't feel like a lion for a while," I said. "You'll have to be very gentle with him."

Maui quickly went back to sleep. Ben looked disappointed that he couldn't play with his kitten but settled down to play with his toy cars. I reminded him to be quiet so Maui could rest.

I had thought about picking up some flowers and a card to thank Aaron and Kevin for helping with Maui. Then I realized that, while Kevin might appreciate flowers, they didn't really seem appropriate for Aaron.

I remembered I still had two of the bottles of white wine left from our Thanksgiving dinner. I didn't have a card, but I wrapped a bit of ribbon around the neck of one bottle to make it look festive. I let Dad know I was just popping out for a moment and to check that he would watch Ben.

"You help out with Ben so much, Dad," I said, "I don't know how we'd manage without you."

"We all help each other," he answered, smiling. "I don't imagine I'd be happy sitting by myself and eating lonely meals for one."

"I bet a handsome man like you would have the women beating down the doors to have dinner with you, if you let them," I told him.

"Well, as a matter of fact, when Mariana phoned to find out about Maui, she invited me over to dinner tonight," he said. "She said it was to thank me for when I took her out to that restaurant a while ago."

"That's nice," I said. "I know she's a great cook."

Dad smiled. "And she's fun to be with. I hope it doesn't bother you, Becky. I mean, seeing me going out with someone who isn't your mother."

"Oh, Dad, I know you loved Mom. But you need to make new friends and get on with your life. And Mom would have wanted you to be happy. I'm sure she'd be pleased if you found someone new in your life and weren't lonely."

"Well, I enjoy talking to Mariana, and it's been nice the few times she's been over for drinks," he said. "But it was a bit strange when we went out for dinner. She described the restaurant as kind of a spaghetti joint, sort of a neighborhood hangout. I imagined big family tables with lots of kids. And there were families there. But it was a bit fancier than I expected, with white tablecloths and candles. I found myself sitting at a candlelit table across from a woman who wasn't your mother, and suddenly I could barely breathe. I just wanted to get out of there. I managed to keep up a conversation with Mariana, but I'm not sure I was making much sense." I could see tears gathering in my father's eyes.

"Oh, Dad, I'm sure you were charming." I patted his shoulder and smiled in a way I hoped was reassuring.

"Well, maybe it will be better having dinner at her home," he said. "I guess I'm willing to try."

"Well, I'll just be out for a few minutes then," I told him. "You'll need time to get ready."

Kevin seemed delighted when I turned up at their door with my gift. Aaron was gruff when I tried to thank him for helping Maui.

"It would take a pretty mean person to not help a poor little cat when he's hurt."

I could have said it took a pretty mean person to yell at the co-op staff and make trouble for their neighbors. But maybe I'd been wrong about Aaron. And Kevin, as Anna had said, was a sweetie.

Before I went back to our apartment, I went down to the lobby to check our mailbox. I was hoping for a check from one of my clients. I didn't really expect it to have arrived yet but, with the unexpected bill from the animal emergency clinic, I could use the money as soon as possible.

The lobby of the co-op building was lined with mailboxes for each of the units. I unlocked our box and glanced through the envelopes. The check I was hoping for wasn't there. It was mostly just junk mail and a few bills. There was also a sheet of white paper folded up. I knew the co-op sometimes just pushed notices through the wide slots in each of the mailboxes. With no staff in the office, the co-op was only dealing with the most pressing business, but the board was trying to keep things running.

I unfolded the paper and glanced at it.

It was done with a computer printer but it wasn't a notice from the co-op.

"Too bad about your kitty," the note said in large capital letters. "Next time it will be your son. Stay out of this."

CHAPTER
Thirty-Four

Dad had changed into a nice sweater and gray slacks when I got back. He was in the kitchen, looking into the fridge where I'd left the remaining bottle of wine.

"Okay if I take this wine to Mariana's?" he called out. "I should take something, but flowers don't seem quite right."

He turned when I came in and gave me a questioning look. Then he noticed how white my face was.

"I found this in the mailbox," I said, showing him the note.

"So it wasn't an accident that Maui got out?"

"I guess not. But it's hard to imagine someone could get in and take him, with you and Ben both here."

"Well, I sleep pretty soundly and so does Ben, I guess," Dad said. "You're the one who wakes up at the slightest noise."

"It's the mother in me," I replied. "And the mother in me thinks we should get out of this place. I know you and Ben didn't want to move, but I think we should start looking for somewhere else to live."

Dad nodded. "That threat is pretty serious. You should tell that D'Onofrio guy. And we'll start looking for a new place tomorrow."

"I'll call D'Onofrio right now," I said. "And I'll ask Dave if Ben can stay with him for a while. That would be safer. I can't risk anything happening to him."

"Do you want me to stay home with you tonight?" Dad asked. "I don't really feel comfortable leaving you alone."

I almost agreed to his offer. I didn't want to be alone. But I had heard him laughing with Mariana this morning, sounding happier than he had in a long time. He needed to get out more.

"No, I'll be fine," I told him. "You go and have dinner with Mariana. You'll be right next door if I need you."

I finally convinced him to go next door. I was glad he was spending time with Mariana. Maybe he would keep on seeing her, even if we moved.

I thought about that. Dad and Ben were happy here. Dad was finding the accessible building easy to get around and he liked the neighborhood. Ben was making new friends. And he'd already had so much disruption in his young life. My separation from Dave, Mom's death, the moves, first into the condo with Dad and then the co-op. I wanted him to have a stable life and a home where he would feel secure. But obviously this co-op wasn't going to be the place.

I knew how hard it was going to be to find someplace else. There were other co-ops in Vancouver, but I knew most of them had long waiting lists. And finding something else I could afford and was wheelchair accessible would be even harder.

I could feel tears filling my eyes. But I blinked them back. I didn't want Ben seeing me cry. And there were things I could do to keep my family safe. I needed to call the police, and make arrangements with Dave to have Ben stay with him. And, if someone had gotten into our apartment to let our kitten out, I should probably have the locks changed.

I was moving toward the phone to call D'Onofrio when I heard Ben calling me from his room.

"Mommy, Maui's awake now but he's crying. I think his leg really hurts."

I glanced at my watch. Maui was due for his pain medication. And he was probably hungry too.

I could hear Maui screeching in increasingly loud and indignant meows as I walked down the hall to Ben's room. Ben was distressed too, and starting to cry because his kitten was hurt. I remembered I'd promised Naomi I'd try to keep them both quieter.

The situation in Maui's kennel was even worse than I thought. The kitten had woken up at some point and tried to use his litter box. He was a good kitten and well trained. But he'd obviously had difficulty climbing into the litter box with his broken leg and then balancing on his three good legs. He'd missed the edge of the box, and the towel I'd used for his bed was wet with urine. Then he'd managed to kick the litter around the kennel, with some landing on the towel and some even in his food dish.

The kitten was obviously ready for his medication and his food, but I thought I should clean out the kennel first.

I lifted the meowing kitten out of the kennel, trying to support his broken leg. The kitten still yelped in pain.

"Ben, go get some of his crunchies," I told him. When Ben returned moments later with a handful of dry kitten food, I asked him to sit on the bed and placed Maui gently on his lap. "Let him smell his food," I told him. Maui was attracted by the smell of his food and interested in the novelty of being hand fed. I could hear him crunching the food and Ben giggling as the kitten nudged his hand for more.

"He likes this," Ben said. "I should feed him like this all the time. But his whiskers tickle me."

I managed to clean out the kennel and fold another clean towel for Maui's bed. I washed the plastic dishes we used for his food and filled them with new water and dry food. I added a spoonful of the canned food Maui loved. I passed a few more of the dry pellets to Ben to feed to his kitten.

Now it was time to give the kitten his medicine. The vet had made it look easy, but I wasn't so sure. I managed to fill the dropper with the liquid and lifted Maui onto my lap. I tipped his head back, pressed his mouth open the way the vet had showed me and squeezed the dropper.

And Maui jerked back. And howled. The yellow liquid sprayed out of his mouth, covering his fur and Ben's bed.

I tried again, this time managing to clamp his mouth together the way the vet had shown me. But Maui still wasn't swallowing, and the yellow liquid was bubbling out of the corners of his mouth. I remembered the vet had stroked his throat after she had placed the medicine in his mouth. I tried that.

That seemed to work. I think he swallowed. I wasn't sure if he had taken enough of the medicine.

I looked down at the struggling kitten in my lap. His fur was covered with the yellow medicine. I hoped he would lick it off and get the necessary dose. I didn't want to try the procedure again, and I also didn't want to give him too much.

I placed the kitten back in his kennel and was thankful when Maui settled down and started to eat his food.

I looked around the room. Sprays of yellow medicine covered Ben's bed and a few drops had landed on the wall. My own shirt and pants were splattered.

Ben was laughing. "That's Maui's medicine, Mommy, not yours."

"Well, I hope he gets better at taking it," I said. "Imagine if Grandpa did that every time he had to take his medicine. Just think what a mess our house would be."

Ben considered this. My father took a lot of medication for his arthritis, both for pain and to reduce inflammation in his joints. "But Grandpa takes pills," he said. "Maybe Maui should take pills." I wondered about that. A pill would have made less of a mess but it would have been harder for Maui to swallow. I'd just have to get better at giving the medicine. He was only supposed to take it for a few days anyway.

I cleaned up Ben's room and changed my own clothes. Then it was time for Ben's dinner and bath. As I tucked him into bed, I hugged him close, remembering the threatening note.

I needed to call D'Onofrio and Dave as soon as Ben was asleep. I was relieved to see that Maui had licked some of the medicine from his fur, although a few sticky yellow patches still stained it in places. I thought about trying to clean it off, then decided to let it go. I'd deal with it tomorrow, if Maui hadn't cleaned himself by then.

Right now I needed to let the police and Dave know about the threatening note.

I grabbed the card D'Onofrio had given me and called him first. I got his voicemail.

I explained about Maui's disappearance and the note I had received. "I don't really know if it's related to Les and Ruth's deaths, but it seems likely. Anyway, now they're threatening my son, so I'm taking this seriously. I can bring the note to you if you need to look at it. Um, for fingerprints or something."

I left my number and hung up. I wondered what D'Onofrio was doing right now. He could be on duty, investigating another crime. Or he could be off duty. I didn't know anything about him, but I wondered how he spent his time off. Was he married? He didn't wear a wedding ring but some married men didn't. Or he could be single and out on a date. With his handsome face and great wardrobe, it was easier to picture him in a candlelit restaurant with a beautiful woman than home alone with TV, pizza, and beer. But, for some reason, I liked the pizza image better.

I called Dave and was pleased to reach him. Maybe he was doing the pizza and TV alone thing.

"Um, Dave, do you think you could have Ben stay with you for a while. It's getting kind of weird around here." I explained about the note.

"Oh, sure, Bec. That's kind of freaky. But you know I'm going to be away for a week or so, covering the Canucks away games. For sure when I get back. But, then I don't know . . . I have to go out to cover games or to the newsroom. I'm not sure that would work. I mean, that's why you decided to stay home when Ben was born. Maybe you should think about moving."

"Yes, I'm planning to, but finding something is going to take time. I just thought you'd want to make sure Ben is safe until we do."

"Yeah, sure, but you know maybe it's just a joke. Maybe the cat just got out by accident and someone thought it'd be a chance to freak you out. Cara told me you've really pissed some people off in that place. You really should try to get along better with your neighbors, Bec. I never have any trouble with mine."

I resisted the urge to hang up on him. Dave reassured me he'd call me as soon as he got back from his road trip. He sounded excited. Maybe it was the hockey and the chance to be out of town for a while. Or maybe Cara was going with him. I realized I didn't care.

But I thought about what he'd said, about people I'd annoyed in the co-op. Could it have been a prank, a mean practical joke to get back at me? Who would have keys to my apartment? Well, someone had managed to get into the office to kill Les and Ruth. It wouldn't have been too hard to get a set of keys. I remembered the filing cabinet had been open the night Les died. Could someone have taken a set of keys?

I thought about the people in the co-op who had reason to resent me. Aaron had certainly been angry and yelled at me. But would he try to hurt us by harming a helpless kitten? I hated the idea of a large, angry man moving through the apartment while my young son and disabled father were sleeping. Aaron had seemed genuinely upset by what had happened to Maui. Was he feeling guilty at a mean prank gone wrong?

Naomi seemed to have gotten over her resentment. But I didn't really know her. Could she have been faking her sympathy?

I picked up my phone to call a locksmith. I wanted to get the locks changed right away. Then I hesitated. It was getting late, and I'd probably have to pay extra to get someone to come out at this time. I really couldn't afford that. Not with the vet bill to pay and the costs of moving again. I decided it could wait until tomorrow.

I jumped when I heard sounds near our front door and a key turning in the look.

I was relieved to find that it was just my father coming home. I looked at my watch. It seemed like this evening had gone on forever, but he'd only been gone a short time.

"Hi, Dad. How was your dinner with Mariana?" I asked as he came in.

"Oh, fine," he replied but he didn't sound very enthusiastic.

"Dad, is something wrong?" I pressed him. "I know you were feeling a bit uncomfortable about spending time with someone other than Mom, but it's really all right."

Like many men his age, my father wasn't great about talking about his emotions. But he was clearly troubled.

"No, it's not that," he answered. "Well, it's still not easy, but that's not what's bothering me."

He shrugged. "Dinner was okay. Well, she'd cooked roast beef and I'd brought white wine, but that was okay. And we were getting along all right."

He took a deep breath. "You know she had these bookshelves in her living room. And I had read some of the books, so I started talking about them. You know, just making conversation. Your mother and I used to talk about books we were reading. I guess I miss that.

"But she didn't really seem to know what I was talking about. Becky, I'd swear she hadn't read a single one of those books."

I laughed. "Oh, Dad, you know not everyone likes to read as much as we do. I've heard of people who buy books just for decoration, although it's hard to imagine that. Or maybe she just hadn't got around to reading those particular books. Or forgotten them. That happens often enough to me, and I'm sure it will get worse."

Dad gave me a knowing look. "Oh, it will get worse, believe me. I know I've carted home a book from the library and realized I've already read it. But this was strange. She looked almost guilty. And then she changed the subject. Talking about some television program I hadn't seen. So it wasn't the most successful evening. But that wasn't the strangest thing," he went on. "Becky, you've been to her apartment, right? Didn't you notice her living room is exactly the same as ours?"

"Well, yes, it's a mirror image of ours. All of the units in the building are similar."

"No," he said. "That's not what I mean. I mean she's *decorated* her living room to look like ours. Same bookshelves, same green loveseat. It looks exactly the same. It was creepy."

CHAPTER
Thirty-Five

I looked at him. "It wasn't like that when I was over there," I said. "She must have just redecorated. I know she was complimentary about our furniture when she was here. Maybe she was planning on making some changes, liked how our room looked and decided to do something similar. After all, people don't invent completely new looks. People are always copying ideas they see in decorating magazines. It's sort of the same thing."

Dad looked doubtful. I remembered that Mariana seemed to copy Gwen's style of clothes, and how she'd switched to a black suit for Ruth's funeral, after Gwen and I had both worn suits to Les's funeral. "Maybe she's just not sure about her own sense of style and copies things she admires. It's the same with fashions in clothing too. People do that all the time . . . wear something similar to what they've seen in a magazine, or on the street. Some people set trends but most of us just follow what we see other people wearing."

"You're probably right," Dad said. "It still seemed creepy. Maybe I'm just not ready to be spending time with other women. I'm still in mourning."

I gave him a hug. "We all are. But I'm sure it'll get better."

After Dad went to bed, I thought a bit about his evening with Mariana. He probably wasn't ready to start dating again and was looking for an excuse to avoid a new relationship.

I liked Mariana. She'd been great to us since we moved into the co-op. But I thought about her son and his criminal convictions, and Amy's actions in running away, and was a little relieved we might not be brought closer to those two through a close relationship with Mariana.

Then I felt mean. She had been so welcoming to all of us.

I was ready for bed. Then I wished I had spent the money to get new locks put on right away. I would call a locksmith first thing tomorrow. But I didn't think I could sleep without doing something right now.

I'd seen people in movies try to protect themselves by jamming a chair under a doorknob so people couldn't get into a room. I had no idea if that worked but it seemed better than nothing. I grabbed one of the dining room chairs and dragged it toward the front door.

I pushed the chair under the doorknob. Then I laughed. The door opened outwards. If anyone tried to get in, the chair would simply fall over.

Still, it would make a noise and that would alert me. I went to bed.

I WAS WAKENED the next morning by the sound of Ben's laughter. I got up to find him sitting on the chair I'd left by the front door.

"Hey, Mommy," he said when he saw me. "Someone left a chair by the door. Can I have my breakfast here?"

I was so often surprised by some of the ideas Ben came up with. "Not unless you want to move the table there, and I don't think you want to do that."

He considered it. "It folds up really small. If we made it small, you and I could carry it."

"And what if someone wants to come in or we want to leave? I think that's why we don't have a table in front of the door already."

"But people already can't come in if we have a chair in front of the door. So we could have a table."

The point of the chair was to keep people out but I didn't want to tell Ben that. I was pleased when he agreed to return the chair to its rightful place at the table without further argument.

Maui seemed to have passed a peaceful night, and I was relieved to see I didn't need to clean his kennel too much. Even the medicine process went more smoothly this morning.

I looked up locksmiths and was about to start calling for quotes when I wondered if the co-op had someone they used.

I was starting to call Gwen, when I remembered the receipt for the clothing store that I'd found in Ben's bedroom. At the time I thought she must have dropped it when she was here for Thanksgiving. But, if that was the case, shouldn't I have noticed it before then. I wasn't a perfect housekeeper, but I did usually pick up things on my floor. Could Gwen have been the person who let Maui outside?

As president, she might have access to keys to the building. But I couldn't think why Gwen would want to warn me to stop looking into things in the co-op. I was the one who had offered to work on the history of the co-op, and she had happily agreed. Surely she wouldn't have done that if she thought there were secrets she didn't want found out.

Still, I thought I'd feel more comfortable talking to Jeremy about getting a locksmith.

"A list of tradespeople the co-op uses?" he said when I called him. "Sure, we probably have something like that, but the staff would have been the ones to call them."

I told him about Maui getting out of the apartment but not about the threatening note. Jeremy had seemed frank when he told me about growing up in the co-op, but he hadn't mentioned it until after I had found out through the files. If the person who took Maui had keys to my apartment, it could have been anyone. The people who knew I was working on the co-op history might have told anyone in the co-op. But I suspected it might be one of the people who had come to dinner at Thanksgiving. I didn't know who I could trust.

"Geez, someone got into your apartment?" Jeremy said. "Are you sure the cat didn't just get out by accident?"

"Pretty sure," I told him.

"Did they steal anything?"

"No, I don't think so."

"Well, that's strange. But stranger things have happened here. I mean, there have been two deaths. I wonder if someone has the master key. The staff had keys that gave them access to all the apartments, in case of an emergency. Gwen was wondering if someone had broken into the office when Les died. But there didn't seem to be anything missing. The petty cash was there. Ruth said she thought some files were missing but who could tell. Who would want the co-op files anyway? I wonder if we should get all the locks changed," Jeremy went on. "Can you wait on this for a while? I should talk to Gwen."

I didn't really want to wait, but he said he would talk to Gwen and get back to me quickly. I reluctantly agreed. I knew from the occupancy agreement the co-op was supposed to have access to all the units anyway. I wasn't supposed to change the locks without giving the office a key. It was necessary for emergencies. A burst pipe in one apartment could cause damage to all the units under it, so quick access was necessary. But right now I wasn't happy with the idea someone from the co-op could get in to my home.

As I put down the phone, the front door buzzer sounded. It was D'Onofrio.

"You mentioned a threatening note," he said, his face grim.

"Yes, I'll get it for you." I had placed the note in a plastic bread bag. "I found it in our mailbox." I told him. "Just the folded piece of paper, no envelope. I handled it so it'll have my fingerprints on it. I showed it to Dad, but I don't think he touched it. I won't guarantee you won't find a breadcrumb or two though. It was the only bag I had, and I thought it might protect it. I thought it might be better than nothing, anyway."

I thought I saw a hint of a smile as he placed the note, bread bag and all, inside a plastic envelope.

"And what have you been up to, to get warning notes, since we last spoke. I thought you weren't going to be investigating on your own? Isn't one warning enough?"

I looked down. "I didn't mean to," I said. I outlined everything I'd learned since Ruth's funeral—finding out that Gwen had brought muffins to Ruth that day, the suspicion that someone else had brought Ruth food, Carol's belief Les and Ruth had been murdered, and everything Cara had told me about Eddie and Amy Cole. "Gwen and Cara said they were going to call you and give you the information. Did they?"

"Yes," he said. "And they might not have if you hadn't urged them to. So I guess I have you to thank for that. And Ruth's mother has certainly shared her thoughts with us. We do interview people close to victims, you know?"

With a slight change in his tone, he said, "I looked into the old case when you first mentioned it. Eddie Cole was a suspect for a while, but he seemed to have a reliable alibi. And they looked into Amy too. But there was a serial killer around at the time, targeting young women. Several teenagers were murdered or went missing in the area. I think the investigators at the time just assumed both Jessica and Amy had been his victims. They did find out eventually that Amy was still alive. And when they caught the guy, they convicted him of three murders, but they suspected he had been guilty of many more. That's still what they think but, with these new murders, we're going to be looking at that case again."

He looked at me, frowning. "But you have to stop poking around. You're putting yourself in danger." He touched my arm briefly and again I thought it might be more than professional concern. Or was that just wishful thinking?

"I'll stop now," I told him. "I know I should have left it alone, but I really will now. I want my family to be safe. From now on, I'm going to concentrate on finding somewhere else to live."

And I meant it. At the time.

After D'Onofrio left I settled down to look for a new home. A scan of the listings online told me what I already knew. It was going to be hard to find something at the same price. Most listings clearly stated that pets weren't allowed. Others were way too expensive or had stairs. I found many of the housing co-ops in the area had waiting lists so long they weren't even accepting applications. Even the few that were willing to take new applications warned that the wait would likely be several years. I was looking at the application for one of them when the phone rang.

"This is Amy Cole," a woman's voice said when I answered. "I understand you wanted to talk to me."

CHAPTER
Thirty-Six

I know I had promised D'Onofrio to stay out of it. But I just couldn't resist talking to Amy.

I explained how Les and Ruth had died and why I thought their deaths might be related to Jessica's.

"Oh, no. Les? The co-op manager? I remember him. He was a nice guy. He'd ask us kids what we wanted in the way of playground equipment, instead of just assuming he knew best. I'm sorry to hear he's dead."

"Cara told me she thought your brother was involved in Jessica's death. Do you think she's right?"

"My brother or my lovely stepmother. They were both there when I left that day. And Jessie was fine. When I came back they were both still there but Jessie was gone."

"What happened that day?" I asked. I'd instinctively pulled my notebook toward me and was writing down what she said.

"Jessie and I were working on a science project together. We'd gone to my place to work on it. I wanted to go to her house, but mine was closer, so Jessie said we'd save time if we went there. Eddie and my stepmom were both there."

"Mariana was there?"

"Oh, yeah, Mar-i-ah-nah," Amy said, drawing the syllables out and affecting a posh, British accent. "She was plain old Marian Cole back then. One of my friends in the co-op told me later she'd started calling herself Mariana. Sounds classier, I guess."

"So they were both there?"

"Yes, then Marian asked me to go to the store to pick up some stuff for dinner. I had lots of homework and Eddie hardly ever did homework, but she didn't ask him. Whenever I complained, she kept talking about how she was raised in foster care, how she was always living with strangers and how I should be glad she was giving me a home with her real family, instead of letting me go into foster care. But she adopted me when she married my dad, and he adopted Eddie. We were supposed to be a real family. But she never let me forget that Eddie was her real child and I wasn't."

I wondered if Amy's anger at Mariana was simply that of a rebellious teenage girl.

"I asked Jessie to come with me," Amy went on. "She said she'd start on the project, and I could look at what she'd done when I came home." Amy was crying now. "I wish I'd made her come with me. I knew what they were like and she didn't. Her parents were always so nice. Not like them. But I thought I'd just go there and back. I'd be quick. And I really didn't think Eddie would try anything while Marian was there. But he did. I know he did."

Her sobs were louder now. "I got back, and they told me Jessie had left. I called her house, but she wasn't there. She never came home again."

"But why did you leave?" I asked her. "Surely, if you knew something about Jessie's disappearance, you should have talked to the police?"

"I was afraid," she said. "At first I just went out to look for Jessie. But when I couldn't find her, I was afraid to go back. If they'd killed her, they'd kill me too, if only to stop me from talking.

227

"So I hitchhiked out of town and I lived on the streets in different places. People don't pay a lot of attention to homeless people. I moved a lot so no one would find me. I really didn't want to be sent back to Marian. Or even have to go into foster care. Marian made that sound really bad."

"But what did you live on?"

"How do most street kids live? A little panhandling, a little drug dealing. Sometimes you can find someone who'll let you stay with them in exchange for sex."

I must have sighed or sounded in some way disappointed.

"Oh, don't sound so disapproving," she went on. "You do what you have to do to get by. Besides, it's not like I was a virgin. Eddie assaulted me the first time when I was ten."

I thought of the hulking teenager I'd seen in the picture and shuddered. "But you could have reported him," I said. "Didn't you tell someone?"

"It was after my father died. At first I didn't say anything. But I did tell Marian eventually. She just accused me of lying and threatened me with foster care. Said I'd be raped by all sorts of people then, by old men, everyone. She said that's what happened to her. So I didn't say anything."

I was speechless. Could Mariana really act like such a monster? I didn't know Amy and couldn't tell if she was telling the truth. But she sounded sincere.

"Anyway, eventually I got to Ontario. My aunt's there, my dad's sister. I got in touch with her. She made me contact the police and tell them where I was. Then she let me stay with her. Marian didn't want me back. And the police seemed to think some other guy had killed Jessie. Marian had told them she was with Eddie the whole afternoon and evening, helping him with his homework. But that was a laugh, Eddie hardly ever bothered with homework."

"I heard he was eventually sent to a juvenile detention center," I said.

"Yeah, for selling drugs to kids at school. But the police didn't know about that at the time. As far as they were concerned, he was just a kid. And if Marian said she was with him . . . I know Jessie's parents tried to keep the police looking into her death and not just writing it off as another murder by the guy they arrested. But after what happened to them . . ."

"Something happened to Jessie's parents?" I asked. "There was nothing in the papers about that." I remembered the nice-looking couple I'd seen in the picture printed in the paper.

"Yeah, Jessie's mother had some kind of breakdown. I heard from some of the other kids she kept hanging around the co-op looking for her daughter. Eventually, they had to put her in the hospital. And Jessie's dad killed himself."

"That must have been even harder on Jessica's mother—to lose her daughter *and* her husband," I said.

"Yeah, she was in hospital for a long time," Jessie said. "I think she's out now, but it's hard to recover from something like that. Anyway, I think she has money, so she doesn't have to rely on the government to look after her. Someone told me there was a public trustee or something to look after the money after Jessie's dad died. They sold the house of course. But I kept in touch with some of my friends from the co-op, and they told me Marian had some of Jessie's mom's stuff—some of her clothes and jewellery, and dishes and stuff. She told everyone she'd inherited things from her grandmother, but I don't think she had any family, except one sister she talked to sometimes, and Eddie. I think she'd just got into Jessie's house and took some stuff when she could."

"Are you sure?" I gasped. I remembered the china Mari-ana had claimed was her grandmother's.

"Well, I wasn't around, but that's what I heard. I kept in touch with some of my friends, people I knew wouldn't tell anyone where I was."

I had a sudden, frightening thought. "Amy, are you sure your brother is still in jail?"

"I don't really keep track, so long as he doesn't know where I am. But I think so. My aunt told me he keeps applying for parole and getting turned down. I guess the police would know. Maybe they'll reopen the old case and find out who really killed Jessie."

"There's a police officer investigating the recent deaths," I told her. I gave her D'Onofrio's number. "You should tell him everything you told me."

"Couldn't you tell him? I don't really like going over all this again."

"I could tell him what you said," I agreed. "But I'm sure he'll have different questions. It'd be better if he hears it from you."

Besides, I thought, as she reluctantly agreed to make the call, I told him I'd stay out of this.

I sat at my desk, stunned by what Amy had told me. And then I saw a figure moving down the street. I had a hunch I now knew who she was, and I wanted to talk to her. But I couldn't leave Ben alone. Then I heard my father's wheelchair coming through the door.

"Hi, Dad. Glad you're home," I said, shoving my feet into loafers and grabbing my jacket. "Can you watch Ben for a second? I'll be right back."

I took the elevator to the ground floor and sprinted through the front door. I hoped I wasn't too late.

I was in luck. The homeless woman was standing across the street, staring at our building.

"Elizabeth," I called.

"Betty," she answered, turning to look at me. "It's Betty."

"Betty is short for Elizabeth. You're Elizabeth Anderson, aren't you? Jessie's mom."

She smiled at me. "So you figured that out. I thought you would. You're smart, just like her. You don't really look like her, but I think she would have grown up like you. She was always curious too."

"I know you've been through some really awful things," I said to her. "But the police are taking another look at Jessie's case. And I can help you. There are organizations, places that help people who need homes."

She smiled at me. "I know. I'm . . . I don't really need housing. I've been in a place since I got out of the hospital. Sort of a halfway house. And soon I'll be living on my own. I'm okay really. I know I went off the rails after Jessie disappeared. I kept thinking I'd find her. Even after I knew she was dead. This was the last place she was seen, you know. So I wanted to spend time here. But then I found out it really drove *her* crazy, seeing me around. That Marian Cole. She kept trying to get the manager to call the police to arrest me. Les Walter—he was a nice man. I think it was him who arranged for me to get into the hospital and get help. Or maybe the police. I don't know. But I knew it bothered her I was around. So when I got out, I came back. Not to find Jessie this time. I know she's gone. But just to keep an eye on Marian Cole. Because she knows what happened to my girl. I know that."

I told her briefly what Cara and Amy had told me. "And I know that Sergeant D'Onofrio is looking into Jessie's murder again, in connection to Les and Ruth's deaths. But," I said, gesturing at her shopping cart. "Are you sure you have a good home? You're not sleeping outside? Are you sure you don't want me to help?"

"You're a nice girl," she said, patting my hand. "But I'm really fine. This thing . . . well, people don't really look at you if they think you're homeless and are going to ask them for money. They particularly avoid you if they think you're crazy. It's an easy way to hang around the building without people bothering you or calling the police. But maybe I won't have to be here much longer, if the police are going to find out what happened to my Jessie."

She thanked me and pressed a scrap of paper into my hand. "The phone number at the place where I'm living. You call me if you learn anything more. You, or that police officer. He's certainly a handsome one, isn't he? And he thinks you're nice. I saw how he looked at you."

I agreed to call her if I learned anything more. And I gave her D'Onofrio's number too. "He probably will want to talk to you," I told her.

I went back to the apartment bursting to tell Dad what I'd found out. I probably should give D'Onofrio a call too, even if both Amy and Elizabeth had agreed to call him. He'd be angry, I thought, but the information might be useful. And I wanted to make sure Eddie really was still safely locked up.

"Dad, you'll never guess who I've been talking to today," I said as I walked through the door.

"Can't wait to hear it, Becky. But can it wait for a moment? I just want to go back to the car for a minute. I went to the pool this afternoon, and I just remembered I left my bag in the car. I should hang my towel and suit up to dry."

I offered to run down to the car for him but he waved me off. "Won't be a minute," he said as he headed out the door.

As I waited for Dad, I wondered how he would react to what I had learned about Mariana and Eddie. Of course, I only

232

had Amy's view of what happened. But she seemed credible. And her story was backed up by what Cara had told me.

It was a while before I realized that Dad had been gone for far longer than he needed to go down to the parking garage and back.

CHAPTER
Thirty-Seven

I called to Ben to come with me. I didn't know what was up with Dad, but I wasn't about to leave my son alone.

As the elevator opened to the parking garage, I saw what I feared. Someone was lying on the floor in the middle of the garage.

"Dad," I yelled, running toward the figure. Had he been hit by a car? The wheelchair meant he was low to the ground and sometimes hard to see. But wouldn't the person have stopped if they'd hit him? And where was the wheelchair?

As I got closer, I realized it wasn't my father. Cara was lying in the middle of the garage, bleeding from a large wound in her chest. I pulled off the sweater I was wearing and put it over her. And I pulled out my phone to call for an ambulance. *Really*, I thought, *I should have 911 on speed dial.*

But where was my father? I heard a groan coming from behind me just as Ben called to me. "Mommy, Grandpa's lying on the ground," he said, sounding scared.

Dad was lying between two cars. His wheelchair was on the ground beside him.

As I rushed toward him, I was relieved to see that he was moving, trying to get up.

"Dad, are you okay?" I called. "What happened?"

"I'm fine," he said. His voice sounded steady. "Some bastard knocked me over. Then I heard a shot. What happened?"

"Oh, Dad. It's Cara. She looks like she's hurt pretty bad. Are you sure you're okay?"

"Yeah, just bruised. The bag had slid to the back of the trunk and I was just trying to stand up to reach it. Then someone came up behind me and pushed me over. They knocked the wheelchair over on top of me. I just managed to get it off me and was trying to get up. I heard someone, but I thought it might be the person with the gun, so I didn't say anything. Then Ben found me."

I gently helped my father back into his wheelchair, checking him for damage. His face and one hand were scraped, and he had a smear of grease on his jacket, but he seemed otherwise okay.

When the ambulance arrived and I'd directed them to Cara, I suggested to my father that he go to the hospital to be checked over. He refused.

"No. I'm really fine. I'll just clean these scrapes off and put some ointment on them. I'm mainly mad. There was a time when I would've been able to fight back, not just topple over. Or at least get up once I was down. I might have been able to see who it was. I guess I'll need to talk to the police. But I don't really have anything to tell them."

As we got into the elevator, I smelled a faint hint of perfume. It was the lavender and rose perfume Gwen wore all the time.

I had been suspicious of Gwen before. There was the food she brought to the office on the day Ruth died, the receipt for the clothing store she shopped at that I'd found in my apartment on the day Maui was let outside, and now the smell of her perfume near where Cara was shot.

"Dad," I asked. "Can you smell that perfume?"

"That's it. I knew there was something I should remember. I smelled it just before I got knocked over. I remember she was wearing it before."

I helped him wheel his chair through the door of our apartment.

"Yes, Gwen was, when she came to dinner at Thanksgiving. She wears it all the time."

"No, I mean maybe she was wearing perfume then. But at Thanksgiving all I could smell was the food. No, I mean Mariana. Last night when I had dinner at her place. I remember she'd put on a lot, and it was really strong. I guess she thought it was sexy, but it just made me want to sneeze. That's what I remember."

"Mariana? Well, she's been copying the way Gwen dresses, so why not her perfume? I'm going to make you a cup of tea. Then I think we need to call Sergeant D'Onofrio."

I settled Dad's chair near the table in the living room and was just heading to the kitchen when I heard a key in the lock. Before I could reach for the phone, the door opened.

Mariana walked in. She was pointing a gun directly at me.

CHAPTER
Thirty-Eight

I focused on the dark hole at the end of the gun barrel. I had to force my attention away from it to listen to what Mariana was saying.

"I guess you haven't lived here long enough to realize you can hear everything from next door," was what she was saying. "Especially if the windows are open a bit. I guess you've been lucky your neighbors are so quiet."

I could feel my vision getting darker, narrower, just like that dark hole in the gun. I couldn't faint. I needed to do something. I realized I'd been holding my breath and forced myself to breathe.

"Mariana, was it you who got in before?" I'd said the first thing that came into my head "You let Maui out?"

"Yeah, well, I was just trying to get you to stop digging things up. Didn't work though, did it?" She looked at my father. "I'm sorry about this, Angus. I liked you."

"Mariana, what's going on?" Dad asked, shaking his head. "Why are you here?"

As if we both didn't know.

Mariana held up a silver key. "The former neighbors asked me to water their plants sometimes when they were away. I don't seem to have given it back. Les should have had the locks rekeyed before you moved in, shouldn't he? He really wasn't a very good manager. It doesn't really matter though. I took the master key after I killed him."

I came close to fainting then. She sounded so matter of fact about killing someone. "You killed Les?" I said. Mariana just shrugged. The look in her dark eyes told me she didn't see it as a big deal.

I had to do something.

"Look, Mariana, Ben doesn't have to hear all this. Let me send him to another room. Come on, you're a mother."

She shrugged again in agreement. I bent down to look Ben in the eyes. "Honey, I want you to go to Mommy's room."

He protested a little. "I want to stay with you, Mommy. I want the lady to go away."

"I know, honey, but I want you to play the game you were playing the day Grandpa fell." He looked puzzled. "Remember in our old house when Grandpa fell down the stairs. I want you to go to Mommy's room and do exactly what you did that day. Okay?" I thought he understood. "And close the door," I told him. I gave him a kiss. "Mommy loves you," I called out as he ran down the hall. I hoped he would realize what I was asking him to do. But even if he did, there was no guarantee I would see him again. Mariana had killed two people, possibly three, if Cara died. She would have no qualms about shooting my father and me. And I didn't really think she'd let Ben live as a witness.

I looked at Mariana. "Thanks," I said. "There's no need for him to hear this."

If Ben did understand that I wanted him to call 911, I needed to keep Mariana talking until the police could get here.

"So you killed Les," I said again, trying to sound like it was a surprise.

"I didn't really mean to." She sounded quite reasonable, as if she regretted it but it had to be done. "At the time, I mean, although it probably would have come to it, eventually. That one was an accident. I just got so darn mad. He'd been asking me and asking me when my son was going to be moving in. How am I supposed to know? He keeps applying for parole, and they keep turning him down."

She looked at me. "You do know he's in prison, don't you? Not working back east."

She could tell from my face that I did know. "I suspected that Cara told you. I saw you going into her place. I guess she told you about the complaint her family made about my boy. She should have been glad he was interested in her. But, no. Well, we won't have to worry about her anymore."

I noticed she lowered the gun a bit when she got distracted. Maybe, if I could keep her talking, I could find a way to get it away from her. "It wasn't like Eddie just had a crush on her," I interrupted. "Cara said he tried to rape her."

She shrugged. "She was just trying to cause trouble. She was a skinny little thing back then. Hadn't had her boob job. There was no reason for Eddie to be interested in her.

She paused as if trying to regain a train of thought. "Anyway, Les kept telling me I'd have to move to a smaller place soon if I couldn't give him a firm date pretty soon. But *then* he said he'd been looking into that old complaint, and he was going to recommend to the board that they refuse to let Eddie move in."

Tears gathered in her eyes. "He's all the family I have. Why can't I live with my family like everyone else?"

I almost felt sorry for her. It would be hard to live surrounded by families when you were all alone.

But then she frowned and went on. "I was furious. I just hit him with that stupid plaque he left lying around. It was his own fault, really. He should have kept the place tidier. I thought pushing the boxes on top of him would make it look like an accident."

I could feel my body start to tremble. I tried to still it, but there was nothing I could do to stop the shaking.

I had to keep her talking, keep her from shooting us both right away.

"But then you killed Ruth too." I tried to stop my voice from trembling but it sounded high and tense. "Why Ruth?"

"Ruthie was another accident," she said. She sounded like she regretted that one. "After Les died, I went through the office, trying to find the old complaint. I took some boxes I thought were from the right year. But it wasn't in there. It was impossible to find anything in that stupid office. The co-op should have hired more competent staff."

I looked at her in horror. She looked so normal, apart from the gun. Just another co-op member complaining about the staff in the co-op. Except she'd just admitted to killing them both.

"I knew Ruth was poking around in the files, trying to find the file Les had been worried about. I didn't really intend to kill her. People don't usually die from bad mushrooms. I did some research. And I tested it on a rat. I guess he did die eventually but not right away. I just thought she'd get so sick she wouldn't be able to work for a while. That'd give me time to find that stupid file and get rid of the copy of the complaint. Who knew the silly thing had a bad heart."

My father had been staring at Mariana in speechless shock. Now he shifted, looking like he was going to intervene. Mariana seemed to be fond of him, so maybe he could persuade her not to shoot us. Or maybe he'd set her off. I didn't think we could risk it. I held my palm up where only he could see it, and went on.

"And then you shot Cara?"

"Yes, now her I meant to kill. And I've found that guns work pretty well."

Mariana seemed lost in thought now. Maybe Ben hadn't understood what I wanted. Maybe the police weren't on their way to save us.

I wondered if I could jump her and grab the gun before she shot me. I was younger and stronger than she was. The adrenalin in my body was supposed to help me fight or flee any danger. Instead, my shaking legs could barely support me.

I tried to calm down, get ready to make a move.

"But how did you get a handgun?" I asked. "They're not exactly easy to come by in Canada."

"Oh, one of Eddie's friends. He has good connections, you know." She waved her left hand, the one not holding the gun, airily. "They were willing to help."

"And you did all of this so Eddie could come and live with you?"

"I just want him to have someplace familiar to come home to," Mariana said. "Is that too much to ask? When he gets out, to have a nice home to come to. And maybe he can get custody of my grandson. You know that bitch Eddie lived with won't even let him see his boy while he's in prison? She doesn't even want me to see him. His own grandmother!"

She lowered her voice again. "Family's so important, isn't it?"

"I think so," I said to the woman planning to kill mine.

I took a small step closer to her, hoping she wouldn't notice.

"I gather you were raised in foster care," I said.

"You have no idea what it's like," she shouted. I thought I had asked the wrong question. Then her voice grew quiet. "Moving from house to house. Trying to find out what each new family's like and trying to fit in with them. Trying to be what they want you to be and never quite succeeding. Never belonging."

For a moment I could see the sad little girl she must have been. I almost wanted to hug her and try to make it better. I could see where Mariana had developed her habit of copying people she admired. But she had more to say.

"And the abuse. Some of the so-called fathers want to have sex with you. So you go along with it. Because you want them to love you. But they don't. Do you know Eddie's father was the foster father in my last placement? We had an affair that lasted several years after I was out of care. But he left me too, once he found out I was pregnant. Didn't want to ruin his marriage, he said, or his reputation."

I knew she was a murderer but I was feeling more and more sympathy for her.

I took a step closer to her. I could almost reach the hand that held the gun.

"But surely there are nice foster families who care about the children. Couldn't you have complained and been sent to a different family?"

"I guess," she said. "I didn't really know what the rules were. They said my mom and dad were unfit, and they took me away. Maybe they didn't treat me right, but they were my family, you know. I tried to find them when I was older, but I never saw them again. I had a baby sister too. When they took us into care, all I really wanted was to stay with her. But they couldn't even keep us together. The family that took her was nice, I think, and they adopted her later on. It's easier with babies, I guess. People want them. We reconnected years later, and she stayed with me for a while. But we couldn't get along. Too different, I guess. We weren't really sisters anymore."

It was a very sad story. I felt tears in the corners of my eyes, but I couldn't tell if they were for her or my own family.

We'd both been so wrapped up in what she was saying we hadn't heard the door open. But I suddenly noticed D'Onofrio in the hall. There were several other officers with him, all holding guns.

Mariana didn't seem to have noticed them. I raised my voice a bit to cover any sounds as I watched the police officers creep closer to us.

"So, Les and Ruth both died by accident. And Cara deserved it. But what happened to Jessie Anderson. She's kind of where all of this started."

"Oh, Jessie was an accident too," she reassured me. "That was never meant to happen."

That was when my father chose the very worst moment to try to intervene.

"Well, Mariana, if it was all an accident, why bother to shoot us." He's been sitting quietly. At first he'd been as stunned as I was. Maybe more, if he had thought he might have a relationship with her. And then he'd followed my hand signal to stay quiet. But now he obviously thought it was time to see if he could do something to save us.

I realized that, while I could see the police from where I was standing, Dad didn't know they were there.

Now he moved his wheelchair in front of her. "Come on," he said. "Put down the gun, and we can have a drink and talk this over.

She swivelled the gun she had been pointing at me and held it to my father's head. I felt all the breath rush out of my body.

"Angus, don't even try that," she yelled. "You pretended to like me but you didn't. You're just like everyone else."

I could see her finger tightening on the trigger.

243

"Oh, forget about him," I said, my voice sounding remarkably calm. "Men just lie. I know all about it. But tell me about Jessie. I don't quite understand what happened"

Amazingly, she complied, pulling the gun a little distance from Dad's head and letting it sink a bit towards the floor. I let myself breathe for a moment.

Then she pointed the gun at me again.

"She was working on her science project in Amy's room," she said. "And I saw Eddie go in there. She should have liked him. He was a handsome boy. But I guess she screamed when he started to touch her. So he had to shut her up."

She said it in such a matter of fact manner. As if killing Jessie was the obvious thing to do.

"He didn't even really rape her," she went on. "He'd been so excited he ejaculated in his pants. So I just told him to clean himself up, and I wrapped her body up and left her in Amy's closet. Amy didn't even look in there before she took off. We moved her to the park after it was dark."

"Surely, the police could tell she'd been in your car," I said. "I mean it was a while ago but they've been able to test for DNA for years."

"We didn't use our car." She looked at me like I was an idiot. "Eddie stole one. And, of course Jessie's DNA was in Amy's room. Everyone knew she'd been there earlier. I just told the police Eddie had been home with me all afternoon and evening. They just assumed she met that serial killer on her way home."

She might have said more. But then Dad finally noticed the police behind her.

I saw his eyes light up and he inhaled. He realized his mistake in an instant and tried to damp down his expression. But it was too late.

I watched the barrel of the gun start to swing away from me and back to Dad's head.

But she couldn't resist turning her head slightly to follow the direction Dad had been looking,

D'Onofrio raced the last few feet. Mariana screamed as he grabbed her arm. The gun pointed towards the floor briefly.

I jumped forward, desperate to move Dad's wheelchair away from her. But D'Onofrio was much stronger than she was, and he quickly pried the gun out of her hand.

I noticed she was crying as the other officers handcuffed her.

CHAPTER
Thirty-Nine

"I did it," Ben said, running down the hall from my room. "At first, I didn't know what you wanted me to do, Mommy. Then I remembered that when Grandpa fell, I called 911. So I called them and told them about the lady with the gun. But, why did you say it was a game, Mommy? Was she playing a game? It wasn't fun. I didn't like it."

"No, honey, it wasn't really a fun game, was it? But I'm so glad you knew what to do." I hugged him. I'd been so afraid I'd never see him again. That Mariana would kill us all. "You're such a smart boy, and Mommy is very proud of you."

"I heard about the shooting in the parking garage, and I was already on my way here when his call came in," D'Onofrio said. "I heard most of what she said when I was waiting for backup. I'll have to get a statement from both of you. But I'm betting this means you didn't stay out of it."

It was hours later, after we'd all given statements and I'd put Ben to bed, that the front door buzzer sounded.

"It's me, Bec," Dave said. "Can I come in for a minute?"

"I thought you were out of town," I said when he got to my apartment.

"I was," he answered. "But I came back when I heard about Cara."

"I'm sorry, Dave," I said. "I found her, and I guess I should have let you know. But things were a little busy around here."

"No, it's okay. A buddy in the newsroom heard about it and called me. And I heard about what happened here. My gawd, all of you could have been killed too."

He'd swayed a little, and I could tell he'd been drinking. A lot.

"I'm sorry, Dave. I haven't heard anything. Is Cara . . . ?"

"No, they got to her in time. She lost a lot of blood, but they got the bullet out. They say she should recover fine."

He swayed again.

"Come in, Dave. You should sit down."

He followed me into the living room and collapsed on the love seat. "I was just sitting there, watching her in the hospital. She just looked so small and pale. And she had all these tubes and things hooked up. And I thought I'd been such a jerk, to her and to you.

"And then I heard about what happened here," he said. "Ben could have been killed, and I remembered you asked me to look after him, and I just blew you off. I just couldn't be bothered, and then I almost lost my son. Well, it's not going to be like that anymore. From now on I'm going to be a good dad and a good husband."

I touched his hand gently. "Dave, you know we're not going to get together again. There's been too much water under the bridge."

Dave laughed. "Not husband to you, Bec. To Cara. I'm going to ask her to marry me."

I was saved any embarrassment because the next thing he said was, "I think I'm going to throw up."

After Dave raced to the bathroom, and I cleaned up the spots where he'd missed the toilet, I said, "I don't think you're in any shape to go home alone."

I glanced at the short love seat and then at my lanky ex. "You take my bed. I'll sleep on the couch."

I had the whole night to discover that the love seat was not that comfortable to try to sleep on. I was awake often enough to be aware that Dave hadn't made any more trips to the bathroom. I didn't think he'd had to make use of the bucket I'd left by the side of my bed either.

So I was up early and walked to Ben's room to check on him. He was still fast asleep, but Maui was awake. The little cat seemed to be feeling better and was moving around a bit more. I leaned down to get him out of his kennel and give him a cuddle.

Then it was back to the regular routine of feeding the cat and getting Ben ready for preschool. I had a brief moment of wanting to keep him close beside me but I decided it was better for him to have things back to normal.

I'd just returned from dropping Ben off when I heard a knock at the door. I was expecting most of the co-op would have heard what happened by now and be anxious to hear the details.

But it was D'Onofrio.

"I just wanted to let you know what's going on," he said. "There's some question about whether Mrs. Cole is fit to stand trial. She'll be getting a psychiatric evaluation. Of course, if there is a trial, you'll be called to testify.

"And I just wanted to give you these brochures. From victims' services. You know, in case you need counselling or anything."

"Thanks," I said, as I took the brochures. "But I think I'll be fine. I'm tougher than I look."

"Yes, I think you are," he said, and his tone softened. "Are you sure you're all right, Rebecca . . . er, Ms. Butler."

"You can call me Rebecca," I said. "Um, I'm afraid I don't know your first name."

"Rafe," he said. "Raffaello, really."

I noticed he was blushing.

"Well, you know, there will be the trial and everything," he said, "and it wouldn't be appropriate, but do you think, I mean, after this is all over, do you think . . . I mean, would you be interested in . . ."

I'd never heard D'Onofrio stammer like that. I could see the color spreading from his cheekbones across his face. There was something very attractive about the flush under his olive skin. Was D'Onofrio going to ask me out? On a date?

He didn't seem able to get it out. Well, I was a modern woman. I could ask him.

"So, after the trial is over," I said, "would you like to . . ."

My bedroom door opened, and Dave stumbled out, wearing nothing but his boxers and a T-shirt. "Oh, hi, Bec. Thanks for last night. I'm just going to get some coffee. What do you have for breakfast?" He stumbled down the hall.

I looked back at D'Onofrio. But he was already turning away. "So, anyway, I'll be in touch about the trial."

"Wait," I said to his retreating back. "That wasn't what you think."

But the elevator doors had closed. I headed towards the kitchen. If there hadn't already been too many murders around here, Dave would have been a dead man.

But, as D'Onofrio had said, we'd be in touch.

Acknowledgements

Crime writers Gail Bowen and Garry Ryan provided advice, mentorship and encouragement during the very early stages of the writing of this book. Vi Ialungo, Pat McClain, Lorraine Robson and Stuart Thomas read and gave feedback on the completed draft. Adrienne Tanner and the Vancouver Police Department answered my questions about newsroom operations and policing respectively.

Thank you all so very much.